D

To my one and only Love
You're the music that makes my heart beat…how do we keep the music playing?

A note for Jeff:
One needs not to see the music to actually feel its impact. Life is sometimes like the Blues.

To a wonderful Author:
A very special "thank you" to Kallypso Masters who has clearly taken me under her wing. She has guided me, educated me, and assisted me on many avenues of writing. A thank you seems a small token for all her generosity.

Prologue – Empty

Oh my god, sinking to the hardwood floor beneath me, I can't breathe, just a slight breath is escaping me, my chest hurts, my head is ringing, pounding and banging inside. Tears are running from my eyes stinging and stinging, this cannot be happening. I cannot move, frozen in my body and pain is taking over a hurt so deep and so raw. God I cannot stop hyperventilating, I hurt so bad, I hurt so badly. I am shivering and shaking and my chest is pumping in and out in a nervous motion as I think or try to think. I reach my quivering hands up to my face to wipe the streams of tears that will not stop.

"Oh god help me," I repeat over in my head or aloud unable to be certain…I cannot stop shaking, I cannot stop the dull ache in my belly, I cross my arms and rock back and forth and drop my head to bob it up and down, while I whimper… What have I done so bad, he was my rock, my safe haven, what have I done wrong, why is this happening to me after all this time, not me, not after all these years…what we had is gone, I am empty, all my love has drained from my body, I am so empty, my heart is completely broken, broken forever. I am so alone…

Chapter One – Meeting

I am in a new part of my life, driving through an early spring day, air thick with falling petals swirling about. I think back to where I was months ago and I remember my marriage ending. It was a horrible cycle of emotions for me, first came so many tears and pain. Then I had so many questions as to why was I suddenly replaced with a woman that he hired to work in his office. I thought we had a solid and secure relationship. His walking away from me was staggering. I then suffered loss of self esteem and later I found anger which was hard for me to release, I kept so much inside. I still carry with me a self-doubt. I'm not sure I can rely on my judgment enough to trust any future partner. My husband ending our marriage knocked me down, but each new road I travel, I will get stronger. I turn on the radio to hear something to sway my mood. The music immediately takes me away on a journey as I travel briefly from traffic light to traffic light through town. Seems like the changing of the light pattern is in a sequence of musical themes like the chorus repeating over and over, red – yellow – green. Go – it is now time for me to go and begin my journey writing about the band. Conveying through my words their passion, their singing, and their playing to becoming seasoned musicians. I follow all the traffic to the concert this evening.

This is my story **Rock Notes**.

"Max, Max, Max Rand excuse me, do you have a moment to talk to me?" I closed in on the far corner of the stage. I had purchased a front row ticket to this evening's local concert to take in tunes and set myself up for the possibility of conversation. "I know you don't know who I am so let me introduce myself. I am Madison Tierney, call me Madison or Maddy. I am a freelance creative writer, once a columnist and now I'm writing a book titled, "Rock Notes" which I follow a band in depth, and I'd like that to be your band "Rolling Isaac's." I didn't want to intrude on his time, so I simply said, "I know you have so many young ladies wanting you to sign autographs and their bodies," I smiled and continued to talk in a confident manner, "but I just wanted to give you my business card in case we can speak in the near future or have your band representation contact me."

Looking up at Max and his combination of youthful and mature yet awesome, truly awesome good looks, I shouted out "Oh and I thought the show was great." I beamed about it trying to remain calm, as I was more mature, rather than getting all flustered by a mere young band playing.

Max looked me over from his vantage point above and smiled a kind brim and nodded. I drank in all his chiseled features and his dark chocolate, delicious hair that had tousled all over during the concert, looking very sexy like he had been rolling in bed for hours. It was then that he turned slightly to jump down and he placed his stunning, well built arms on the edge of the stage and the tattoo under his sleeve peeked briefly through. He was wearing a tight white long sleeve tee pushed up onto his forearms, and he was completely soaked with his sweet sweat from singing to the crowd. I wasn't certain what was inked on him but I knew it drew me in. It was colorful and his tee shirt sleeve was stuck to him. I could see his firm, fit stomach also as the tee clung to his torso. I looked up, startled to see he was now standing in front of me and still smiling tenderly. He took my hand gently and slightly slid his finger over my fingertip as sensation ran through me, it was only for him to take the business card but it left me sort of out of breath, scattered my thoughts for a moment. His eyes pulled me in like an inviting Caribbean ocean, they were a deep tropical blue and his dark eyelashes swept over them. I had to rethink and tell my body to blink as I was captivated. I thanked him and hoped to hear from him and as he walked back I stood and stared at his tall frame and truly awesome body…he did not turn around. I went to finally leave when my feet would allow me to move them and I glanced back to take in the entire empty, darkened stage only to see him leaning on the far side and sending a smile and wink my way. I looked around to see if it was meant for someone else and then back to him where he laughed and nodded his head to me.

I walked to my car and thought about Max Rand and our brief meeting and I was concerned about my attire for some odd reason…as it took me hours to decide earlier what to put together which was very unlike me. It was like taking time to prep for a date. I kept reselecting pieces from my closet to make me look a bit more hip and trendy. Finally I had chosen simple jeans, black boots and a black top with open shoulder areas. The appliqué on the shirt was a striking detailed cross with hearts that seemed to dance across the top and wrap to the back, almost like a hug, I added a black gem belt. Checking my look in the mirror, I was content and headed to the concert. I was just about to take hold of the car handle when my cell phone sounded, its timing making me think I set off my car alarm. I reached into my pocket and was surprised to read:

> *I watched your nervous smile, and caught a glimpse of the top you wore, one of my inks looks like it. I sing yes, but I am also believe it or not, involved in the band's representation…can we continue our conversation at a quiet space tomorrow? Max Rand*

I fumbled for a reply to him, could this actually be happening, he was contacting me in mere moments? I sent him a voice text as a reply –

Yes, sure. Under my breath I said absolutely.

That was so stupid of me, an adult to say yes, sure, and he probably heard me say absolutely…what was I thinking, I had to be in control of this proposal for my writing and I should not feel like a school girl, shy and nervous, my phone sounded again.

> *I can meet you in Philly. There's a coffee house there. It's the 2nd Street Coffee Café. I began in the biz there and I hang out there upstairs. Meet you at two o'clock. The address is the name. I got the first cup.*

Wow was this really happening, I decided to take control of my life for once and go after the stories I wanted to write and now I was going to possibly have my foot in the door per se. I replied:

Sounds great...I'll be there

Of course I would be there. That is all that I could say to him without sounding too over anxious. I smiled to myself and opened my car and positioned myself behind the wheel ready to start to take control of my life.

I drove out of the city skyline to my townhouse. I had just begun to make it my new home over the past few months. The collapse of my marriage was devastating. My husband of ten years, Thomas, came to an epiphany that he just wasn't in love with me anymore. He had taken me to bed and poured his heart out about how we were soul mates and destined to be together in the end, but there was something missing for him. As we made love that evening trying, I thought, to save or recapture what he felt he was lacking, I was unaware that this was his goodbye to me. He held me in his arms until dawn, but when I awoke he had left and moved out. I broke down and since I was always the one in the shadows of him, I had no real confidence to stand alone or walk tall. I was lost and lacked all confidence in my ability to love another. I didn't find out right away, but the dark, ugly truth eventually made it out into the open. The fact was that Thomas found someone else, but apparently did not want to come right out and tell me that himself.

We met in college, as I was deciding to be an English Major to write or do something like that with my degree; he had all his ducks in a row and set goals and was heading for the big business world. He had followed in his family's steps and was soon interning with a leading financial company and heading for the top. Great pay, high-rise condo in the city, convertible automobile of the latest year and me as his wing person, just along for the ride and always in the shadows. He loved me I know but I always felt he could do better with someone showier, someone that wanted the life that he sought after. For me hanging in sweatpants and cami tops all day and writing different poems and stories was pure satisfaction. We had been in love and enjoyed so many memories together for ten years. He kept striving for the top so we put off any plans of starting a family and I was content with that as I had come from a slightly dysfunctional family that the peace and calm of just him and I was perfect.

We had a beautiful over the top wedding with all the trimmings. Thomas's family planned it all and the only say I got was that I loved crème tea roses with dark pink edges and so on my wedding day the only thing I remember smiling at was that there were a few of my favorite flowers. I really just wanted it simple but he wanted to show the world that he was getting married, only for me to find out later that the company he was working for wanted their employees married to show a secure status and responsibility. Now I wonder if he was really in love with me or was it a business tactic.

Pulling into my driveway, I was finally reaching a comfort level in my life that took so long to get to after my breakdown. My townhome was quite comfortable with several extra rooms. One of the rooms held my desk and all my writings strewn about and another was filled with music for me to enjoy as I wrote. It also contained various art pieces, treasures I carefully selected. These rooms became a source of comfort for me, it became my tiny slice of heaven, a safety net for me to be in and feel secure.

I threw my keys on the table in the entranceway and entered my bedroom and saw all the clothing choices I picked through earlier for the evening all over the floor. I laughed at my mess and climbed up onto my bed. I reached for my notebook, tucked my knees comfortably and began to write a handwritten note for Max Rand.

Max Rand:

As I sat this evening in the front row of your Philadelphia Concert, I was all too captivated by you. I am not certain in my lifetime that you will ever read this, my first love letter to you, nor have the opportunity to read my words as I write them. I just knew that something touched me deep inside as I sat below the stage and watched you and the band begin to perform. As the show progressed I could not take my eyes from you, not in a star struck way, but I felt I was pulled in by some force to you. I know this is crazy as I had just met you but I felt I knew you for such a long time.

My heart is not in a good place right now, I still feel something tugging inside and I knew that you started that pull. Let me tell you that your blue eyes are so warming, they searched the crowd and landed on mine and I felt them envelope me. So many fans were on their feet tonight dancing and singing all the words to your songs. I sat firmly in my seat, mostly because I felt if I stood that my legs might weaken mainly due to how your passion was coming through in your music and it made me crumble.

Max, as I handed you my business card I wondered how I could love you and fall for you. It was almost love at first sight. I guess this is pretty sappy for me writing about you like this, and it feels as though I am gushing with my first never to be read love letter. This will be added to my Love Notes and be like my secret diary. For now I will await our next encounter and see what feeling comes to me at the sight of your face or the sound of your voice.

Maddy xo

My eyes tired from writing and I drifted into thought. I am not sure if I'm still awake daydreaming or if I have actually fallen asleep. I was again at the concert from this evening and as they announced the band, Rolling Isaac's I was looking and searching to connect with Max's eyes and there they were. He sought me out and winked and never took his deep blue eyes from me…he reached out on one song, his hand stretching toward me and almost touching me as I reached toward him. Wanting that touch, wanting that feeling…wanting a brief passing of his igniting sensation. He got on his knees and his hands were clasped around the microphone as if in prayer. He was deep in a ballad and pouring his heart into it. He looked at me and I sank, it was so very crushing, it tore at my heart.

I was all wrapped up in the sheets and woke to music coming from my programmed ring tone on my cell phone, a tune from Tenth Avenue North called *Love is Here.* I exhaled and for that moment in my dream, love was there. I was still in my clothes from the concert, twisting in the sheets. Who was calling me now, and what time was it? I glanced at the clock it was already after eight in the morning. I slept through and Jillian called. I missed meeting up with her at eight to head to the gym. I reached out and dialed her back, and told her I was so tired and slept in but would meet her later in the week.

Jillian had become my rock over the past months. She was the first to enter the door to the high rise condo my husband and I shared after he left me. She had to pick me up, carry me and take care of me for many days. She taught me to lean on myself and take control and never be so dependent on another that I would lose myself. We shared so many girl talks and girl days together. My phone now sounded with a text that she would catch me later and hoped my tiredness was because I met someone and had fun and a late night. Although she knew that had not happened over all these months and she knew that I was not seeking that she asked anyway. I had been so deeply hurt that I didn't think I could go that route ever again.

Now that I was up I stripped down and decided to take a shower and see what was ahead of me for today as I had to meet Max Rand. Just then while in thought for the afternoon my phone sounded and a text came through. I thought Jillian was reaching out again to make the gym a little later but it was from Max.

Good morning Madison, hope you're free later tonight. I have rehearsal and if our conversation goes well, you can come meet the band. It'll give them a chance to decide about you writing about us. Hope you slept well.

Wow, I stood there, completely nude, reading this and the water in the shower continued to run, if only he knew how great I slept. I dreamt of him. This was chilling to my naked body, but in such a good way.

The rest of the morning seemed to drag; it is always like this when you want to be someplace. I caught up on cleaning since my clothes were all over and also prepared an outline for my writings in hopes my project was approved.

Soon it was time for me to leave to meet him. As I was driving into the city it took me back to Thomas and me living there before. I was happy and in love then. Thomas still lived downtown, and still almost like it was written on his calendar, would call me and leave a message of how he was thinking of me each month that has passed since he left and since the divorce. Each time he would leave in the message that he knew that we would be back together sometime in the future but he needed time to find himself, or he'd say he wasn't there yet. He never admitted to me that he left me for another woman. I heard he moved on real quickly with a new office intern, that he handpicked for the position but I heard it wasn't all that wonderful lately and there was trouble early on in their new paradise. I never took his calls because as angry as I felt inside, I admit I was weak and I would have broken down and taken him back. I would have liked closure, to hear him tell me his side of what happened. After all the time that has passed, I still felt something for him for all those years together as man and wife. We all make mistakes or wrong decisions and I always believe in second chances. I think he may have been convincing and I would have crumbled.

I was going round and round on the city streets hoping to park close to the coffee shop, but luck was not on my side for parking. I finally managed to take a spot as someone was leaving but several streets over, so my afternoon arrival time was delayed by about fifteen minutes. When I arrived I walked in and was greeted by the employee behind the counter in a very friendly manner. Before I could tell him I was meeting someone he told me that Max was upstairs already. Upward I went and smiled at the idea that Max already alerted the coffee staff of my impending arrival.

Max was deep in thought and writing in a journal as I approached. He wore cool looking silver rimmed reading glasses that he had not worn on stage and a hat that snuggled down covering his ears. He looked so everyday, average, but still very breathtaking in his normalcy. I was surprised as he seemed reserved and not exposed as when he was up the stage last evening with screaming girls surrounding him. He looked simple, still drop dead good looking but he camouflaged it this afternoon with not having a tight tee, tight jeans or the cuff bracelet. He had worn a leather cuff bracelet last evening that he had kissed before raising his hand to the crowd at the end of the show. I wanted to ask him about that gesture but figured I would in time if I saw him do it again in concert. Today, if I didn't know I was meeting him, the same Max Rand from last night, I would have passed this guy by on a street. His attire was toned down, plain loose black tee with an open buttoned shirt over top, loose and worn and torn jeans and it appeared work boots. I pulled out the chair across from him as he looked up; he was really lost in thought there for the moment.

He paused and then complimented the color of my shirt. I felt the heat as he was staring at my chest. "Madison, wow, you look so warm."

"I'm not warm, I feel fine."

"No, I mean your shirt color highlights your dark hair and sends a warm glow. I guess I am stumbling here for something nice to say. But you look good. You're good looking and you remind me of the warmer days coming." He also sniffed in the air and said, "You smell good, really good."

"I guess thank you and thank you, you may make me blush."

Wow, did he just floor me with a compliment, and he actually smelled my Light Blue fragrance, even though I only applied a trace of it. I felt shifted in my thoughts. I had to gain composure and so I blurted out nervously, "Glad you could meet me so soon." I spoke in a professional manner trying to sound more and more confident.

He smirked and simply replied "Yeah, sure absolutely." Sounding just like me last night. He asked how I liked my coffee and took the liberty of ordering some lunch selections since if this went well, he wanted me to head to meet the band so there wasn't time for food until much later.

We began talking and I explained to him that I was following my dream of writing and had certain pieces that I wanted to complete and put together in a collection. One was to get in depth with a band. Why his band? Well I had heard them play a tune months back called *Missing Ash* and during the lowest time in my life, I had downloaded it and played it too often as I wrote at home in my writing room. I dared not tell him that, all I said was, "I have heard great chatter about the Rolling Isaac's." Also, since they were a local band from Philly. I could easily attend a lot of their shows and perhaps get stories from them to write about.

I drifted in thought for a moment; here I was trying to start a conversation and hearing Thomas in my head telling me that my writings were good, although he never really cared to read them. They weren't making him the big bucks in the corporate world so he just seemed to pass me over. But I had been so in love with him, perhaps I should have ignored my passion of writing and been more in tune with him.

"Madison, hey come back"…Max was seeking my reply. I jumped as he lightly touched my hand as it lay near my untouched coffee. It felt comfortable, safe and he kept fingers on top of my hand.

"You zoned on me, where did you just go?" He asked. I apologized to him as I slid my hand out and took a sip of coffee. I told him that I drift often into thoughts that take me away for a moment but not thoughts I want to stay in.

I started the conversation explaining that if I wasn't going to be an intrusion or bother tagging along with them, I wanted to cover them and get some real raw, natural experiences of the band. The talent, their hopes, and what they gave up to have their dreams. I told him it could be for a few months or longer but that would depend on if it became bothersome for me to be with them. I knew they played in Philly often but knew they traveled about as well. I told him the travel wouldn't be a problem and would be at my own expense. In between my speaking with him I managed to take in some bites of food, but I was still nervous. I felt like I was on a first date. I was trying to settle myself and continued to tell him some of my story.

My husband Thomas made a lot of money and he thought to leave me a nice divorce settlement. He did this despite saying that we would never be over. I guess his leaving me for someone else helped him to not have the guilt of carrying on an affair and staying married. I think he felt that he could try out this new woman and if it didn't work then he would have me in the wings. I lived a simple life so the monetary agreement would surely carry me far. But I didn't tell Max any of this, I just looked into the dark blue eyes that I had dreamt of and was stunned that they were the same blue as in my dream. I told him I was in a position to do my own travel and would not be any burden to them. I did then produce for him several pieces of writing that I published in the past from being a column writer for years at the city paper and then to a few books that were out on the shelves of several bookstores. None were best sellers, but to me, humble accomplishments. I had so many confidence steps to climb in my life now but I think I was feeling like I was on the second step.

Max glanced at the portfolio of items I brought supporting my occupation and smiled. He said, "I know exactly who you are, I followed your weekly column. You wrote the editorial piece a few years ago supporting bands. It highlighted a new, up and coming band, our band the Rolling Isaac's." Max continues "I still have the clipped article someplace back on **The Wall.** That's what we call it where we rehearse and where the band tacks up our memorabilia.

You should see this wall it's freaking awesome!" He flashed me a devilish smile and said. "Slapped all over are new items about us, photos of our loved ones, and many we have loved and left the next day."

I shook at that last statement; I had been drawn in by his keepsake of the article, but then stunned by the morning after thought. Thomas had left me the morning after, left me after ten years. I had been so caught up in him that I lost me.

I could feel his eyes, warmth focused in on me and I moved around in my seat. As we talked I couldn't help thinking about the other girls. I was trying to convince him to let me follow the band, but I knew I was different from them. I knew that I was about eight years older than Max Rand. Nothing that he said or did made me feel old, but that was just one way I was different than the rest of his followers.

"What the hell, a pretty, smart lady asks to write about me and the band, I say yes, and you can start by calling me Rand. I'm done with hearing the girls scream "Max". I tune them out. You though Madison I would listen to. It also gets confusing with me being Max and my Uncle Maxwell. Rand makes it easier. So I say, it's a go," Max said.

"Then Rand it is, thank you." I cheerfully sounded, and I nodded to agree.

After a few more bites of food from Rand's lunch selections, I started to ramble a bit. I paused only when he would eat as I followed the food to the edges of his lips. I was getting easily distracted, but then I calmed myself and told Rand a little about why I was pursuing this project now. I explained that I'd been through a painful divorce and I was beginning a new chapter in my life. I offered little in the way of details, hoping to make it clear I didn't want to revisit this subject. I needed to take a moment in my life to recapture my dream and goals and was hopeful that he could help me with that. I talked innocently to him about losing love and wanting to fill my days now with work and keep busy – that love wasn't something for me anymore. Rand looked and closed his eyes for a moment and there was something else that appeared in the blue when he reopened them, something in his thoughts but I didn't press. He knew I sought out approval for this venture with them, so he again said it was no problem.

Rand said, "Madison, all of us hurt and have been cut deep. We look for a new start, if we can ever find it." I wasn't sure where that part of our conversation was heading but he smiled warmly at me.

"Ready? Let's go" he said and grabbed my hand and tucked his journal under his other arm. I felt his fingers just hold the edges of my first three fingers lightly. He never paid a tab, but left a large bill under my unfinished coffee cup. He led me down the steps, waved goodbye to the staff, and we walked out to the black Hummer parked in the very front space. He released my fingers very slowly, in a way that made me shiver. I reached in my portfolio case and pulled out my voice recorder and hit record. I began to say with excitement in my voice, "This is the start of my writing Rock Notes." He opened the door for me, as he walked to the other side, in my whisper voice that began to shake on my recorder; I added "OMG!"

We drove about forty five minutes to where they had their space to rehearse. It was out in the suburbs of the city, in Bucks County. As we pulled up onto the location I stared at the oversized, completely redone barn. It was a sight to take in. I had seen many old barns, but this has a modern twist to its exterior. The architecture was beautifully done, not where I expected a band would rehearse. There were several acres of cleared, rolling green property that surrounded it and there was a custom built home off in the corner. It was such an awesome home; it looked like something from that television show on HGTV would have built. I wondered if their rehearsals were a nuisance to the neighbors. When I questioned him on it, he simply replied that he knows the owner and the owner never complains. We had exchanged brief conversation in the car, mostly about how much mileage does the Hummer get, weather and stupid, yes stupid, conversation topics from me. I had blundered through the conversation, but most of the unspoken communication came from Rand. He often glanced over at me and smiled, just simply smiled. I put music on and when it was their music on his playlist I said stupidly, "This is a great tune." Again, Rand flashed me his simple smile, not telling me how dumb I was coming across.

When we pulled into the open area to park in front of the barn, he told me to wait. He came around and opened the Hummer door for me. Thomas had not done this in years; I always let myself out of my side. It was such a nice gesture from Rand and the start of our business together and I hoped that the band would be as comfortable and welcoming to me.

Where do I begin? The band, all too charming, and hot looking, not as charming as Rand, and definitely not the heat of Rand's looks, but they were like a band of brothers to one another. Don't get me wrong, they talked up their stories of the girls they won and tossed. Yes tossed, and their words pitted in my stomach but I knew I had to suppress that and be calm. Rand even said, "Madison, good luck with us, you may not like us, other days you may, but don't fall for any of us, we're dysfunctional."

"Who's not functional?" was shouted by one of the band members from behind us. That gave us all cause to laugh and then I then began to meet each of the band members.

Introductions began with none other than Isaac; the person the band was named after. He was a local to the Philly area, and from what I had seen one incredible guitar player. I was introduced to him as *my front row.*

I asked, "Why was I named that?"

"Rand saw you in the front row of our show and he never took his eyes off you." Isaac's answer tugged at my heart.

Isaac seemed to be the loudest of the members and oh so ready to party. He already had a few girls waiting for him. Hoping for a kiss and that he might stay with them. I'm not sure if he needed this attention as he was a confident guy. My first take on Isaac was he was the life of any party.

I was talking with him about what I do for a living, and Rand came and tugged at him for a moment. Rand said something to him and then Isaac replied, "Hell yes, to the front row chick." Just like that, I was approved to follow along with them.

The other members then came over and were introduced to me. Next I spoke with Raeford who played the drums. He was from the Midwest, Decatur, Illinois. He was the silent one of the band I was told, and he looked so much like Usher. Rand had filled me in that Raeford brought the funk and soul to some of their songs. To me, he seemed mysterious, quiet but when I saw him on the drums the evening before he went off, so I knew he had another side.

I was introduced to Ron and Kent last. Ron was their keyboard player, wearing sunglasses indoors – in the evening. I wasn't sure what that was about but he was very friendly. Ron welcomed me aboard and told me he was from the south. He had a slight southern drawl and was very kind. Kent was from upstate in Pennsylvania, from a small town called Clarkes Summit and he was the bass player. He was the most muscular, or should I say overly muscular, he would intimidate any person at a gym. He was very solid and fit and had a shaved head and a few piercings. He said he was destined for the military until he met up with these guys and music took over. As Kent approached me, he did not hesitate to pick me up and twirl me about and then he planted, yes planted, solidly a kiss right on my lips. I was shocked for the moment and they all laughed and he released me. The only one who seemed annoyed was Rand. He shook his head "no" to Kent and then Kent smirked at him as he simmered in his joyous greeting.

Rand told the rest of the band that I was going to write about them and to be themselves and pretend I wasn't there so I could capture them raw and real as much as possible. Rand then took me over to an area that was the loft of the barn, completely furnished with sofas and chairs and a bar that overlooked their practice stage area. As he left to head down to practice he said "Madison there's beer, help yourself and get writing. I believe it will be very interesting."

I pulled out my voice recorder and spoke into it a lot of my initial thoughts. I also pulled out my portfolio and laptop and began to type and type. The title read alone on a full page – *Rock Notes.* The band practiced for several hours, I periodically got up and stretched. I turned away and decided to help myself to a beer, well a few in the timeframe and then I walked over behind the sofa area to see **The Wall** up close and personal. This was amazing; it was huge and had a backdrop on it like a brick wall. I scanned over all the contents and in the center was the band's name, Rolling Isaac's and in each area of the wall a band member had a large area of their name and keepsakes. I saw Rand's area and there were photos of him with many, many young girls. So many photos of him with his microphone, on his knees singing and it looked like he was on the verge of crying. Next to one of these photos was a beautiful photo of a girl, so model like in looks. She had dark hair similar to his in color and shoulder length like his. She also had the most beautiful blue eyes. Next to this picture, were words signed by Rand, it read, *I will forever love you Ashley.* It took my breath away for a moment and I thought that perhaps this was the love of his life. Maybe it went bad, or perhaps they were still together, although I wasn't about to ask.

I saw many newspaper clippings and articles about all of them posted all over **The Wall**. I searched to see if my column was there and it was. I reread what I had written several years ago and I was surprised at the end of the article to see a circle around my name. Yes, just below my column photo, there was a definite circle around just my name, *Freelance Columnist – Madison Tierney.*

It was a good piece of writing if I say myself and it brought the band a lot of attention. I had done research on different bands in the city and had listened to their earlier music and critiqued it and wrote a piece about their sound and their following, although I never met them. So here I was now after meeting them, and I smiled that here I was a piece of their famous **Wall**.

Throughout their rehearsal I caught many moments of Rand staring at me. He was singing and it felt as if he was driving his voice right through me. I was always a fan of Rock music and when Rand began to sing a slow ballad, I was unable to move, I felt weak as it tore me up. It was about love lost and the emptiness you undergo and time spent on love that was gone in a moment. I wasn't sure if he had glanced my way then to see the tears in my eyes but I hoped he hadn't because I didn't want him to think I was that pathetic. Love lost was definitely where I was. He glanced up to me in the loft as soon as he finished the final melody, adding another verse without anyone playing the music. It was then that I turned away with tear filled eyes and I walked over to choke down another beer hoping to dissolve the lump in my throat.

As their evening rehearsal, or should I say early morning rehearsal came to a close, he headed up to me in the loft area. Some of the band guys had earlier invited some of their friends which were girls, to come hang out near the stage during their rehearsal. I stayed up in the loft the entire time away from them putting some of my thoughts to notes. I was watching Rand as he had stopped, yet again, to kiss another pretty young girl and patted her on the ass.

When he reached me I said, "So are you spreading the love?"

He replied, "Madison, I have no love, I just make them feel good. Actually, I feel nothing." He said, "I lost love for anything long ago." I felt bad for starting this conversation and told him I was sorry for the intrusion into his personal life. I had a few too many beers and I know I tend to get all curious and weepy when I drink. I gathered my belongings and then he pulled my hand toward him but I wasn't certain where we were going. I thought we'd go back to get my car in the city, but then he said, "Madison, come with me," in a serious, sexy tone. A few girls were hooking up with some of the band members. Isaac was loud in shouting out to two girls that they were both for him this morning. Rand never said goodbye to them, he just waved a hand up and we walked from the loft to outside into the morning darkness and then down the path toward the house just beyond.

As we walked I asked him if we were going to wake anyone at this house. I also suggested to him that I only lived out by the National Park, only about a half hour away so if it wouldn't be a problem he could just take me home instead of all the way to the city for my car. He did not answer; he simply took hold of my hand and led me closer to the grand front door. When we got in front he removed a key and opened the door to a beautiful, lavish wooden foyer. Rand then spoke. "I've had too many beers and you look beat, I say we get your car when the sun comes up." He then said as he brushed past my ear tucking a fine wisp of hair behind my ear, "Madison, make yourself comfortable in my home. You can crash down in any of the rooms upstairs. There are plenty of boxes of the band's tee shirts if you want to change, help yourself. He continued with, "You're now part of our band" and his eyes sparkled and he smiled and then he headed toward the kitchen.

"Madison what can I get you?" he asked with an intriguing tone.

While what I really preferred is to spend more time with him, even at this late hour, I replied, "I don't need anything but thank you, all I really need is some sleep." He laughed and replied, "I'm getting cases of Red Bull for you to keep up with us on the road."

"Don't worry I will keep up, today was just a long introduction."

"Madison we have only just begun, but sleep well."

It really had been a very long afternoon and evening, and I was mentally exhausted trying to process all that had happened today. I headed toward the upper level and went in the very first room to crash. I laid my body on the first bed I saw not bothering with my clothes. Since it was spring and the evening weather was nice, I had worn a crème colored lace cami top with a floral sweater over it and jeans, but I barely recall slipping the sweater over my head.

Once my eyes closed, my thoughts turned to Rand, lost soul, lost love, so similar to me but then on stage he was so confident and sure of himself and his place in the world. That confidence was something that I lacked. He attacked the stage and all his charm and stunning looks dissolved those that set their eyes or minds on him. My mind kept trailing over and over about him. His deep blue eyes, his messy dark hair that just swept over his shoulder, his towering height, his hidden inks. I could think of nothing but him.

I tensed for a moment when I felt someone hovering over me. I felt a breath and caught the scent of Rand fresh from a shower. I was lying on my side and I slightly opened my eyes. I knew I was seeing him, not dreaming. I could see him getting closer and I shut my eyes, remaining so very still. He reached down, took his curved fingers down my cheek, so slowly and tenderly and then he leaned in and kissed me on the forehead. Trailing his mouth down from my forehead he placed a soft kiss on the side of my neck and then moved upward to the tip of my shoulder and he lightly bit at my cami strap. I was so completely shocked and although I wanted to reach around and tell him I was awake, I couldn't move. I had hopes that in the darkness he didn't see me see peak out at him moments earlier. He then whispered, "Night Madison" and he tugged off my boots and pulled a light blanket over me.

When the sun appeared in the bedroom I awoke all nervous, I got up and went to the bathroom. I had to search my purse for items to make myself presentable. It had only been about four hours that I slept. I gathered my boots and put my sweater back on and went downstairs to find Rand already wide awake and in the kitchen making us some breakfast.

"I'm starving," he said looking at me like he was ready to devour me. "Madison what are you hungry for?"

He made me hesitate to answer him, I was definitely hungry for him. "I think I could eat something." My stomach was excited and jumping inside just from seeing him so relaxed and cooking.

"Your phone has been vibrating all morning."

"What's vibrating?" I was too focused on his body and didn't hear his words.

"Your phone, you left it on the steps last night with your computer."

"Oh, okay that's what was vibrating." I was still watching his body in motion, and was thinking of how I would like him to make me stir. He caught me staring at him and I looked away and then I remembered I had silenced my phone during their practice and then powered it up when we walked over to the house. I had to pull myself together so I went to retrieve my phone and I looked at all the missed messages, they were from Jillian. I hollered back, "Rand, I just need a few minutes to check my messages." I went into his main front room and dialed her back.

"Where the hell are you?" Jillian yelled. She was so worried that I hadn't called her and she stopped by my place having her own key and I was no where to be found. It took some effort to calm her but I told her briefly what had happened since the concert.

"Jillian can you take me to Philly today to get my car? I don't want to put Rand out anymore. I'll just see if he can bring me back to my house."

"I'll agree only on one condition, I want every single detail, don't leave anything out, I want all of them!" I had to put my hand over the phone as she said this. She was so loud and I hoped Rand did not hear any of this.

"Hey, I should go, I don't want to be rude, he is making me breakfast," I whispered to her.

"No I bet you're his breakfast…but I'll come get you at noon. You can tell me then how great this sexy man is."

I didn't get to comment, as she hung up too quickly. Rand flashed me a sexy smile when I returned to the kitchen, I wasn't sure if he heard any of our conversation. I did look up at the high ceiling in his house and knew each word spoken echoed.

"Wow this smells and looks so good," I commented but wanted to say you look and smell so good.

"Madison, take notes, you can write this too, I can cook and I am very good." Again that sexy smile pursed on his lips.

Before me was a breakfast feast. There were berry filled pancakes, sliced fruit, fresh squeezed orange juice and turkey sausage links and of course coffee made just like he had ordered for me at the coffee shop and it was in a large to go cup that read 2nd Street Coffee Café. I bet he had tons of these to go cups, he said he was a regular there.

As we sat at breakfast Rand was still writing something in his journal.

"Rand, this tastes delicious, thank you."

"Madison you seem so easy to please."

"I am a simple person, but I want to know about you, can I ask you a question?"

"Ask away Madison."

"Well this is a lovely home" I began and "well did you always live here? Was it your parents'? How did you and the band meet? Who inspired your music?"

Rand began, "Hey slow down, you said a question" he paused, "and that's several questions. But, yes, this is my home; built the year after our band got our big break. I figured since my mother, Angela had passed away from cancer right before then and she left me money I would do something good. I had the recording studio built for our rehearsals. It honored her as I continued with my passion for music."

I looked at him and smiled tenderly and then wrote some notes. He continued to answer my numerous questions. "My inspiration was my grandfather Archer, he taught me music from as far back. He was great but he left this world before my mother." Rand continued, "If I ever have a son he will be called Archer after my grandfather." And there was a smile on Rand's face like a child at an amusement park for the first time. I held his look of pure love that he displayed as he mentioned his mom and grandfather, it was so endearing and then doing what I do best, I blurted out, "What about your father is he proud of you?"

"Well," Rand replied in a serious tone, "not someone I want to discuss, to me he is Paul and right now dead to me. He never really acted like a father. When my mom got ill, he couldn't handle it, he left. He hated I played music. Hated I was the singer in a band. He hated that Ashley was my biggest cheerleader. I'm young, I stayed out late, I drank and he told me I lacked responsibility and purpose. He told me to get a real job in the business world, but not be a singer in a band."

I looked at him as he answered and mouthed silently that I was sorry. I was sorry to hear about his mother passing and his dad's desertion. I saw his eyes swell but not break, perhaps this was his love lost.

I wanted to change the subject and said, "Rand, I have lost too, most recently, my husband, Thomas. We were married ten years. He just one day up and left me, for someone at his office. The one good memory that I have from my wedding was the flowers. They were my favorite – delicate crème roses with dark pink edging. I don't want to bore you but Thomas had become my life and world for a long time. As for my family life, it's only me. I was an only child. It was lonely. I guess that is why I love Jillian so."

I never stopped. Once I got started, I kept right on going. "And, to make my life crazier, my mother, Grace left my father, John and I for my father's younger brother Jake. She and my uncle moved off to Galveston, Texas. I haven't heard from her since."

Rand responded, "Wow your mom leaving with your uncle that's hard."

"It was, and I found myself swamped with the memories of her abandoning us, of how it felt and how I knew that I'd never truly understand relationships again."

"Do you miss her?"

"I do, she is my mother, but I never knew how to reach out to her. Since I was still with my father, I didn't want to add to his sorrow of her departure. The only saving grace, per se, for my father during that awful time was that he didn't need to raise me as I was already a teenager."

"So tell me about your father."

"Well, he was a police officer; he was a little tough on me since I was his only child. He recently retired but back during his days on the beat, he was strong like a Robocop. Everyone looked up to him. His fellow officers called him Mick, but everyone else called him Mr. McCormick out of respect. He was a very strong man but her leaving us really broke him I lived it and witnessed it."

"I miss my mother and uncle being part of my life. My mother was a true romantic and very creative so I think I have her to thank for my writing traits. But the romance part I no longer have. I hope I am not boring you with my story?"

Rand looked happy that I was sharing stories with him, "Madison not at all, I like when you talk to me, you're very…interesting."

I decided to continue and told him how I met Thomas after which I took a deep breath and then let out.

"My father adores him, and when we divorced my father blamed it on me. He told me that I didn't try hard enough to love and stay with Thomas. I haven't had the chance to repair this relationship with my father, if there is any to fix. Even now my father and Thomas talk and get together, that hurts me."

"I'm sure he adores you, what's not to like." Rand took my hand into his and began to stoke his thumb over my knuckles. "Maybe in time you and your father will reconnect." Rand could see me pushing through this with pained eyes so he changed the family topic rant of mine to geography. I was immediately grateful for his attempt to distract me and got lost in Rand's story as he kept hold of my hand with his soothing light touch.

He began to tell me that he always lived in the city and loved the vibe. He also explained how his music career all began by singing at the 2nd Street Coffee Café. Later, he ran into some other musicians and it was Isaac that shouted one drunken night for them to form a band. They all agreed to pursue this venture and their dreams of making their music together. It allowed them to combine their individual musical talents. They all fell into it quite nicely and the band in turn took off from local venues to now statewide venues. They decided together to name themselves ***Rolling Isaac's*** as Isaac always rolled into the practice sessions late. They didn't have a demanding schedule since they tried to stay grounded in normal life, but they did have a manager to oversee their schedules and travel and bookings.

Rand told me about his Uncle Maxwell, who had been hired to be the band's manager. He was Rand's mother's brother who took a special interest in Rand after is mother died and his father left. Maxwell was very good at the finances and the other business aspects of music. Rand's Uncle Maxwell had never had any children and never married. He had built himself a nice bank account from working in the music industry early and no one to share with, except his nephew Rand. Maxwell took care of all the schedules and arrangements from the band's equipment, to venue. He kept all the big things that went into a performance with the band low key. Maxwell took care of his guys and wanted them to focus on the music. Maxwell let them do what they did well; create their tunes while he ran around behind the scenes.

Rand continued to tell me that he had been named after his uncle and always felt a strong bond with him. His uncle always encouraged Rand to write his own songs. He was very proud and never disappointed in the career path Rand chose. He believed Rand had such talent and his music was a true art form.

The knowledge of his losses pained me since I too knew that feeling of loss. Rand then started on an upbeat note to change the tempo of our conversation. "This book is going to be great! You're a good luck charm to our band when you write about us. Plus this time I'm looking forward to hanging with you." I got up to help him with the dishes and he said, "Madison, leave it, go crash in the sunroom. I know you only slept a few hours." I wasn't about to disagree. I turned to head to the other room, as we were standing very close, he brought up his hand to the side of my cheek and touched me gently. Just as he did while I lay pretending to sleep last night. I gushed inside, I could not wait to share this with Jillian, but then I stopped. If he could not love then what was this? Just to make me feel good like he had with kissing those girls last night and many other nights in the past? I was confused and so I walked out into the stunning, bright sunroom.

The décor was masculine but eclectic. Several music themed items were in there and the rays of sunshine warmed the room as I curled up in the taupe colored leather loveseat looking outdoors and taking in the property from this view. My eyelids got heavy and I drifted.

My phone sounded and I jumped up. It was Jillian heading to my house already. Rand was lying at the other edge of the loveseat with me, leaving only about eight inches of separation between us and he was writing in his journal.

"Can I bother you? I need to get home Jillian is coming to take me to get my car. I left it parked on 5th Street yesterday."

"No bother Madison, I can take you all the way to your car."

"No, Jillian is heading to my house anyway and she lives in the city so it's not out of her way."

"Oh, that's right you have a story to tell her, she wants to hear all about us." He started to laugh.

"Oh, I guess you heard our conversation." I was blushing.

I diverted that topic and said. "I just bought a new white Audi. I just didn't want to leave it in the city too long."

"Hey don't worry I'll get you back and I'll meet Jillian." He laughed and then said, "If I don't get you to her soon your phone will never stop ringing."

Jillian was already in my driveway when we arrived. Just like so many others, she knew who Max Rand was, but she's never met him. When he jumped out and came to open my door, her eyes got large. And then, when he took my computer and belongings into his arm, she smiled brightly. When he walked up to my door and met with her, he took her hand lightly and introduced himself, and she melted. He had that way with all the girls and lately the grown women as well.

"Rand thank you so much for the ride and the writing opportunity. I will talk to you later to go over your travel schedule." I gave him a quick hug and started to move away.

He pulled me close and said, "Madison, we leave in the morning. It's going to be a packed schedule, first Florida, and then we come back to Philly for a few weeks. Then we have Atlanta, Texas and back here to Philly to regroup." He then moved one hand to touch the side of my face as his lips lingered on my cheek what seemed a very long moment. I nervously pulled my face away, and then Rand said, "I spoke with my Uncle Maxwell and all arrangements are done. We will be by around ten tomorrow morning, so you better get packing!"

He pulled me in for a hug and smiled to Jillian who was standing behind me. When he released me, I was still leaning toward him even after he had left and driven off.

Jillian whispered, voice quivering "Holy Shit!"

Chapter Two – Traveling

Thank God for Jillian again in my life, I was frantic, talking incomplete sentences. Filling her in on the past two amazing days and trying to pack for a few weeks, when I had so much trouble dressing for just the other evening. Jillian was shocked that I had gotten up enough confidence to approach Max Rand. She didn't know that I had on other occasions attempted to reach out to his manager Maxwell, but had not gotten a reply. I hadn't shared this will Rand either.

Jillian worked for an advertising firm in the city and we had become close over the years when I wrote for the city column but so much closer when I had died inside and needed someone to bring me back to life after Thomas's exit. She helped me so. She was like the sister I never had. She was always fiercely supportive of me. She understood my goals and my passion for writing and encouraged me. My father was not supportive of me becoming a writer. He thought I was a dreamer and wanted something more from me.

After Thomas and I divorced, my own father questioned me about what I did wrong that lead us to divorce. With all my insecurities this only brought me down and so I wasn't really in touch with him anymore. I felt as though I didn't measure up in his eyes, that perhaps it was my mom he saw when he looked at me. I always saw his disappointment.

As I started to pack Jillian was going over and over what I should do, not do, what to wear, not to wear and she was still beaming about the meeting and seeing the handsome Max Rand. Actually, a thought had entered my head that Jillian would have been a girl I could see with Rand. Why with her stunning good looks and long, straight, always perfectly placed reddish hair, she knew how to take over a room of people. Her smile captivated all, and I know that she had the biggest heart in the world, and he surely needed heart. But then I thought here I was, just plain simple Madison, I too needed love, but couldn't go there again. I was trying to be calm playing off that I too was overwhelmed by his great looks and his new found kindness toward me.

Jillian said shaking her head, "Madison, he is so freaking hot why didn't you sleep with him? I would have jumped in bed with him, you're crazy."

"I felt him come near me last night, but nothing happened," I thought about last night and licked my lower lip.

"Madison, there's a vibe coming off you two."

"Girlfriend something is here, it feels really good," I smiled; I too had a feeling but didn't want to act on it knowing Rand emphasized he could never love again.

While finishing up packing, we decided that we would go for a drink and a bite to eat in the city when we headed in to pick up my car. I don't know how I did it, but packing wasn't that bad. Perhaps all those business trips I packed Thomas for came in handy, as I got it all done in a few hours time. Jillian spoke all the way to get my car. "I want you to check in weekly, not daily that would be too much, but girlfriend if you have great news or sex, especially sex I want to hear it right away." She told me perhaps we could meet up. It would surely be fun for us to catch up for a girl's weekend while I was on the road and take in the show.

I decided on the way into the city that I needed a haircut. It had been a good few months; my hair had grown out longer and lacked shape. I wanted it styled nicely to have it take less time to style while on the trip. Not that this mattered but I was thinking I wanted to look better, perhaps because I was finally feeling a bit better about myself. For so many months I simply pulled my hair back and wore slight makeup, not out to impress anyone anymore.

Jillian said, "Great let's get you beautified. I have wanted to get my nails touched up and we can talk, because I have missed you the past few days."

After our girl primping we stopped to grab a bite at a local eatery called, Matyson. How appropriate. We loved this place. Their lunches were good and their dinners better. We chatted and had a few glasses of wine and finally I told her I really needed a decent night sleep so I was going to go. I only had a few blocks to walk to get my car and before I grabbed my purse a few familiar faces stopped by our table.

Jillian could not contain her excitement for me and blurted out, "Maddy's leaving with a band to write about them, isn't this exciting?" The faces were familiar because they were old friends of both of us, but one was still friends with Thomas and I hoped this would not get back to him. As we hadn't spoken in months, I kept out of any gossip about him and expected that he do the same. For awhile from friends, I had heard Thomas and the woman he was seeing weren't working out. I also know he was asking what I had been up to. I know I wasn't dating, considering it or even trying to find love. It's not that I can't love again, but I wasn't sure I would pick wisely. I was still trying to understand what happened to Thomas and me. I then spoke, "It's really not a big deal about the band" and tried to downplay it and asked them what they had been up to lately hoping we could change the conversation.

Jillian got up and hugged me and said in a whisper, "I love you girlfriend, be safe and I'll call you in the morning. Oh and try to have a great time." She stayed behind at the restaurant as I left and struck up conversation with the others.

As I walked toward my car, I suddenly got pissed even as I was still several feet from the car. I saw a ticket on my windshield. I knew I parked in a spot that wasn't metered, I was sure. I was getting angry, wondering why I would have a ticket. I looked at the signage near my car and it surely was a spot with no restrictions. I grabbed the ticket and threw it on the seat and climbed in. I set my purse on the seat and glanced down to the ticket. It read –

> *As I leave this note on yet another White Audi parked on 5th Street, I'm not sure this will get to you or at what time, but I may be at the 2nd Street Coffee Café so if you want to stop by maybe we can talk. I'd like to see you, Rand*

Another heart stopping moment, from pissed that I got a ticket to the thought of catching up with him. I wondered if I should I just pass it up, or should I go. I had to do something first, so I got out of the car and walked the entire block to find the other white Audi and remove the note. I didn't want any other person to get the note and be meeting up with Rand.

I walked in to the coffee shop smiling and heading upstairs. I looked about and saw that he was not there, I checked downstairs as well then I asked one of the employees carrying coffees and desserts to a table and she told me she thought he just left. Oh well, I guess I missed him, so I started back to my car. As I rounded the corner to 5th Street there he was leaning against my car. He looked so incredibly good, as my eyes traveled from the sidewalk level of his feet planted on the ground in front of me, to his chest, then to his lips smiling on his face. I felt the urge to run up and hug him, but who was I to even think that? He wasn't that way with me; we were barely anything, just friendly.

I smiled and as I came close to the car. He moved toward me and took hold of my hand and pulled me into him. He kissed me, and it felt like my first kiss, a passion in his lips as he gazed directly into my eyes. As I shut my lids taking this in, I knew I wasn't dreaming this, or over thinking this. I kissed him back with a sweetness and softness and nervousness. It was an amazingly sexy, long, lingering kiss, and he trailed his lips up over the side of my cheek and he said, "Madison, love the new hair." He then nuzzled his messy dark hair into my head and breathed in. "You're beautiful, so beautiful."

My new hair style was going to be much easier and it was more sophisticated the stylist told me. I now had a look where long pieces trailed along the sides of my face and it was much shorter in the back.

He remained pressed into my hair and then started to lick at the piece at the side of my face. That turned into to a kiss on my ear, down my earring dropping off to my neck and then trailing on my neck to my collarbone area. I got lost in him as Rand continued lightly placing delicate kisses all around my neckline. His mouth was so warm on my skin. He was making me wet and aroused so quickly. I had forgotten I was on a street near my car. He felt so good, he made me feel again. I hadn't felt like this for so long. He suddenly pulled back and I stared at him in surprise. I wanted more, I wish he didn't stop. He then spoke, "Drive safe and be packed, we'll see you tomorrow morning." After a pause he said, "Good night my Madison." His voice had taken on a low, sexy tone with these last words.

I was stunned and sat in the car and had to remember how to put the key into the ignition, how to actually start the car. Still shaken I had to turn on the headlights and move from the parking space to go home. He walked down the street and turned, I guess, to find his vehicle. Just before he was out of sight he turned and smiled. I had not taken my eyes off of him, watching him through my windshield. On the ride home I wanted to call and tell Jillian but didn't because I didn't know what this was. Was it a game, or was it real? Why would he kiss me if he feels nothing for anyone? So many questions were going through my head and then so many things I needed to get accomplished in just the next few hours. I had to send a reminder text to Jillian to get my mail. I had to pay my upcoming bills online before I left and, and I am sure I was forgetting something else.

The limo arrived on time the next morning and I felt like a princess or a prom queen as the band all got out welcoming me with hugs. Again, it was Kent that turned his tight bear hug into a stolen kiss, and Rand pulled him away. Then it was Rand that snuck a kiss into my hair inhaling deeply at the back of my head, and a lick to the lower part of my neck just where my hair fell, as I entered the limo. We loaded up and we were all heading to our first stop, Florida.

Thoughts were spinning in my head with travel and excitement and so much of this was out of character for me. As Rand led me to the seat next to him I noticed a tall pile of items on top. The band members chuckled at me, I picked up the pile and there were a few Rolling Isaac's tee shirts, tank tops, a hat and a VIP Access Pass for me to have backstage access and/or the front row access to all their shows. Rand spoke, "Anytime you want, you can bring someone to our shows. Just give us a heads up and we'll hook you up VIP Access passes for them." I thought this was going to be great and perhaps Jillian could come to one of their shows in the future. A touch of sadness was creeping in on me as I realized how much I was missing my sister friend already and then I had to break into a laugh as at the bottom of the items there was a case of Red Bull with a note attached that read:

Madison, please take once a day to keep up with the band and me, Rand.

Rand pushed the items aside smiling and I sat down beside him startlingly aware of his hand around my waist the entire ride to the airport. His thumb made little fluttering circles on my back, slightly lifting my shirt and touching my bare skin. His thumb moved in a pattern, as if he was tapping out the rhythm of a song, making little circles and shifting the beat to go in reverse. I tingled, chilled and smiled and lightly licked my lips in anticipation of the trip and how he made me feel.

Our arrival in Florida was sunny, first stop was Jacksonville. I was told we would be going down A1A on the coastline to Fort Lauderdale and then to South Beach. The band had mentioned a surprise awaiting me in South Beach, but with guys talking you never quite know what they are implying. Maxwell greeted us all at the airport and was very kind to me as well. He never let on that I reached out to him, perhaps he never received my inquiries to write about the band or put two and two together as to my identity.

Maxwell explained that there were two vans to take us to the hotel, but when he told Rand to go with the band members, Rand shook his head and took my finger tips and lead me to the other van and shut the door once we entered. From the limo, to the plane, to the van, all the way to the door of my hotel room, he never let go of my finger tips. It was endearing. I felt his softness, just like I was being caressed and taken care of, and I thought that I was maybe helping him feel something back as well. As we stood in the hallway of the hotel before I entered my room, I leaned on the wall waiting for the bellman to exit the room after taking in my luggage. Rand still had a hold of two of my fingertips.

Turning toward me, he placed both of his hands on the wall. With me pinned up tightly against the wall, he stood looking down at me, holding me captive as he tilted toward my lips. He did not touch me at first, just slowly leaned down and then came in to kiss me. First, he nudged my forehead, and slid his nose down mine and then pulled back. He looked into my eyes and then came in and took one passionate kiss. My arms hung at my sides and his arms still remained firmly overhead leaning above me on the wall. Isaac was coming down the hall and hollered, "Oh, please get a room you two!"

Our lips together chuckled and we let out a breath from our noses, but we continued to kiss. I was so consumed by his lips and his unrelenting kiss. The way he kissed me, it was like he hadn't seen me for a while. I opened my eyes only to glance at his wrists and saw an inscription on the inside band of his leather wrist cuff. This was the same wrist band that I'd seen him wear at the concert and that he rubbed and twirled on the entire trip here it read, *My Love, Ashley.* I pulled away from his lips and ducked under his strong arms. The bellman was exiting at this moment so I think he thought that was why, but as I entered my room and looked back, I smiled and said calmly, "Rand I will see you later."

I shut the door and fell apart, how could I compete with this beautiful girl, Ashley, his love? Where was she? Did I dare ask or open this wound to him? I liked being kissed by Rand but with another woman holding his heart, I knew this would end for us before even starting. I figured when the time was right perhaps he would mention her, or the band would. I stood behind the door for several moments tracing my lips over and over where Rand's lips had just been. Despite my worry about Ashley, I felt like I never wanted these lips washed or touched again. Well, touched by anyone else at least.

With all of us checked in, Maxwell told the guys that he was having them practice for a bit and wanted to go over their upcoming schedule of shows. This would take a few hours and he also offered that he had food coming in for them. Men always respond nicely to food. For me, I decided to just stay back and catch up on my thoughts and writings and enjoy the amenities of the hotel. I also wanted to catch up with Jillian and let her know I arrived okay and all was good. With the band all gone and Maxwell too, I walked the hotel and toured the property taking in the pool area that was so nice and peaceful. Since it was spring and quite warm here in Florida, there still weren't too many travelers here. I believe Maxwell knew that when booking the band here to stay.

I sat for awhile, out by the pool in my clothes but started to get warm with the early afternoon sun. I thought I would head up to my room, grab my notes and change into one of my bathing suits, a bikini, that *yes*, Jillian packed. Actually, she jammed them into my suitcase saying, "Madison you have a rocking body even if you don't show it, you're heading to the South. You're going to have hot weather, sunny days, and hopefully heated nights!" I stopped her train of thought. Today, I was glad I hadn't stopped her before she had packed it for me.

As I sat by the pool, I wrote a bit and then dropped my notes next to me and lowered my beach hat to relax and take all this in. The next few hours flew by and when I looked up through the design of my hat, a thatched pattern appeared with a face just beyond. In a whisper I heard, "Madison please cover up, these guys will go crazy." Then as his voice lowered, "Please cover up now you're driving me crazy." I tilted up and lifted the brim of my large hat and adjusted my eyes realizing that I was within inches of Rand's face and he was handing me one of the hotel's large pool towels. "Here, please put this over you." He said as he actually laid it on me. Normally, at this moment I would have been so nervous and embarrassed and probably shy to be lying in my bikini, but I think it was my knowing that the young girls' eyes were on us that allowed me to remain calm and mature. I knew that I had just totally climbed two more steps of my confidence ladder.

"Rand, I must have crashed. I thought you guys would be gone for hours, and I wouldn't catch you until tomorrow at breakfast." As I spoke those words, I realized how glad I was that they returned.

Even as the sun had warmed my body outside, I knew something simmering between Rand and me was responsible for the warming inside. And for a moment, taking in the sight of him there poolside, in his shorts and tight tee shirt, I think he was the one who needed the covering up. A few young girls had already switched their lounging pool chairs to get closer to where I was and I know it was not to get a glimpse of me.

I got up and wrapped the towel around my waist but my bathing suit top was still on display. I leaned back down into the chair letting out a sigh like Rand had just won in succeeding in getting me covered up. I had definitely taken in some color in the past few hours out here at the pool and I looked at Rand as he touched my skin in between my chest and neck and said, "You got color," his fingers drifted up and down my sun soaked skin between my breasts, and traveled up to my throat, then he slowly outlined my entire bathing suit top like he was memorizing the shape. I was breathless; I had to actually bite the inside of my cheek to keep it from quivering. He said again, "Would you please cover up you can't do this to me." I know I wasn't doing anything; he could have any girl as they were all there for the taking and ready to be with him anyplace and surely at anytime. I was just lying in the afternoon sun relaxing, but to make him happier I pulled on a Rolling Isaac's tank top, and he smiled while we walked back toward the hotel.

Their first concert in the sunshine state was great, although I expected nothing less. The band left together and I stayed behind to ride over with Maxwell a bit later. I was excited to have my backstage pass, but when we got to the venue, I soon found I would rather be in the front row with them all singing out toward me than seeing their butts all night, not that that wasn't a nice sight either. While they were setting up I was back stage with them all and felt like a part of their team.

Isaac was loud and commenting about the huge crowd and loud again as he talked about all the hot girls. He was even calling them out by their clothes. "The one in the purple tank top," or "the one in the yellow halter." Obviously he didn't know their names, only their clothing color and description but for him that was enough. Raeford, he was kind and seemed in thought a lot and took the shows seriously. He brushed past me and said, "Madison you looked great at the pool." I blushed as I didn't hear him talk too much yet and I didn't even know he was out there. I thought it was only Rand with me.

Kent, well he was another story. He again spun me around and when I turned so he could not plant a kiss on me, he turned and grabbed my ass tightly and said, "Hey you can write this." It was all funny – he didn't mean any harm. He was just being Kent and, well, it seemed to slightly ruffle Rand's mood. Rand took a few steps back and headed over to talk to Maxwell briefly, but still kept his blue eyes on me.

It was Ron that surprised me this evening. Again in his sunglasses, and it was dark out, he came over and raised his glasses before speaking. "I've played some music at our practice to lyrics Rand's been writing, it's sounding pretty cool. It's a ballad with him singing and me playing the keyboards. He and I will have to perfect it before we perform it. I think you are a good influence and inspiration for him. Thanks for being here."

A tear welled in my left eye, but I quickly said back, "God these lights are so bright don't they make your eyes tear?"

Ron replied, "Why do you think I'm always wearing sunglasses?"

As they took the stage, the crowd roared, the lights started to dance all over and the fog covered the surface of the stage. Rand shouted to the crowd, "Hello Jacksonville, we are Rolling Isaac's!" Rand turned and mouthed me a kiss, I was pretty certain it was to me, but the many girls surrounding me in the crowd before him all let out sighs and screams. I watched how truly captivating he was and how he just pulled in your every emotion as he sang.

It was midway through their playlist that I saw the lights dim and Rand took a corner position toward where I sat in the front row, or actually stood as I was on my feet almost the entire concert. He hung his head, gently cradling the microphone and a tear fell from one eye. He did not wipe it, and I just followed it down until it hit the stage below in what appeared to me, slow motion. The crowd was silenced and then Rand did what he did best. He used his incredible voice and sexual moves to tug on every single girl's heart including mine. Then as quickly as a ballad had slowed the audience down and saddened us all, they ramped up the next tune and were back to rocking the house.

"That was awesome!" I shouted at Maxwell, mostly because I think the loud music deadened my hearing a bit. Maxwell smiled and said, "I'm proud of Rand even with what has happened in his life he still pours his soul into the music." Maxwell was to be my designated driver back to the hotel, so we did not linger back stage at all. Actually he wanted to head there and so I figured seeing the band off in the distance high fiving and opening up beers that I would slip out with him.

It was when we went to get in the van, I was taken aback. I viewed a large group of very pretty young girls, heading back to where the band was hanging out and drinking. I only saw a few seconds of Isaac reaching out and lifting one young girl up onto his shoulders and walking off with her and then Rand leaning in and kissing another.

The evening of Jacksonville, now became a repeat scenario a few days later in Fort Lauderdale. Another hotel and more practice for them and I actually stayed a bit distant from Rand since I still had his face so clearly in my mind. Reaching out and bringing that lovely girl close to his thighs, grabbing her waist tightly and pulling her in for a kiss that evening. When he asked me why I was quiet lately, I just told him I was pouring myself into my writing. He continued to lead me about with finger tip holds a few quick breaths to my ear, and cheek kisses.

In Fort Lauderdale, I actually emailed Jillian a very lengthy email and let her know my writings were coming along and I enjoyed their first gig. I did not mention the butterflies in my stomach in Rand's presence, nor did I tell her about the way it felt when he touched me. That he could lead me almost any place and I'd follow. I definitely didn't tell her I saw the kiss that twisted my stomach, very effectively smothering my butterflies. I sent her their upcoming schedule highlighting the Atlanta date, and since she had family there it might work perfectly. Jillian and I could visit her brother Jason and after seeing him we could go to a show together. I told her to let me know and we could work out the travel details. I told her I loved her and did miss her, and yes, I was totally having fun.

While I usually ate most breakfasts with the band before they headed out to practice, I was usually on my own for lunch.

I walked along the Fort Lauderdale Marina for a bit enjoying the sight of the vast yachts and the day's beautiful weather. I visited a few shops on the well known Las Olas

Boulevard and then I finally stopped at a restaurant that faced the water from across the street and ordered some lunch. I was enjoying these quiet afternoons. Just then my phone sounded.

I've missed you since breakfast, sorry Maxwell held me up talking. Kent didn't hesitate to jump in and take my seat next to you this morning. You handled Kent well. Please wash that left side of your face before I come to kiss it later – Rand

My heart pinged, I exhaled on a long breath. I stared at the beautiful beach, this lovely day and thought this is a wonderful life. I texted him back.

The breakfast that you make is sooooo much better and so is the company. I am beachside taking this all in. Have a good rehearsal. Oh and I'm wearing shorts and a tank top; yes I am clothed even though I'm beachside so you need not worry.

My phone sounded once more.

Madison I always worry, always where you're concerned. Shorts and a tank top, still to skimpy. You have no idea how us men think.

I replied back,

At least it's a Rolling Isaac's tightly fitted tank top, which should make you smile.

I received a yellow smiley face back on my phone screen.

Well tonight was another concert in Fort Lauderdale. Again in a repeat fashion like the movie Ground Hog Day where things kept taking place over and over, I went to the show with Maxwell. I think he enjoyed my company because he really had started to open up with me and talked about his passion with the band. He wanted them to succeed, but not burn out or sacrifice their lives for this, but to enjoy it and live it and really experience it. That night after the show I did not look back to the band at all. I got in the van with Maxwell and we headed back to the hotel.

I stayed up rather late as I wrote a nice piece on Maxwell taking me in and opening up to me and how he was so unlike managers taking control. He was letting them all go on a long rope, keeping them in line but not strangling them with a too demanding concert schedule and letting them enjoy their music and successes.

A slight tap came to my door, I was unaware it was almost three in the morning. I got out of bed and looked into the peep hole and there, across the hall, leaning on the wall was Rand. I opened the door and I could smell beer over the distance of several feet.

"You okay?" I asked. "Do you need me to help you to your room?"

His room was only next door to mine. He smiled, he walked to me, actually stumbled, and as he laid his head down on my shoulder he said "Madison you have no clue, no clue what you do to me. I hurt Madison, I hurt."

Not knowing if in his current condition he hurt himself, I asked "Rand what's wrong, what hurts? Where do you hurt?"

He pointed to his heart and leaned on me and handed me his room key. I walked, leaning over to get him and his drunken weight into his room. As we entered he began singing a tune that I never heard. He was singing, "My sweet nervous one, oh my sweet." The tune wasn't half bad for his state of mind. I helped him to his bed and he pulled me down with him. He laid there and didn't move too much, only to point to his heart and he kept a low singing voice and pointing to me, "My sweet nervous one." I slowly slid off the side of the bed and he did not stir, only mumbled a bit. I leaned near him and I took off his shoes and undid his belt, I tried to take it off but could not, so I just left it undone. Then, I slowly tugged on his tee shirt to loosen that up a bit to enable him up to sleep more comfortably. He reached out to me and took my hands in his and placed them up under his shirt near his heart. I curled my body right up next to the heart side of his chest and actually felt heat.

Steamy thoughts poured through my head, as my shaking fingers were touching his awesome, ripped chest, and I remained there until morning. I think it was the beating rhythm of his heart that put me to sleep.

This morning was pack up day and only a short drive further down the southern coast. The band was really excited as they would have several days off in South Beach before their next scheduled concert. So when the hotel door flew open to Rand's room and all the members entered, I was completely embarrassed and stunned. There I was tucked into Rand's chest and I believe they all assumed that something happened. I was certain of it. They could not contain their excitement and they said "Good morning Maddy," like this was nothing at all, like they were all entering their morning class and acknowledging their teacher.

As I worked my way up from being cramped to the side of Rand's body, Rand sounded, "Guys, get out, give me a few minutes I'll meet up with you at breakfast, and Madison what the hell are you doing in here so early?"

I knew he probably did not remember coming in drunk this morning and I need not fill him in, I simply said "Oh, I wanted to know what all the excitement is about this morning since we are heading to South Beach. You told us all that there was a surprise in South Beach." The guys all looked at me confused at first that I hadn't answered Rand's question and I had actually been on the bed next to him when they arrived – and all night – but they then quickly changed their morning topic. They were all glad to be heading to South Beach, and as they were exiting and they shouted that I would have to wait for the surprise until a bit later and they laughed.

Rand commented, "God I smell like crap, a brewery… I need to hit the shower." Before he left the bed though, he pulled me back into his chest, I could stay right there forever, it was so welcoming, I felt needed for that moment. As he hugged me tightly he said in a very sexy whisper, "I know you were here with me, thank you for taking care of me".

I was the latest to the breakfast feast this morning, and I do mean feast, these guys can eat. I guess since they played their hearts out once again last night and sweated pounds off singing and playing under those lights and dancing on stage, and let's not forget their after the show romps, that amount of food was probably necessary. When I walked in to the hotel's restaurant, Kent jumped up to give me his seat which was next to Rand. Rand kept his head tilted down, but I did see a smile on that face.

Maxwell started to speak, explaining that today we were heading to South Beach and pleading "Guys PLEASE go easy there…I know temptation is always around with so many beautiful women, take it easy. Madison, no offense to you, you're up there too with our list of beautiful women." I heard a low voice agree, "She sure is."

I totally blushed and then I noticed they were all heading out that they were all done their breakfast but me, as I had just taken my seat, I gave them all a wave goodbye. Rand continued to sit next to me and he reached under the table to caress my hand, he looked in my eyes, he was piercing into them and said, "It was nice feeling you close to me last night, I slept great."

I wanted to ask him about the song he was singing to me when he was drunk but I let that go. I smiled back and let him caress my hand while I ate with my other hand.

Chapter Three – Bejeweled

South Beach was a very short drive down the coast of Florida, again we were split into two vans for the ride, with the guys in one and Rand and I in the other. I wasn't sure if Maxwell was okay with this arrangement, but he seemed to enjoy his time with the boys. He never complained, he was like a coach preparing the team for their next game. He always appeared proud and didn't rattle easily. So far in my writing I was seeing some really crazy stunts by all band members, yet Maxwell never seemed to notice.

We pulled up to a nice boutique hotel as most in South Beach are which make them smaller, quaint, not your average chain hotel. This décor was vintage and from the entrance into the lobby, I felt like I had gone back in time. After we all checked in I wandered out to the property which was directly on the beach. I walked gracefully at the edge of the very long, thin rectangle shaped pool, and headed toward the huge, wooden gates that opened to the South Beach sand. Beyond there I viewed the beauty of the swaying palm trees waving to the blue ocean waters. Flanking the pool were the private, comfortable cabanas. Since it wasn't summer, a few were still empty. I walked back and climbed up into one, and felt like the Princess and the Pea. Totally surrounded by white fabric sitting within the comfortable pillow cushions, I took out my writings and put my reading glasses on and began to transcribe my latest thoughts.

There was a nice breeze carrying through the cabana and the fabric doors were tied back leaving the entrance open. I looked up several times and glanced at the few people in the pool area and at one point the server from the pool bar popped his head in to see if I wanted a beverage, so I ordered a frozen Mojito. When my drink arrived, I did not watch him set it down as I was in deep thought on my laptop. Then I noticed the lighting had decreased in the cabana, and I looked and saw Rand before me with the cabana's drapes drawn.

"Mind if I join your private cabana?" he asked.

"Not at all, it is so wonderful, I'm just taking it all in," I replied but then he stopped my voice. He sat down next to me and turned my chin toward him, he held my chin in his hand and leaned in and took over my mouth. Kissing me softly and slowly he licked my lips in between, his hands played with my hair and then he rubbed my neck and shoulders. As quickly as this began and I started to feel excitement inside, he ended the kiss. He climbed up next to me, took out his journal and put his glasses on and began to write. This was nice, but I can't explain it, he would tear me up with a passionate kiss and then be so close but, as a friend, next to me like we were growing old together.

I didn't want to give any of it up; I started to realize I felt a need for his touch, his kiss, his just being near me. As we both were off in our thoughts and writing he reached over and stroked my leg a bit, always in a drawing, artistic manner and tapping so I assumed he was writing music.

What a wonderful afternoon this had been with him, tonight would not be as serene. The band asked me to hang with them as they went out in South Beach. It began with me meeting them in the lobby. I chose to wear a black beaded halter top and lower rise jeans, and strappy sandals with a very high heel. I was thinking that if we were hitting clubs that would keep me cool, when the elevator opened to the lobby they were all clapping at how I looked, seeming like my biggest fans. During this moment it was like I had a family, a band family and I felt very warm and appreciated.

Rand was not there yet and they said he would be down shortly. Moments later Kent came up to me when we were exiting the lobby and remarked on my sexy bare back. He said that he just had to kiss it. As he leaned up to me to plant his kiss, his lips were swiftly blocked my Rand's strong hand. That was so funny; Kent actually had closed his eyes and kissed Rand's hand. All of us were hysterically laughing. We all dined earlier so we decided get some after dinner drinks.

We were staying in the heart of South Beach and bars are at every street corner. We walked up Lincoln Drive and sat for awhile ordering some shots and beers. I looked over to see Isaac having fun with the ladies there and then I saw Kent chatting it up as well. Ron, he was actually out walking about the Lincoln Drive area, which is several blocks closed off from traffic. The area contains plenty of shopping, coffee houses, restaurants and bars. I think he was crushing on a girl back in Philly and he wanted to talk to her some more. I caught him several times this week speaking to her while we traveled. Young love, so cute I thought.

Raeford, he surprised me this evening. He stayed by my side more than most nights and made certain other men didn't come up to me. It was like he was a back up for the nearness of Rand.

We all drank a lot; the shots went down too smoothly. The guys were all singing, hell I think I was singing too. Not that I was a bad singer, I sing in the shower often. A few times I saw Rand speaking with some stunning women at the side of the bar and he would glance back to me, and if Rand was away, Raeford was close to me. I decided to head back toward the bathroom, it was necessary after all these drinks. As I walked past I heard the one stunning girl at the bar that Rand was up near earlier rave about him taking her telephone number. I felt a pang of sadness hearing that but he wasn't mine, I guess I was his friend. I know I hadn't seen him lately kiss too many women or take any of them back to his room, but I also was not naïve that I only spent a few hours a day with him leaving him plenty of playtimes.

When I got back to the bar, lined up was another round of shots. I think, I know, I was way past the legal limit, we all were. I was leaning my head on Kent's shoulder and he actually did not try anything funny with me. Isaac yelled, "Let's put these down and get the hell out of here…it's a surprise you'll like, Madison!"

Rand lifted my head lightly from Kent's shoulder and took my hand, wrapping his fingers over it. We all headed a few blocks down and then I saw where we were heading, I froze even in my altered state. It was a lit store front Bejeweled Body Piercing & Tattoo. The band was excited; they were all shouting what they were going to get done. Then they turned to me and asked what I was getting done.

"No, no, I have no tattoos, no piercings, not happening to my body," I proclaimed. Next thing I know I was lying on a comfortable table in a private, back room with curtains drawn and Rand handed to Russ, the owner and skilled tattoo artist, several hundred dollars to cover the evening's piercing party for the band. The guys were all out front flirting with the female employees and selecting their piercings.

Rand stood next to me and said, "So which belly ring is it going to be?" Somehow, I had agreed to get a navel piercing. Did I really agree to this, was I crazy?

"Rand, why don't you pick it out for me," I answered. "I like how you taste, I mean I like your taste, I mean you taste good." I wasn't speaking too clearly, still feeling my head swaying with all the alcohol we consumed. Rand laughed and walked over to the counter that had hundreds of choices and I heard him select one and he handed it to the tattoo artist. As I felt the artist, Russ, coming toward me I panicked. I was so nervous and getting scared.

Rand came and took my hand and calmed me. He looked at me with those deep blue, sea calming, sexy eyes and said, "Madison trust me, it won't hurt, I think you'll really like it."

"I really don't take pain well, I like pleasure not pain, I'm sure I'll scream."

"Oh I'll take you screaming with pleasure but not here. It's going to look great. Russ here's a pro he's done all my tattoos."

Russ then asked me to undo my jeans and pull them low, and he went to move my halter top up off my stomach. Rand took over and did that, just resting my beaded top under my chest. Russ moved in and marked my belly button. Then I saw him thread something onto what looked like a fish hook.

I yelled and squeezed Rand's hand, "Oh, God, there is no way, I can't do…" Rand plunged into my mouth so deeply he swirled his tongue and traced my teeth, he remained deep in my mouth, tasting me, kissing me and not at all releasing me.

"All done, you did great!" Russ spoke and our lips parted, Russ gave a firm pat to Rand on the shoulder and exited the room. I was certain I had just stepped onto the fifth rung of my confidence ladder.

I suddenly felt a current go through my body. No pain just a rush, can't explain it. The kiss was a rush but different from this other feeling. Proud of myself for doing this, I looked down at my belly to see a tiny music note dangling. Rand bent down and kissed the area around it, saying aloud, "Madison you're now my secret musical note."

It looked great; I was staring back and forth between the piercing and Rand. He kept me lying there and continued to kiss around my navel and then brought his hand to where my beaded halter was piled and he started to push his hand so lightly underneath. Feeling my nipples, swirling each one, giving equal attention to them as he let out a deep sigh. Rand traced the outer sides of my waist with his finger tips, stopping for a moment to reach back to my face and take my mouth with his once more.

I murmured, "Oh Rand…" then he kissed my nose and I was actually trying to slow my breathing.

I pulled his tee up over his head as he was now half naked above me. It felt so amazing to look up at him and get lost in his eyes. I lowered my glance and stared at his chest, his incredible chest, and his remarkable ink that was there in front of my eyes. It was a large, very detailed cross with a lot of scrolled designs swirling and surrounding it. Entwined in the cross was an open heart outline. The ink artwork traveled down along the right side of his rib cage and waist. On his right arm from his bicep to just below his forearm is the tattoo I only got a glimpse of when I first met him. It was written ***dream of music, my beloved***. This was surrounded by detailed design work that made each of the words beautiful and endearing.

I rose upward from the table and traced the heart on his chest with the tip of my tongue and placing sweet, light kisses as I moved along the cross above me. I licked the edges of my tongue over his artwork and tasted the flavor of the skin on his chest. Oh, God, help me, I thought as this felt so good. Rand, then went back down to my belly and lightly hit the jeweled music note to make some movement, it did not hurt. I hoped my hands didn't hurt him as I began to rake at his back and his bare skin moved beneath my finger tips, and continued down and traced the tops of my fingers down his back to his hips. His hands went lower to the opening of my jeans that had been pushed out of the way and were resting just below my hip bones. He slowly and ever so lightly took his fingers to the top of my panty lace and lifted just under the seam and traced along my naked folds with his fingers inching lower.

My belly and my hips tingled with sensations and started to rise up, I felt shivers in me, and I was unaware that I could feel like this again. It was amazing. It occurred to me that if he kept this up I would shatter into a million pieces.

Lying there, I was moving my lower body to his tender tracing movements. I could feel my nipples peaking and my pulse quickening and God, I wanted him to go further. I did not want him to stop. Rand spoke in a light, sexy voice, "I can't do this, I mean I want to, I really want to, but I can't give you what you need…" But he kept kissing my stomach in between his every whispered word. I lifted my hips up off the table to meet his kisses and they became more firm. He lowered his head to my thighs and dropped it slowly into the deep fold of my jeans. He slid one arm under my rear and lifted me, pressing me more fully into his face. I fisted his hair and tightly pulled some dark strands through my fingers. The only sound I could make was, "Please, just please don't stop…"

Isaac pulled back the makeshift curtain and looked at us in our intimate position. In a low growl he said, "Now that's the kinda piercing I want." The intimacy of the moment was abruptly lost. The band guys were through having their piercings done and were ready to leave.

Rand told them to go ahead; he knew they wanted to go to the clubs until later in the morning. He wanted to hang back and return to the hotel and snuggle in the fabric covered cabana and watch the evening stars and dream – with me.

"Jillian, Jillian, pick up your phone, do not text me, I need to talk to you…" I nervously left her this same message already six times this morning. I had to talk to her, I could not sleep. It was very early in the morning, and I couldn't breathe in and out like I used to. What was happening to me? Was this an illusion or was all this really happening? I could feel something again and I didn't want to have it begin just to lose it, I was so torn. Oh, Jillian please call me, I need you sis…

Mid morning I got her call back. "Maddy what's up? You okay, your messages sounded urgent?"

"Oh Jillian, you will not believe what's happening." I rattled on and on. "I so think I could fall for him, I hope it's not a game. I feel for him, and I wish I knew he felt the same." We talked for at least two hours and she had calmed me and told me to go for it and see where it leads. She said she hoped that he would develop real feelings for me. She was glad I was out having fun and doing what I wanted with writing, but we both knew and did not say it, we knew Rand had a history with the ladies.

We talked about the calendar of concerts that I sent her. She would arrange to head to her brother Jason's and we could all meet up for a few days and she would attend a show with me in Atlanta. As we were winding up our lengthy and necessary girl talk, she paused and said, "Listen, I have something else to tell you. Thomas called your home and called me. He recently heard through the rumor mill that you're traveling around with a band. I couldn't help myself and told him they are all gorgeous hot guys and they love you." She continued with, "You owe him no explanation for what you do, but I told him that it was about your writing and you were doing great. He wants you and him to catch up and thinks maybe he can invite himself to take in one of their concerts. He went on about how he was missing you now and really wanted to see you. I guess girlfriend he isn't with anyone and suddenly wants what was best for him that he gave up. I told him he should just move on, but he needs to hear that from you. I don't ever want him hurting you again. I know this is not what you want to hear, but he ended the conversation telling me he loved you, he never stopped loving you."

My heart dropped, now he says all this after his long absence, and the finality of our divorce. I couldn't answer her, I was speechless. I fought back the tears that swelled in my eyes, but then they began to drip down my face and across my lips. "Madison, talk to me, I didn't want to upset you. I had to be honest with you and not keep this from you. I think Thomas was an idiot for ever letting you go but I believe he loved you while you were married."

"Oh, I know he loved me, and I loved him, it's still so hard to understand why we ever parted after all those years, and he moved on so quickly to another, that hasn't lasted."

"Who knows how guys think, but totally his loss I say. I hate what he did to you. I support you in whatever you decide. If you decide to talk to him let him see you're strong and that you've moved on. Maybe seeing him will bring you closure. I believe you need that. I know girlfriend that you're torn and that's tragic. My heart hurts for you, please know that I'll be there for you as I always have been."

I cleared my throat, "Jillian I could never thank you for being with me through all my drama and I will always need you. I'll think about what you said. It's a lot to think about. Let's catch up soon; I'll be home for a few weeks after we wrap up the show here in South Beach. I'm excited to plan Atlanta and I think you saw on the schedule after that we'll be off to the Alamo. You'll have to go shopping with me for cowboy boots and a cowboy hat." I laughed. "I really miss you!" Jillian replied, "I miss you too."

I gazed through my tear clouded sight to the phone for so long, I looked at the back of my eyelids as I sealed my eyes closed. My phone sounded:

> *You awake yet? Not sure you're up sleepyhead. I couldn't sleep; my thoughts kept seeing a music note nestled on one naked sexy belly. Stop me now… hope you aren't sore. We have practice today and Maxwell asked us to meet up with some promotional marketing sponsors. It's going to be a long afternoon. I was thinking do you like tapas and art? I'd like if you would join me tonight to visit some galleries in the Art Deco District and I know a great tapas place?*
>
> *Rand*

I wiped my eyes, and a smile came to my pursed lips. I replied:

> *I love art, I like the body artwork I had the rare opportunity of viewing last night. Actually I collect different pieces of art, so yes that would be really nice, and tapas for dinner sounds so*

much better than dining with the entire band, not that I don't enjoy them all, but this evening sounds nice.

I sent that response, and then paused and sent this next one but, before I could finish typing it my eyes filled with cheerful tears and I hit send instead of rewriting it. I didn't want him to know that I was crying and had been upset, it didn't have to do with him.

Thank you Rand, I really need this. This will make me feel ……much better. I was upset…but

I knew in a moment he would surely respond, I waited, and I waited. No response came back and I released a big breath, maybe he put his phone away, then his response came. I heard a light tap on my door, "Madison, it's Rand open the door…I'm here for you."

I walked to the door; I held the door handle and then opened it wide. Rand looked at me, noticing my tear streaked face and wiped away my last tears. He did not question them; he just knew something wasn't right by the way I said I really needed this night. I looked up at him and he kissed me and firmly grabbed hold of my waist. He pulled me into him, but then set me back and lifted up my pajama shirt, and looked at my belly piercing and smiled.

"Madison let it out, don't write this, we all carry sadness, but I'd rather see you smile," He tugged at my waist twisting me side to side playfully, "Anything you want to share with me?" He seized my jaw, tilting it upward toward his lips once more.

I shook my head no as I trembled and let out a smile.

"I'm looking forward to us going out tonight." he changed the subject to a happier thought.

"Rand, I am too, I'm good, thank you. I'll be fine. Sometimes I think too much."

"I can take your worries away for awhile," he proceeded to kiss and lift my pajama top higher.

"Oh I am sure you can keep my mind occupied, it's just that Jillian and I were talking about my ex."

"That I can't help you with except to keep him as your ex," Rand grinned.

"I'm going to be just fine, but thank you for your concern," I smiled.

"See that's what I like, seeing you smile." Rand added, "Hey, this will make you laugh. You should see the guys since they got their piercings…Kent added another brow piercing. Raeford actually got his tongue pierced and said it hurts to talk. Ron got his nipple pierced, and Isaac, he went down low with a Prince Albert."

I could actually picture all these and laughed aloud. I asked, "What did you get?"

He replied, "Me? I got a secret musical note," as he pulled me in, and tucked me under his arm. I felt this warmth and decided to hold on to it for the rest of the day even though I knew he had to leave soon.

The Art Deco District that evening was amazing. There were so many galleries and as I enjoyed this time spent with Rand, I wondered if it was a date or just a friendly outing. Either title of this scenario I wouldn't change how wonderful it was. We stopped into several of the art studios and one gallery had such wonderful canvas paintings. One in particular we both felt a vibe from was titled, "Separation." It displayed two lovers, a man and a woman each walking away from the other and in a field of colors and high, wild weeds sweeping across the landscape and the sky was a setting orange and grey hue. We stood in front of it and took this all in. It was so innocent and yet powerful and seemed appropriate to our friendly, uncategorized relationship.

Rand seemed like he was really appreciating the art as we toured in and out of the district. Never once did he separate his hand from my fingers except when I excused myself to the ladies room. When I returned, I found him talking and smiling with one of the artist's agents, and she was tall, built perfectly and simply lovely. He was quick to glance at me and halt his conversation, but not without a quick kiss to her cheek, at least it wasn't to her lips. I did see him signing something for her as well so it appeared that she had asked him for his autograph, which was not uncommon at all, it happened very often when he or the band were out in public.

We enjoyed a great meal of small plates and conversation taking us deeper into what each other's goals and hopes were in life. I had gotten the feeling that he didn't open up like this to many. I felt like a sister sitting across from him just listening. I found that looking at this super fine-looking man across the table from me that there was such depth and emotion. Whatever love he lost saddened me but he was still such a kind person with substance. These were my mature thoughts but I also looked at him and just wanted to fall apart. All I wanted to feel was love but this could be a tragedy waiting for sure. He moved me inside without even knowing. He knew nothing of what I was thinking as he kept talking about the band's funnier antics and I just smiled and wondered what we would be like if we were truly a couple. Would we be good for one another, or would we shatter one another? Could we trust each other? I know we could lust after one another. I was contemplating what would happen after I stopped traveling with him and the band…

"Madison, you want another drink?" He asked and interrupted my reveries. I nodded back and wasn't sure what I was agreeing to. Rand took my hand and felt the inside of my palm and stroked his hand to my wrist. "Let's get out of here", he said deeply.

That evening I slept so well, no worries, no bad dreams, no thinking of life's yesterdays, looking at life with all the tomorrows ahead. I awoke very refreshed. I grabbed my phone and sent Rand a text:

> *Rand, this morning I was flying high from our outing last night. Thank you for not letting me fall like I did earlier with the tears. I'm ordering room service since we are only here in South Beach one more night and I never order room service, do you want to join me?*

I did not receive a reply; I guess he was still sleeping. He did need to rest because it appeared that he never slept. I got myself up and put the hotel robe over my pajamas – a cami top and underwear. I dialed the room service line and placed an order. Room service was really quick and as I heard the knock on the door I grabbed some money to tip the server. I opened the door and there stood Rand with a bottle of Dom Perignon and a quart of orange juice and a single rose. As he entered my hotel room, he hung the do not disturb tag on the door knob outside and tucked a fifty dollar bill next to it.

I never did receive my room service food order but sitting in bed making mimosas with Rand was fine. We played around, laughed, cuddled, tickled one another, had a vicious pillow fight that got out of hand since we started to use the heavier sofa pillows that were in the room and they hurt. We laughed so hard. I think we both worked up such a sweat that as we breathed heavily on the floor after our play the thought of a shower hit us like we read one another's mind. Somehow, through playtime I lost the hotel robe and he lost his shirt so we just stared at each other's chests rising and falling. Rand sat up and pulled me into the bathroom. We didn't speak, we entered the shower. Steam filled the bathroom like the fog fills their stage and I felt that Rand was about to perform as the most romantic shower partner.

We stepped into the shower still in our few pieces of clothing, soaking them to our bodies like a second layer of skin, we laughed. Rand then began to lather my hair and washed my exposed neck. Before he spread the body wash all over me, he kissed each breast, and his teeth tugged at the thin drenched fabric covering me. I reached up and placed my hands around his neck, knotting my fingers together and dipped my head back to let the water spray across it and rinse my hair. He pulled my head back toward him and brought me close for a kiss. Our water soaked bodies swayed up against one another. My nipples tingled and hardened in my soaked cami top against his naked glistening chest. I am not sure who stopped this first but the water could have run all day; finally we were toweling off and still laughing.

I felt a dull ache as he said he had to get going and he would look for me at the show. After one more stolen kiss, I shut the door to him and went to change from my damp pajamas.

The South Beach show was again a hit. I again was taking mental notes to write down after the evening concluded. Maxwell watched over me and came out to the front of the stage and stood with me and I actually saw him make movement to the beat of some of the songs. He told me we all would check out in the morning and we would be back in Philly for a few weeks. He said he looked forward to me traveling with them to Atlanta next; this was the perfect opportunity for me asking him for passes for Jillian and her brother Jason. Maxwell said he would make any and all arrangements for them and it was no problem at all. I hugged him for some reason. Perhaps to thank him, but I was feeling a really nice bond with him and maybe out of appreciation for how nicely he took care of Rand. I felt him hold me tightly in the circle of my hugging arms.

I traveled back to the hotel with Maxwell and we shared a drink in the hotel lobby. I hung out there after Maxwell went up to his room, hoping the band and Rand would come in but it got even later, I headed to my room.

The Rolling Isaac's never returned to the hotel that night, not until the morning. All of them wearing the same clothes, and very tired eyes. They chatted about their very, very long night.

On our travel back, Rand leaned his head softly on my shoulder and fell asleep but in his napping he spoke here and there, saying, "No I can't…oh, I really do want you, we could be great." I shuttered and could only imaging where they all went and what happened. I glanced out the airplane's window into the sea of clouds; I was floating on top of the wispy, white puffs, but could see the squall colors brewing below. Was all this wonder I felt with Rand just the calm before our storm? I looked out into to the vast open sky beyond the wing of the plane, we would be home soon. With Rand now quietly sleeping, I lightly touched my stomach and felt the jewel underneath. I pulled open my notebook, not disturbing his sleep and I began to write him another love note.

Rand:

As I dangle my little music note from my belly, I get yet another rush. I have to pause to breathe and I keep my eyes closed and see you as clearly as you touched me so gently, so seductively. I feel this little gem on my navel sparkles like a little hidden secret between us. I want to be your musical note, one that plays a tune in your heart endlessly. I see in the darkness of my lids, you barely touching my body and yet it instinctively moves toward your touch, craving that nearness. I feel you and want that touch again; I want you to continue with the course your finger tips were heading. I don't know what is occurring in me but there has certainly developed a hunger like no other.

I want to tell you in just this short time we have spent together that it has all been such a different feeling for me from my past. I know in my heart that it will probably go no father than my travels with you and the band, but it's intriguing and unknown and perhaps that is part of the pull that draws me near, but I know that I can't seem to get enough of you right now. I hope you don't know my fears - the fear of never feeling your touch again. I tread lightly not to speak out to your actions for you have given me both the opportunity to write again and to feel again. Until you came along I was uncertain I'd feel such emotion once more. I know you won't read this, you won't know my innermost thoughts but that is fine as if this is to be it will, if we are to be one we will. Somehow our two different worlds may collide and I await that. I will wait and hear, feel the hairs on my skin prickle sensing your presence.

Maddy xo

Chapter Four – Heartfelt Friends

Our time back in Philly surely grounded us all. The band kept up with their rehearsals. One evening when I called Raeford to get some detailed information about his musical upbringing, he told me that the band was really working hard on some new material, and that Rand was finally getting around to writing. I got caught up on my home stuff, all my phone messages, my writing notes and I tried to make sense of them and organize them. I had to open a huge pile of mail and all those things that stack up whenever you're away. Rand and I still talked and texted one another but hadn't seen each other for a week. Jillian and I set a date night tonight for the two of us to catch up and for me to reveal any and all details to her of my first travels with the band and everything about Rand.

With a big hug like life itself, I wrapped my arms around Jillian as soon as she crossed into my doorway. "God I missed you and it's only been a few weeks," I spoke as my eyes filled up.

"I missed you too girl, how was it? And don't keep out any juicy details," she replied.

Well I couldn't say enough, I told her I thought I was falling for him and that I couldn't believe this could be happening to me. I told her that we shared quiet time, fun time and very exciting time as I pulled up my shirt to display the dangling music note that hung from my navel. She laughed so hard, her shock apparent that I let myself get talked into a body piercing. I continued to tell her how I drank so much, braved my bikini (thanks to her) and was asked to cover up. I told her I had times my heart was so happy, but then I recalled her phone conversation with me about Thomas and those moments saddened with my reflecting on the past. I hadn't forgotten that he really wanted to talk to me so I told her I decided to return a call to him even though it was against my better judgment. I wasn't sure I could face him, but something in me still wanted to hear what he had to say. I had to stop feeling so conflicted.

We were talking at each other so rapidly, she was asking me all about Atlanta and she was excited that she would see her brother Jason. She told me she had looked up the information on the band and she had a spiked interest in Raeford. This was odd as he was the quietest of them all and Jillian was the polar opposite. She said his photos on the website showed him in a great light and he was very handsome. She asked if he had a girl in each town. I told her he was a sweetheart and really watched over me, and as for girls in each city, it was me that he mainly stayed near. I made a promise to her that I would definitely tell him about her in advance and introduce them both when we all would be traveling to Atlanta in a few weeks. Jillian said, "You promise?" I said, "Absolutely!"

I promise, oh I remember those words. I had promised my love to Thomas so long ago. In my whole life I never broke any promise. I remember Jillian coming to the front door of my condo and leaning on the outside and talking me through my tears and crying voice that she promised if I just let her in she would make it all better, that she would be by my side and she would make it all right. It had taken every ounce of my strength to open that front door and allow her to come in and join me on the floor and comfort me. At first she reached over to me to offer a hug and I flinched and pulled back.

Thomas had broken my very soul. Slowly she gained my trust and as she promised over and over that this would, one day, be much better. I felt somewhere deep inside that there was a part of me that may have believed her. "Maddy, are you still having wet dreams about Rand?" She broke into my thoughts.

"I wish I was, no I was just recalling the importance of promises." I said to her as I pulled her into another hug.

We had ordered Chinese delivery, and requested they send plenty of fortune cookies. After the food arrived we girls did what we do best and we talked well into the evening, sitting on the floor with an array of white take out containers and then we ripped through all the fortune cookies to select the best fortune for each of us. I found one that I liked and claimed it, it read: *A wish for true romance will happen in your life when you dream rose petals.* Jillian selected one she liked and it said: *Your smile brings happiness to everyone you meet.* We were laughing and I got paper and pens and suggested that we write our own fortune cookie saying. Heck I am a writer, how hard could it be? We wrote the following, mine read – *Hold on to the past but eventually let the times go and keep the memories and move oneself into the awaiting present.*

Jillian wrote – *No distance is too far for true friends bonded together.* I was really happy to have spent this time with her and told her we would hit the gym this week because I had missed too many days lately. Her schedule this week was going to keep her a little busier than normal but we could work it in, we hugged it out and I had just shut the door to her and my home phone rang. Thank god for caller ID, it was an incoming call from Thomas and I really didn't want to start in on this with him at the moment. I let it ring and he did not leave a message.

Being back here had me missing Rand and I wondered if he was missing me as well. I decided to text him –

Just wondering if you're awake? I had a nice evening with Jillian; by the way she has taken a liking to none other than Raeford! Believe that? We had Chinese food and rummaged through fortune cookies to select the one we wanted, we don't play that fair.

Seconds later he replied:

I'm up, and I've been thinking about you. Hey, can you pick through your fortune cookies and choose one for me? Wow, Raeford that's good news. He keeps his whole life quiet. I know he's not into any one girl right now. Maybe in Atlanta they can get to know each other. Maxwell told me you asked for some passes.

I went back into my kitchen and there remained the opened Chinese containers and many fortune papers lying on the counter and I looked through them.

Rand, here's one for you: Listen to the music in your heart and your happiness will dance and be intertwined with your outlook on life. I thought that was fitting for you.

Rand didn't reply back, then my telephone rang again on the home phone and I didn't want to pick it up thinking it was Thomas, but then I saw the caller ID and it was Rand. I picked it up, "Why are you calling?" I asked.

"Madison, I just had to hear your voice. I wanted to feel you speak to me."

Our live conversation lasted for a long time to follow. I remember trying to end it.

"Rand we should hang up, I should let you go now."

"I'm not letting you go, I don't want to."

"It's late, we'll talk soon, I'm getting very sleepy."

"Don't hang up, just put the phone next to your pillow and that way I will hear you breathing while you are sleeping."

"You're a crazy man."

"Maybe crazy about you, but I will feel like I am there with you, so go to sleep now Madison, take me with you as you dream."

As I closed my eyes to sleep I was content, first I had hugs from Jillian earlier, and then comfort through the open phone line from Rand that held me tenderly as I slept. I dreamt in color and it was so vivid. His blue eyes were upon me and he was lying next to me in thought, he began to admire my body, mentally taking it all in. I was so caught up in his look of desire that I inhaled him as well taking in his purely awesome body and sensual mouth and, oh how I wanted to be kissed in my dream. My fortune was coming true as in my dream I felt the touch of soft rose petals that were falling down and spreading on my bed. I leaned in toward him only to find my extra pillow in my face on the other side of my empty king sized bed. I really needed to get it together. I was falling for him like a high school crush and although I know he enjoyed my company he also backed away, keeping me at arm's length.

I slept well and felt refreshed this morning. I had to re-charge my phone as it spent the entire night on my pillow. I hoped I didn't talk in my sleep or snore through the phone connection to Rand. I was proud of myself as I had gotten all caught up from the previous traveling and knew I could handle this next journey to the Atlanta concert. I never heard my phone as it must have gone off while I showered, and Rand left a message:

I don't like separation, what can we do about it?

I was about to return a text, and my doorbell rang. I looked out and there was a delivery truck and as I opened the front door, there was the delivery man standing in front of me with a huge wrapped item marked fragile.

"What's this? I haven't ordered anything."

"Are you Miss Tierney?"

"Yes, I am but…"

"Miss, I just need you to sign this delivery slip."

"Is there an address from who sent this?"

"Miss it's just my job to deliver this to you this morning and it was noted high priority."

"Sorry, can I use your pen?"

The delivery man handed over his pen so I could sign for the package.

Just as I was signing the release slip, I saw a black Hummer pull into my driveway.

"Thank you Miss and have a nice day."

Rand walked up the driveway, stunning in his everyday, simple appearance, in his jeans that fit his hips perfectly and a tight black tee shirt as usual. He stopped first to talk to the delivery driver and I saw Rand tip him. I was really confused. As he came up to my door, he was smiling and said again to me, "I didn't like being separated, I missed you." I melted inside, and hoped he wasn't playing with me. I, for some reason, couldn't help myself from reaching out and hugging him like I hadn't seen him in months.

We walked in, his arm draped across my shoulders and mine wrapped around his waist and he said, "So let's see what this is, shall we?" First, though he walked around my home curiously taking it in since he'd never been past my doorway. He didn't come in before when he dropped me off to meet Jillian. He was humming and walking around.

"Do you want a tour?" I asked.

He said, "No, I'm just trying to figure something out."

"What's that?" I asked.

"Well, where to place your package that just arrived" he stated. It was then that I knew exactly what it was before even opening it. It wasn't an autograph he gave to pretty artist's agent; it was an order, an actual sale. He had bought me "Separation."

We decided to place it right over my bed. I had a large open wall there and the colors of the painting popped against the light yellow walls. We stood in front of the bed and were admiring our successful handyman work in hanging it and Rand nuzzled into my hair. He smelled so good. It wasn't a particular cologne, just the scent of Rand. I was getting so drawn in and used to his smell. I thanked him for the gift and I knew going forward every time I looked at it I would think of us. Was there even an us?

If I had even a slight doubt at this very minute, it escaped me as he cupped my chin and pulled me in slowly laying me down on the bed. Here we were in my bed, I never would have thought I would have kissed another man, much less in my bed, but that is what we did. We remained wrapped in one another's arms and he gently stroked my face and we passed the morning into the afternoon quietly, sensually and beautifully, only taking a break to eat some leftover Chinese food.

My home phone rang and I chose to let the caller leave a voice message. I did not want to take a call and interrupt this warmth of our being together.

"Maddy, pick up if you are there, please I just want to talk to you, we need to talk. Maddy, I still love you. I know I messed up but I miss you, I miss us. I'm sure you miss us. Don't give up on so many years we had together," Thomas pleaded. My body tensed, I was shocked the message sounded so loud in the quietness that had absorbed Rand and me.

I sank into his chest, did not know how to cover that up, how to handle that, how to respond. Rand simply leaned up, took both his hands and pressed them to the sides of my face in a capturing way and took my lips to his once more. He did not speak about the message, but did tell me it was getting late and he needed to escape this beautiful afternoon and head to meet the band. He said he would talk to me later.

As Rand was pulling away from my driveway I cursed Thomas and cursed his timing. I knew I would have to call him to get him to stop this. I reached out and began to dial his cell phone.

"Maddy, thank God you are returning my calls, I know I have no reason to worry about you but I miss you and I actually called Jillian when I was unable to reach you," his voice happily sang.

"I know, she told me. Listen, I want you to know that we will talk, perhaps we need that." What I wasn't saying was that I hoped the talk would be the closure I needed if I had enough strength to follow through with that. "Right now though I am deep into a concert schedule with the Rolling Isaac's, but you already know about that."

"Yeah, I looked up their schedule and I have a business convention in Austin, Texas the same time they have a show, I'll meet you then. I think this will work and it's a change of scenery for us both."

He just invited himself. I guess I now had to finally meet up with him to be able to move forward. I think I heard in his voice that he thought this might mean reconciliation, he sounded so hopeful. I told him I would get passes to the show and I knew without saying to him that with the loud music we would not get to converse too much.

I spoke without emotion, "Thomas, I'll call you when I have the passes and let you know where we can meet for the show. Take care, I really have to go." I did not say goodbye only hung the phone up and started to cry, this was my first conversation with him since we sat across the table with lawyers going through our assets, although even that went smoothly as our lives parted. I wasn't sure what tears I was shedding. Upset that Rand heard the earlier voice message, or upset at the wanting in Thomas's voice that I had longed for the months after he left?

As I tried to clear my head with a workout at the gym, I found myself sitting on the stationary bike and pedaling for so long that I could have reached another state. I had called Jillian and left her a message about my conversation with Thomas and also for her to get packing since next week we were heading to Atlanta. Maxwell was great. He had already sent me confirmation that he was having Jillian fly with us to Atlanta and he had bought her ticket. To date, I hadn't paid out any of my money for all the traveling with the band. Jillian and I had agreed and confirmed with Maxwell that we were going to stay at her brother's so there would be a cost savings for that. I had the VIP access passes on Rolling Isaac's lanyards for her and Jason and me to enjoy the show.

Today had been like a salad for me why, after what started off as a lovely day, was then mixed with some awkwardness in between and then a dash of self pity and dressed with intimate thoughts and naked images of Rand. I was exhausted. My phone sounded, it was Rand, and I smiled –

Glad I got to see you earlier today, I'm writing new music and keeping busy but my thoughts keep taking me to you. I'll talk to you soon.

Rand did not call me after that nor did he the next few days. As I had gone over to their rehearsal studio toward the end of the week to take some notes and a few photos to inspire my writing about **The Wall**, I ran into Ron who was working on some notes. Ron filled me in that Rand was out late every night and still hadn't returned yet this morning from last night when they all were at a club. Ron said, "I don't know how he does it. Rand is like that bunny commercial, he just keeps going. He parties all night long, and rarely makes it to his bed and…" He stopped speaking as he looked at me and could tell he probably had talked a bit too much already.

I took several photographs and headed out telling Ron I would see him soon for the Atlanta trip. I was so upset as I left, in my heart I thought Rand felt something for me and in my head I could hear that he was out and having fun, late nights, later mornings and with who I was wondering, but I knew it could be with any girl, anytime. Was I going to be satisfied with whatever playful extended friendship with kissing benefits I was sharing with him? Or was I going to have Thomas, who was saying he still loved me try to restart our past relationship?

Atlanta was already here, we were all set for the limo to take us, and Rand was not in attendance. As Maxwell reached for his phone, he told us that Rand had just called and would be here shortly. When Rand finally did arrive, he looked tired and not his lively self. He did come right up to me, took me by the waist, pulled me in and gave me a kiss on my nose. Jillian smiled and said, "Oh too cute." Rand then gave Jillian a quick hug and welcomed her to the weekend for the show. She was putty when he released her from the hug. But I couldn't focus on anything except for where he'd been. He looked like he just strolled in from yet another evening of all night sex and drinking.

Although the traveling for the trip was uneventful he did sit next to me and offered conversation to Jillian throughout the first hours of flight. He was mainly asking her questions about me in front of me. They covered all my likes, dislikes and yes, insecurities. Jillian kept up with answering him and the entire time they talked I watched as Raeford kept glancing at her with a look of anticipation. Raeford usually was laid back but there was a fire in his eye starting to manifest. I think Rand must have said something to him about Jillian, because abruptly Raeford leaned in and jumped into their conversation and then swayed her to converse with him the next hour of the flight.

Rand never took his hand off of me on the plane. I had covered myself with the provided flimsy, navy airplane blanket and underneath Rand slowly stoked my hands and rested his hands in the seam of my thighs. His head settled in on my shoulder and I could smell that Rand scent again. He breathed in and let out a sigh.

Our arrival in Atlanta was rainy and stormy causing all of us quickly scramble into vehicles to depart the airport. It was a messy morning there. Rand stopped me just as I was entering the cab to take Jillian and me to her brother's as the rest of the band, Maxwell and Rand were heading to a hotel. There we stood in the rain as it was still coming down and stared at one another. He leaned into me and kissed me really hard, taking the back of my head and holding it tightly pushing in to his kiss, he said "I'm going to miss you're not with us, but I'll look for you at the show".

Jillian had to pull me into the cab as the rains were intensifying and I was already soaked. I looked to him and felt sad and I wanted to turn and go with him. His long dark hair captured all the raindrops and glistened as he shook them off. He smiled at me through the closed window and I lost it. I told Jillian I felt something for him but with the other girls and his lifestyle who was I kidding. She held me all the way to her brother's home. I realized later that I hadn't even been a good friend as I meant to ask her about what she and Raeford talked about while in flight.

Jason waited very patiently while Jillian and I dressed like school girls in a dorm room, getting ready for the show, changing our clothes and laughing. We were acting so silly, it was so much fun. I had given Jason a Rolling Isaac's tee shirt when we arrived and he was quite excited about us being there but more about the concert. As we all got ready to leave Jason told me, "Hey thanks for the getting me in the show! It's great to have both my girls." We walked into the show that evening arm in arm with Jason. Maxwell had come up to us and invited us to go backstage after the concert. I was always welcome back there but usually did not attend. But for this evening with Jason and Jillian and my thoughts of perhaps Raeford seeing her again, I certainly agreed that we would all go.

Their concert was amazing again and as they stepped onto the stage, I saw Rand search the crowd, his eyes scanned it and then he came directly to me. He smiled, he tilted his head down, he kissed his cuff bracelet. He adjusted the paper play list in front of him and then looked back to me and pursed his lips and blew me an air kiss. I looked deeply back to him but was taken back for a moment knowing he kissed his cuff with Ashley's name on it just moments before. Was he filling me with softness while he awaits her return, had he been with her for all of his late night trysts? I was full of questions and worry.

Backstage was fun. I was hesitant to join them, but this night back there was like a family reunion. Kent had picked me up and kissed me again on the lips; he even picked up Jillian and kissed her too. Raeford was so smooth though, he just reached out and caught her hand in his and pulled her over toward him and kept her standing talking to him in between his legs. I think I saw Raeford kiss her too. Jason was in deep conversation with Maxwell talking all about the music business and drinking a beer and having a blast. Raeford introduced himself to Jason and they both talked quite a bit as Jillian smiled at them both. Isaac said, actually shouted, he really missed me lately. Rand took my hand and whispered to me, "Not more than I have." He licked the side of my cheek and moved in toward my ear and continued to whisper, "What you do to me, you have no idea. I breathe you in. I hold my breath. I wish you could stay tonight."

I was wondering if he meant with him, or the band. I was planning on staying here with them as long as they were hanging out, but then Jillian and I were going to return to Jason's and stay on in Atlanta for another day while the band was returning to Philly tomorrow afternoon. I was so happy this evening. I was right here, by the side of the stunning Rand. It was wonderful to have my dearest friend Jillian here on this experience with me, and seeing Jason smiling happily with the band made it that much better. At that moment, I felt such happiness having this family of people surround me. I looked up to Rand and confidently said, "I'm here now, let's not talk, just kiss me." I had openly invited him to take my lips with all these people in our company. There, backstage I was now the girl he was kissing this evening. I had climbed another confidence step in taking him on. I wasn't the young pretty girl tonight hand picked from the new corral of girls that so often came back to see the band; I was asked to be here, I was invited and I knew as his tongue slid into my mouth and circled my teeth and licked at the roof of my mouth that I wanted to be here this evening. The feel of him making me prickle inside, I definitely wanted to be here with him.

The lights were shutting off one by one backstage and we were all going to move out. I pulled from his embrace and he pulled me back in, saying aloud "We'll be out front shortly." As the last light dimmed and then faded in the darkness backstage, he took his fingers from tracing my already sensitive lips, tender from all his kisses, and he opened my mouth slowly and placed his two fingers on my lower lip and to my teeth. I began to suck on his fingers almost immediately, rolling my tongue around them and gently sucking them in and out. He gasped and let out a long sigh. He took his fingers from my mouth and traced a moist line to my nipples just under the strapless top I was and wearing. Then, he placed his other hand just under my skirt to the inside edge of my bare skin and lace panties. My thighs began to shudder at the touch of his hand.

"Come on guys!" Isaac screamed. I went to reach for Rand's hand in the darkness but before I found it, I took hold of what I though was his solid, muscular leg but, that is not what I touched. I found that he was very, very hard and very aroused. I laughed; we laughed and slowly walked out to the front of the arena to allow Rand time to calm down. I had hoped that this wasn't how Rand was each night back-stage. I had hoped it was only with me.

Chapter Five – Ashley Revealed

We were all safely back on the ground in Philly and returning to a few weeks of normal life. Things were a bit unsettled for me though. Atlanta had been a great weekend and even the extra day Jillian and I shared with Jason was fun. It was nice to see such love and interaction between a brother and sister and they included me too. But something was missing here at home, I wasn't being included.

Rand wasn't calling or texting as much, and he just seemed preoccupied and very busy. When I had conversations with him I wasn't certain he was actually listening to me. One day I even said to him, "What do you think about the purple lemons that have taken over the world?" He simply replied, "Oh that's cool!" I wasn't sure what was going on but I felt a distance with him that I wished I could bridge. I missed him, my friend, and my stunning rocker. I just wasn't sure what to do or if there was anything for me to do.

I had been contacted to speak at a local writing seminar so that began to take up some of my time keeping me busy as I had to prepare a speech and some ideas to discuss in an open forum. I also had been trying to put the band's road traveling notes together, so eventually days and hours flew by with all the time I spent writing. For a few days, Jillian and I actually hooked up at the gym and all we seemed to talk about was the band. We seemed like the two oldest groupies.

Each night though, I looked up toward my bedroom wall and would smile at the Separation portrait, and yes Rand and I lately seemed to be separated. I said a silent prayer that my life would be fulfilled and that I would perhaps be happy again one day and possibly learn that I could give love. During these past days I had gotten another voice mail from Thomas who was again overly happy in his tone, and he looked forward to our upcoming meeting in Texas.

As I put my head to my pillow rehashing all that had happened in the past few months, it exhausted me. I was happy thinking that Raeford and Jillian were talking a lot and planning to meet up at some of the band's rehearsals which she was getting excited about. I too had inner excitement just thinking of all the times with Rand, and I began to go over in my mind every detail of Rand, from his head to his eyes, to his…I stopped at his lips. I traced my lips and thought of him. I wanted his lips over mine so badly, and this was my last thought as I drifted off to sleep. I dreamt that night about him, seeing him standing there looking over at me, gently touching my face. I must have been deep in a dead sleep, because when I did wake up once during the night I saw I had a text message and I never heard it sound when it arrived. It was from Rand –

Good morning Madison, I can't sleep and haven't been good company with you or anyone. I've been in a funk and I don't want to pull you into it. Just know all I can give to you now is I'm missing you. I was thinking if you have this Friday night open, maybe we could get together at the barn. I can play you what I've been working on. Let me know and if you are sleeping as I write this, I hope I'm in your dreams.

I had been dreaming of him and I was getting the impression that he could actually read my mind lately. I picked up my phone and sent him a reply –

What's better than waking up to your words? I felt something bothering you but I didn't want to pry. You can talk to me about it if you want to share. And Friday sounds great, what time? Miss you too.

Rand's reply was quite simple –

Definitely do not want to talk about it. I am too drained already thinking about it. There are things you don't know about me and we aren't going to discuss this tonight, but for now I hope you can fall back to sleep. Even though you don't need any beauty sleep. I'm looking forward to seeing you Friday, at ***The Wall*** *at seven?*

I read his text and knew that there was no way I was going back to sleep because I wondered what he was going through. I was overthinking that he maybe wanted an out and needed to tell me that he was back with Ashley or someone else. My head was going to hurt thinking so much, but first I did send him my reply. –

I hope Friday comes quick….at seven you will see me, I'll even wear a Rolling Isaac's tank so you can play to me like a fan. Goodnight.

I had been right about one thing and that was I never did return to sleep that night or the following nights. I did doze off during the day here and there but not a sound sleep since his words had me questioning what was going on. I did know that my entire body was anxious and hungry to see him again. I had thought of how close we became in Atlanta. I had held onto the hopes that he truly wanted me close to him. Even as I wrote about the band, as I ate meals, showered, cleaned my home, he was all that I saw in my head. I looked so forward to just the sight of him again. I thought about him over and over the next few days until finally it was…

Friday finally arrived. I had been pacing about all week like any girl does waiting for the guy to call her after she has given her phone number to them. I decided that I would take plenty of time to get ready so I would look attractive for him, I took a little extra moment to do my hair, and I put on a little more Light Blue perfume as he mentioned he liked that a few months back. I spent time picking out the perfect outfit, I was feeling like this was a date. I don't know what it was going to be. With Rand, you never knew, one moment he is swooping in and keeping me close and the next I am alone.

Since the weather now was warmer this time of year, I thought I would wear just a plain white, long, sheer skirt, which flowed to the floor and it had an underlay fabric stopping at the knee and of course the Rolling Isaac's tank top I promised. I wore white wedges, as I could wear high shoes, Rand had at least seven inches in height on me and no heels in my closet would ever be that high. Since my hair style had exposed my ears a bit, I put in long dangle earrings that hung below the edges of my hair. I refreshed my makeup several times and as the hour got close to seven I headed out the door.

When I arrived at their rehearsal barn, it was pretty dark. I didn't see Rand's Hummer there and no other cars. I parked and walked up to the doors, it was open as they left it open most days because someone was always rolling in. I did though turn more lights on when I entered. I walked up to the loft area near **The Wall** and sat to wait for Rand. I walked up and was looking at some of the additions to **The Wall**; time began to pass and no Rand. I went over to the bar and took out a beer, surely something must have held him up, he would call if he was going to be too late I thought. Or could he have forgotten? I sat there for quite awhile and when I looked up at the clock down near their studio it read eight twenty–two. I had tried to text him, but didn't get a response and I was just about to give in and try to call him to see if we were still on when I heard the door below open. I looked down below to see that it was Raeford coming in and I waved from above. Raeford left the door open and he yelled up that he was going to be bringing in some new speakers. I figured maybe Rand was coming in behind him to help. Raeford first, though continued up the steps and hugged me and said, "Hey Madison what are you doing here all alone?"

I answered him, "I was supposed to meet Rand here to-night at seven, is he with you?" There was a moment of that dead silence, that horrible pause and Raeford said, "No sweetheart, he left earlier for Ashley…"

Raeford could see immediately my face drain and my eyes fill with tears, I said between my sobs, "I knew he was in love with her, I knew it was Ashley. I'm not a stupid person and I knew he was acting distant and strange all week. I know I can't ever compete with her."

"It's not a competition," Raeford looked confused.

"But, I've heard his ballad *Missing Ash* and it is so heart-felt. I've even saw the leather cuff he wears with her name and he kisses it after completing his shows. I can see in front of me how young and beautiful she is in this picture here on **The Wall**." I slammed my hand against the wall. "I'm definitely not as young or as beautiful, I can't even com-pare."

"Oh you are beautiful Madison, I think you're con-fused."

"I bet him asking to meet with me was so he could let me down easy tonight. I think he was going to say goodbye. And, Raeford I was falling for him. Now he's gone to be with Ashley. I feel like such a fool." My eyes pooled with tears.

Raeford reached up to my face and wiped my tears and then he took my hands together and sat me down and said, "Madison, let me tell you about Ashley." I was shaking with tears and looking at him not sure I wanted to hear him speak.

Raeford was always a calm person, and didn't talk very often. At this moment he seemed to want to share what was going on because Rand failed to enlighten me. While a part of me dreaded what he would say, I was all ears and poised to listen as Raeford began to speak.

"Ashley brought a personality like no other to the band. She actually brought all of us with our crazy, off the wall personalities together and she has been able to keep us grounded. She's taught us what is important in life."

"I don't understand what you're trying to say?"

"Growing up without love from her father, Ashley and Rand formed a very close bond. She became his biggest cheerleader for all his music."

"I don't think I've seen her at the shows lately, she's lovely, I think I would have noticed her."

"Madison she's actually always with us, and you're right you have never seen her."

"So you're telling me that he chose to be with her to-night and not even let me know?"

"Madison, he has to be near her tonight, but he should have told you why. Madison, after Rand's mom passed away which was very hard on him, Ashley picked him up and they became inseparable. She was here for almost every rehearsal and was at all our shows." Raeford paused and said, "Madi-son, please don't let this hurt you but Rand will never stop loving her." I let out a sob and started to cry again. Raeford paused to hug me so tenderly and again wiped my tears. He then continued to speak. I was barely listening as my heart was beginning to break.

"A year ago tomorrow, we were in the Finger Lakes of New York wine tasting. We hired a limo that drove us to the wineries of Seneca and Cayuga."

"Where are you taking me Raeford, on a wine tour?"

"Madison, let me finish. We drank a lot that day, and hit the hotel to chill before our concert that night. We had a show at the Glenora Winery. It was awesome our stage looked out over tons of vineyards. It was a packed crowd and right down in front was Ashley and her friends. Rand took hold of the microphone as he does and welcomed New York and thanked all the wineries for the spirits they supplied to us earlier in the day. We were all feeling good and played one of our best shows."

"Raeford where are you going with this?

"Well, after the show Ashley praised Rand on his newest song, which she'd been pushing him to complete. I remember her hugging Rand tightly as she kissed him and shouted to us that she was heading back with her friends to the inn."

"I don't think I really want to hear about him and her kissing, I feel upset already."

"I know how you feel but let me finish. We were staying to sign autographs. We were on such a high from our show, while we were at the autograph table signing away, there was a terrible accident just a few miles away."

"Raeford what are you trying to tell me?"

"While Ashley and her friends were driving back to the inn, another car flew through the intersection in Watkins Glen. It was like something out of a NASCAR race. The other car crashed into their vehicle and the impact flipped them into oncoming traffic."

Raeford paused and, I had to close my eyes, my mind was racing thinking that either Rand lost his girlfriend tragically or she survived and he was with her now. I opened my eyes to see Raeford tear. He took a deep breath. "Ashley's life was so bright and promising and then suddenly in a moment it darkened. She hung on for days on life support. We cried and we took turns talking to her, singing to her, and we prayed."

"Raeford, I am so sorry."

"Something had to be done to save her, but the doctors told us her brain was going to bleed out. The decision was made to remove her from life support. Rand was the only person to do this. Rand let her go, and something died in him at that moment too. Ashley was his twin sister."

I suddenly gasped and then broke into tears, the breath left my chest, and I felt like I couldn't get air. Raeford comforted me and he continued to rock me, he held me to his face as tears rolled down into my hair, and we both cried. We remained holding one another for a long time. I heard Raeford choke up and sob, only it wasn't Raeford, it was Rand standing in the landing to the loft. How long he had been standing there neither of us knew. Raeford rose up slowly releasing my hold on him and as Rand walked up I heard Raeford tell him in a low voice, "Man, she should know." Rand reached out and pulled Raeford in for a man hug and walked to me, he sat; he pulled me in, he cried, so hard. All I could do was hold onto him.

He whispered to me in between his tears that he received a call to go to attend a candlelight vigil in Ashley's honor and he had silenced his phone during it. He thought he would get back here to see me a little late but then he mentally broke down and couldn't compose himself for the longest time. He had arrived on the loft landing below the moment I had melted down about him being in love with Ashley and carrying on about all the signs I was seeing. He didn't have it in him to begin to tell me the story of this love that he lost, when he heard Raeford begin to tell it, he let him go. If it was any comfort to Rand after all this, I at least know he may have heard I was falling for him.

Rand walked over and stood near **The Wall**, he removed the cuff that he wore for Ashley and kissed it and hung it next to her beautiful photograph. He turned toward me and came over slowly, he pulled me up into him and as we held each other, I now knew what had been taken from him that had hurt him so badly. I wasn't certain that I could ever repair this. He looked at me and asked, "Madison, please stay with me?" I didn't say a word as I simply slipped his hand in mine calmly and walked with him, his arms around my waist out of the barn and across the moist grass up toward his house. I took his keys from him and after a try or two found the key that fit the front door and I led him to his grand bedroom at the end of the upstairs hallway. I climbed into his bed, and he settled in next to me. He wrapped himself around me and didn't let go, he cried, he sobbed and all I could do was remain there holding onto him. I knew my being there was helping him. I also knew that when the sun rose in the morning it would not be a brand new day, it would be a worse day for him as it would be the anniversary of Ashley's passing. I was grieving for him; I held in my tears and bit my lip to pass the crying urges. He need not worry about me right now.

As morning came, I woke to Rand sitting up in the bed writing in his journal with one hand resting above my head. With each pen stroke he would look down at me. He came in close to me and kissed my forehead, I closed my eyes and he then licked my sleepy lids, my insides seeped with a pleasant tingle. He then said in an intriguing way, "Thank you for last night." His tone sounded like we had just completed a night of sex and we hadn't but it's not that I wouldn't have wanted to. Rand rose and headed to the kitchen to again make me a great breakfast. Several times while we ate, he apologized and I just shook my head side to side to relay to him silently, "no" as he had nothing to be sorry for.

"So thank you again for my great breakfast. Is there anything you need today?" I wanted to begin this day on a happier note knowing the sadness he was surely feeling.

"I need you, Madison can you stay here with me today?" He continued, "I know I need you and want to give you so much, but I don't know if I ever can. I'm glad you know what happened and I wish I had been able to tell you."

I told him I would stay for the day only if he would get me to my home for some much needed clean clothes. After breakfast he took me back to my home for a bit so I could change and as I was in my bedroom he walked in and took my travel bag from my closet and began filling it with some other clothes of mine.

Laughing he said, "You can leave this at my place so I won't have to bring you back here anytime soon." I walked over and I pulled him into me and kissed him. I started to kiss him on his lips and trailed downward. I leaned into his tee shirt and said, "I'm here for you, this is going to be a very hard day for you." He tightened his hold on me.

The band members, one at a time had phoned him today to share their memories of Ashley and share with him his pain. I held his hand through all the calls and I wiped his tears after each one. During the afternoon, I went to the sunroom and phoned Jillian and filled her in on what happened. She actually surprised me by saying that Raeford called her last night when he left me and Rand and stopped by to see her and opened up to her.

"Madison I know your heart is hurting but I know you can feel enough to help Rand through this. From what Raeford told me you are the one to help Rand." The fact was, I was falling hard for him, but I was certain he didn't have what I would need; I didn't think he would ever commit or even move forward with me. For now I just had to take him in and I was on the other side now, I needed to help another.

Early evening we were in his study and I was seated on one end of the large sofa and he was at the other. The doorbell sounded. Rand got up and went to answer the door; Maxwell had been away all day and stopped in to see how he was coping. Maxwell seemed pleasantly surprised to see me there when he entered the study. He sat with us and got us up to speed with the itinerary for the Texas concerts and then said after a brief break it would be off to the west coast.

This took Rand's mind from the present day and he looked like he was finally coming back to the Rand we loved. I sat with Maxwell for while and shared with him some teasers of the writings of the band that I had. He laughed at some and others he said that I nailed the storyline. I felt comfort in being there with him and Rand; I felt I was supposed to be there. This day was surely just as hard on Maxwell since he had been Ashley's uncle. When he tired and felt he should head out, Maxwell said a goodbye and hugged me tightly. He told Rand to take it easy for a few days and then get to rehearsal. I heard my phone sound while they were saying their goodnights at the front door.

I received a text from Rand?

I can't begin to thank you for staying. I miss texting you. Can we head to bed? I just want to hold you. I'm relieved I made it through this day and I couldn't have done it without you.

I pulled my notebook out and knew I had to write at this moment, another love note to him quickly, while Rand and Maxwell continued their conversation in the foyer.

Rand:

My heart is so broken for you right now. I have now been told who the lovely Ashley was and I cry as I write these words to you. I cannot believe what sadness you must contain within yourself. I only hope I can somehow, someway bring in to you some ray of hope that you can feel for another. I am glad that Raeford told me the entire story as I would never have wanted to put you through such pain again. I am here for you and I don't think you even know that.

Funny how life is, my ex-husband shattered me and now is trying to come back into my life. Something though changed after he left that I cannot recapture...but also since he left and we divorced I've found you. I know we are not a couple, but then again I don't know what we are to one another; I just know I don't want this to end. Since I cannot label what we are, I don't ask you to answer to me, I seem to take what you can give me and for now it is more than I have felt and I will gladly accept that. But I would love to be more assertive and ask you things more openly that I'm thinking but you are so empty inside that I back away and I walk on egg shells and treat you so tenderly to not loose this taste of happiness you've allowed me to sample.

Fate is a funny meeting place of many and our paths have crossed at this time for a reason. I hope one of us figures it out. I hope it is an essential crossing of our lives to perhaps join one path together. Rand as you play your guitar on some songs; I feel every stroke you pick with. As you sing, your words and eyes pierce through me like an arrow.

My mind aches at the love lost and sadness you and I both feel, but can we rebuild our lives when it seems like there's no foundation to build on? Can either of us take a chance on the other trusting and believing?

I only seek to find what lies ahead, and I hope it is you Rand standing at the crossroad for me to venture forward. I give you a sweet, tender kiss as I write to try to display there is love out here and hope.

Maddy xo

I stayed that night with him and I didn't leave for the next few evenings. Each passing day got a bit sweeter. Rand would snuggle up to me each evening and although we didn't have the passion sweep us away yet, I kept him calm and feeling warmth during the darkest days that he was dealing with. We were now on another level, we just seemed to hold onto one another, and savor the time spent in each other's arms. Rand did become more affectionate, kissing and hugging me more. A few times when we were in public he seemed to play down or actually ignore some of the lovely girls that were always hanging around.

I wasn't sure where Rand and I we were heading but for right now I was back on board with him and the entire band and enjoying my life.

Chapter Six – Thomas's Return

We were all heading to Texas and I arrived this morning with a cowboy hat and boots to match, ready to kick up my heels in this next state. We had received a briefing from Maxwell which contained a schedule of three concerts to come, along with some added free time in between each. The first show was in Austin, then off to San Antonio, and then lastly to a resort in Galveston. Rand was in a very good mood this morning and as we sat together on the plane, he tilted my cowboy hat down low and came underneath for a very long, drawn out, lip smacking, wet kiss. Even though we had kissed a lot recently, I was still missing his lips and the past few weeks had been full of love lost memories and a lot of painful emotions. This felt good as he took my mouth to his and gently swirled his tongue with mine. He reached under my chin and cupped it, never breaking our embrace.

Raeford tapped me on the brim of my hat, and handed over his phone, just before we were about to take off. "Hello" I answered.

"Well I just wanted to tell you to have an awesome time. You go girl, write your story and make sure it's juicy." Jillian said. "Oh, and aren't you meeting up with Thomas at one of the shows?"

I answered, "I'll make it very descriptive just for you and I'm not meeting up with him, we're just going to talk." I hadn't wanted to think about this at all. Thinking of meeting Thomas had my emotions all over the place and I certainly didn't want to bring it up to Rand. Rand wasn't following my conversation with her which was good, although I was choosing my words very carefully. I had already obtained a VIP access pass for Thomas from Maxwell, telling Maxwell I was meeting an old friend to take with me to the concert. I didn't think I really had to tell anyone any more about who he was. With Jillian still speaking to me on the phone she continued, "Oh, and Madison can you…." in a whisper voice like someone would over hear her on the phone in my ear, "watch Raeford for me. I really do like him." I laughed and said, "I certainly will, love you Jill, we're taking off now." Rand pulled me into his chest and I remained there until we landed.

We arrived at the Driskill, which was a legendary, landmark hotel in Austin. It was a breathtaking site to take in. The hotel design was very luxurious and historical; it was built in the 1800's. I was told too that there was a lot of ghost activity here at this hotel. As the band settled into their assigned rooms and I was in mine, I heard a knock at the door, but when I opened it no one was there. Perhaps it was one of the ghosts of the hotel. I then returned to unpacking my clothes and heard the knock again, but it was coming from the door in the sitting area of my hotel room. It was a connecting door to the next room. Perhaps this was for families that stayed here, the children could be in the other area. I opened this inner door. Standing up against the frame was a sight to behold.

Rand was standing there in jeans that rested just below his hips and he was shirtless and barefoot. I didn't speak, I just had to swallow and exhale slowly, even his naked feet got to me. Rand lifted his face up and sent me his electrifying smile. Already in my room when I arrived was a bottle of champagne, a bowl of ripened strawberries, and some selected cheeses and crackers on the table in the sitting area.

"Madison, I think we are missing something we both need right now."

"Like what?"

"How about these?" He pulled from behind him, two champagne flutes. He then took the champagne bottle from the ice bucket walking proudly to the bed in the other room. He sat on the bed and tapped the bed for me to join him.

The rest of the afternoon we drank champagne, ate strawberries and cheese intermingled with kisses and licks to one another's lips. We had created our own type of edible treats; appetizers that definitely whetted our appetites for more. Rand made use of his talented fingers and traced them along my face and then pulled my chin upward to meet his still hungry mouth. I found being in his arms and the taste from his lips that I could hunger for more. Although Rand and I could have stayed in my bed there, in that room for a long time, we decided to head out and walk about the hotel. Since previously hearing of ghost encounters in the hotel, my interest was piqued. Being a writer, I thrive on that, and was intrigued.

Our afternoon stroll took us down through the massive columns that lined the lobby and then we settled ourselves out on the mezzanine. Here we sat in the deep brown wooden rocking chairs looking beyond the white railed posts on this outdoor patio retreat. Just before we left my hotel room, I grabbed my voice recorder and Rand went through our connecting door and retrieved his journal, shoes, and thankfully a shirt. As we rocked, I softly spoke into my recorder and Rand was drawing and writing on several pages, I was certain creating new music.

The band had tonight off and Rand had chosen to remain with me here at the hotel. We saw Maxwell and the band as they were heading out into the city of Austin to eat. We waved from the mezzanine to them below. Rand leaned over me in the rocking chair and took my hand leading me back to my room where the dinner he preordered for us was set up. He ordered so much food, knowing the hotel's restaurant was very highly rated. We started with a roasted beet salad, moved on to a wonderful plate of butternut squash risotto, and then a huge Texas style aged rib eye. We both practically dove into the apple tart and whip cream topping without using our forks. We broke pieces of it away and fed one another, taking tiny bites of each other's lips, licking fingers savoring the taste of the delicately flaked pie crust and the sweetness of the topping. I had a tiny piece of apple near my lip that Rand was to gracious to leave there for a moment and then he came in and removed it very seductively. I believe every meal should start with dessert.

This evening was wonderful, with our appetites satisfied and precious moments like this that we shared. It was so nice to have this calm with Rand in his busy lifestyle. I liked this side of him. During times like these, no one else existed. But the return of the band reminded me that they did. My hotel door was knocked on loudly and soon all the guys were marching in. They said they were stealing him from me for awhile and as much as I wanted to protest that he wasn't mine to steal, I didn't. Before he left my room, he looked back and he stole a deep, sucking, swirling kiss from my lips.

My hotel phone rang the next morning which was odd as I wasn't sure who would use that phone to call me. "Good morning Maddy, I'm looking forward to seeing you tonight, I miss you," Thomas said with such confidence it was clear he felt like he'd be getting exactly what he wanted out of this meeting.

"Oh, Thomas, hey, you can meet me here at the Driskill Hotel Bar about seven, and then we'll go to the show." I replied. I didn't linger on the phone with him and I really wasn't looking forward to this as I just had such a lovely day yesterday with Rand and finally felt Rand and I were making baby steps with one another.

I headed for the shower hoping that the warm spray would help to wash away the feeling of uncertainty that I had about tonight. I knew I was seeing Thomas after all these months and wasn't sure how that was going to go, I had my hopes of getting some closure. The timing for Thomas and I to meet again was very close to what would have been our eleventh wedding anniversary. Some of our wedding vows were replaying themselves in my mind… *I Madison take you Thomas to love, cherish and grow with in all our days ahead. I promise to be by your side for as long as you will have me.* That seemed funny to me now as I was by his side actually only until he decided to leave me. As I lathered myself beneath the showerhead and thought of Rand's touches and felt deep within my belly, warmth envelope me. I closed my eyes and let the water beat lightly at my face preparing myself for this day.

After I showered and dressed, I went to the connecting door and tapped lightly hoping Rand was awake. My knocking was not answered, so I reached down and wrapped my hand around the doorknob and paused, then slowly twisted the handle and opened up the door. From where I stood on the threshold I could see just his messy bed sheets in his room, some of his journal notes on the nightstand but he wasn't there. I lingered there for a moment. It was as if I could actually feel him, and as I traced a finger over my lips, I could still taste him. I knew I could definitely smell his scent and I closed my eyes and drew in his aroma. My phone sounded a moment later and it was from Rand.

> *Good morning. Sorry the guys pulled me away from you last night. I was looking forward to the next part of dessert. I've already left this morning. We all got in late, I'm beat. I have a meeting today with Maxwell and some people in the music industry from Austin. You know these meetings can go long. I'll search you out in the audience tonight. I'll lock onto your beautiful dark eyes, and imagine that I'm tucking a strand of your hair behind your ear and singing. I'll be singing to you like you are the only one in front of me. Later I will pull you toward me and kiss your ear and then travel to your welcoming lips.*

I was star struck, I was in awe and I missed him, I knew I did. I wanted to let him know.

Hey, I was just standing in the doorway between our rooms breathing you in. Although you aren't here I feel like you are, I'll miss you today, but I'll be looking forward to seeing you tonight.

I leaned on the doorframe with my phone to my chest and tapped my head lightly on the wooden surround. I was beginning to feel something with Rand, something so alive and warm, so new, so fresh and yet so unknown, but what I knew somehow was I wanted more.

I had seated myself at the bar several different times just before seven o'clock. Once I sat down and then hurried to the bathroom being nervous. Another time I sat and crossed my legs and looked as if I was waiting for one of the surrounding Texans to kindly buy me a drink and then finally I sat myself at a small table off to the one side of the bar, in a bit more secluded area where the fabric of the chairs made me laugh as they were a cow print. My laughing made me relax as Thomas arrived and placed his hand to my shoulder. "Madison, you look lovely. Please don't get up, let's sit here for a bit." I was surprised, I had been so distraught and angry with him for so long, and now seeing him was like meeting him all over. He was very pleasant to the eyes, his sandy colored, short hair and light grey-blue eyes, pulled me in. I actually got up and slightly placed my arms around him and tapped him slightly.

"Thomas I'm glad you made it, I know you're really going to enjoy the show."

"Oh, I am already enjoying just being here with you."

I wanted to keep our conversation as friends. "Thomas, I am really having a great journey with all of them. I know you've heard many of their songs."

We were able to keep our conversation light and friendly. We spoke for the next hour about the business convention he was attending and how my writings were coming along. We didn't get into anything deep about what happened to us, and that was fine for me at the moment. He did speak to me about my father and said that my father missed me. Thomas told me that he believed my father was pulling for us to make it back together, but I let that topic brush over and asked him how long he was going to be in Austin. The time flew by and I looked at my watch and knew we had to get to the show. Thomas said he could drive as he had a rental car. We left the bar, I felt him reach down to take hold of my hand, but when I pulled it back up toward me, he rested his hand at the small of my back following me out of the hotel to his car. I felt his hand near my back and a few times he raised it and gently stroked at my lower back, but emotionally, I felt nothing. I felt his hand but no longing or wanting sensation.

When we arrived at the concert I thought of possibly taking him back stage and briefly introducing him as my friend to the band and even Rand, but we got tied up in the traffic to get to the venue as only one lane of traffic was open. Since it took us so long, I only briefly caught up with Kent in the side corridor for a moment as he was rushing backstage and told him I was with my friend Thomas and we were going to quickly find our seats. The band opened up with the usual from Rand, "Good Evening City of Austin, we are Rolling Isaac's." His eyes did a once over of the crowd below and he quickly scouted me out. I had on my cowboy hat so I tipped it to him when our eyes met. As the band started playing, a few times Thomas leaned over and said that it must be really fun traveling with them. He seemed genuinely happy for my new occupational venture. The band played so well and was received by Austin greatly. I knew most of the songs by now, I always had a copy of the night's playlist and sang along and even Thomas knew a few verses.

At one point as I stared at Rand I saw him smile, and I was overwhelmed with happiness. As I turned to Thomas, he leaned in and took the opportunity to kiss me on the lips. Thomas smiled gently at me and then reached to the back of my neck and pulled me in once more. I kissed back, thinking of Rand. I quickly realized what was really happening and pulled away abruptly. My first thought was to just run away from Thomas but I didn't want to leave in the middle of the show. So I sat there and gave Thomas a kind smile and then focused back on the show.

After that song was done the band took a moment to wipe their sweat, quickly chug some water and glance at their playlist for the next tune. I saw Kent go over to Rand in a brief conversation he was telling Rand something and they both glanced in my direction. Rand turned when he was done talking to Kent and he stared at me with fire in his eyes; he knew who I was seated with. I saw the sudden change in his sweetness to a conflicted look. He then went to the other band members and suddenly changed the next song on their playlist. I knew this because when they took a moment to play a few cords I could tell it was a different song.

The stage darkened completely. I wondered what was going on as they rarely do this in their shows. When the lights came on, there was only a single light shown in the corner of the stage on the side where I was seated. Rand was kneeling with a tight grip on his microphone. Rand closed his eyes and said loudly, "Ladies and gentlemen this is a brand new song titled *My Empty Heart*."

The song began –

I've been watching you for oh, so long,
For me I know you are my only one.
Though, I am scared to give you my empty heart,
I hold tightly onto you so deep within.

You are my light, in my life, that I can truly see,
I have to pinch myself to know this is reality.
You are so unaware of what I feel in my aching
heart,
I watch your every move from the stage above,
I have remained so captivated by you from the
start.

Oh god, I thank you and you I cherish,
I feel again, something between us that is ahead.
I give to you all my thoughts unconditionally,
I want to show you someday, as my tears shed.

You are my light, in my life, that I can truly see,
I have to pinch myself to know this is reality.
You are so unaware of what I feel in my aching
heart,
I watch your every move from the stage above,
I have remained so captivated by you from the
start.

In all our days please remain my center stage.
May you take me completely for what I am?
May we look back and surely both know,
This feeling has made me your favorite fan.

You are my light, in my life, that I can truly see,
I have to pinch myself to know this is reality.
You are so unaware of what I feel in my aching
heart,
I watch your every move from the stage above,
I remained so captivated by holding you in my
heart.

The music stopped and Rand stood up and he opened his teary eyes and silently he mouthed, "*I don't want to lose you, my front row,*" and then he placed both his hands cupped to his chest over his heart, he glanced just past my eyes and it looked like he lost his soul. The audience roared and gave him a standing ovation. I sank with every word that he sang. I had never heard that song, and knew each of his written words was directed to me, written about me and that I was actually somehow in his empty heart as he sang it. It pained me inside to see him like this, I wanted him to open his eyes and look out to me. I knew he must have seen Thomas kiss me and I wanted to tell Rand it meant nothing. That it was him I was thinking of, seeing in my head so clearly in that moment when I kissed Thomas back.

Thomas glanced over to me, "That was a great tune, he's really singing to someone he cares about. I think I know exactly how he feels." I nodded at Thomas agreeing about the song, thinking to myself that Thomas had no idea what was happening.

At the close of the show, I looked to Rand and he still had not met my eyes. I decided to leave with Thomas to take me back to the hotel. As we were leaving the stage area I glanced back to see the band all excited about their performance and shaking hands of the fans that had lined up for autographs. I saw Rand pull a young girl toward him, the only thing separating them was the makeshift fencing for the fans and he pulled her in for a kiss. He kissed her and then turned in my direction. I realized she looked similar to me. He did at this moment lock his eyes completely onto mine. We were separated by many aisles of people, but our eyes spoke. It had pained him terribly, seeing me with Thomas, and I could see from his clouded deep blue eyes that he was clearly hurt.

On the ride back to the hotel, Thomas was speaking on and on about the show. I rested my head on the window and looked out through the glass as a tear left my right eye. When we arrived back we said we would have a drink together in the bar. We were right back where we started our evening. I had hoped sitting at the bar that I would see the band return from their concert. I seated myself on the barstool so that I could see just beyond into the hotel lobby. I also so hoped that I would see Rand return soon.

As Thomas and I sat at the bar, there was an older bartender with his nametag displaying his name as Will who asked for our drink order. The hotel had a very nice staff; some were very seasoned and knew all the history of this place. Will told us a few cute bar jokes and Thomas took the liberty of ordering us each a double Bailey's on the rocks and then he began his plea. He spoke about how we met, how we had traveled together, how I decorated our city condo, so many memories were going through my head. We downed one round of drinks and then asked Will for another. Thomas again spoke, "This was nice tonight, us enjoying each other's company. I know you had a great time. I felt you kiss me back. It was warm and inviting. Madison, I know now that we're to be together. Can you give me the chance once again? Even though I know I don't deserve it. But I am or was, I want to be a good husband to you."

I stared blankly back through him. Here he sat wanting me back and I was remembering part of his wedding vows to me: *I Thomas, take you Madison, to be my wife, become my life and to follow where ever our dreams may take us*…I felt saddened and I reached up to take hold of his handsome face and I spoke softly, "Thomas in the ten years we were married, I thought of no one else but you. I'd completely given myself to you. You are a warm and kind person, and you and I shared a great marriage. I'd still like us to be close."

"Madison I want to be close to you right now."

"No listen, I was actually so scared to see you tonight, but now I am relieved. This has brought me closure. Thomas, when you left something died in me and I cannot bring that back. I may never feel again like I did for you but I know that I am finally in a different place in my life and within myself. After ten years of marriage, I wanted to believe that we wouldn't avoid or hate one another."

"Madison I could never avoid you, I want you, and I still love you."

"Oh, Thomas I am sorry but that's not what I want anymore." I pulled him into me and kissed him close to his lips, on his cheek as this was my goodbye to him. I knew we would be alright if we were in a room of other people. That he and I would continue to be nice to one another and check to see how the other was doing now and again. But we would never be back to a couple where we were long ago.

Thomas reached into me and held me closely. He took his hand and pulled my head in toward his chest and held me. I heard loud voices entering the bar and turned back to see the band had arrived. Maxwell had turned in for the evening as we all were scheduled for a late check out and then it was off to San Antonio. The guys all gave me a happy wave from the table that they settled into for their drinks. Kent gave me an uncomfortable glance perhaps he had seen my kiss and embrace with Thomas moments before. I felt self-conscious and looked away from him. I did turn my eyes to their table a few times and Rand was never with them.

I slept that evening with peace that Thomas and I could move forward. I was now confident enough to not cave into him, not return to him just to be with someone. I had made my decision to be on my own. Knowing this morning we were again packing to leave for the next show, it was nice that Maxwell set us up for a later check out time. I ordered room service, a large pot of coffee and orange juice and an English muffin with strawberry preserves and sliced cantaloupe. I was sure that would carry me until we all stopped on the road for lunch. I reached into my purse to find my phone to text Rand and I typed – *Can we talk?* I wasn't sure if he was still sleeping so I hit send and waited.

I pulled out my laptop and was finishing some of my recent notes on the band. My room service came quickly and as I was finishing my coffee which was so welcomed this morning after a few too many drinks last night. I heard a hard knock on my hotel door. I opened the door and was stunned to see Thomas. He looked beaten, like he was sad, like he had not slept. He took my hand and said "Madison, your father had a stroke and is critical, we need to go." With that he told me he got the call just an hour ago, and he would get me back to see him in Philly.

I packed all my things in the room; I shut my phone and laptop off and threw them into a carrier. I was speechless throughout the packing process only stopping to hold Thomas in my arms and weep in between. As we left to the lobby and checked out, I glanced over to the newsstand area to see Kent picking up a morning paper and saying good morning to me. As he started to walk toward me, he could clearly see I was crying, Thomas had turned in my room key and checked me out and reached back to take my hand. Kent stood at the lobby entrance and just watched as I left with Thomas's hand in mine and my head on his shoulder. I didn't look back as we exited the hotel and rode off toward the airport in Thomas's rented car.

Chapter Seven – A Love Lost

Everything was happening so fast. Before I knew it we were on a plane already bound for Philly. Once we landed we were heading right to the one of city's top hospitals. My father, was a recently retired police officer from the city and he had been born there, stayed there, met my mother there, and never left. I was hopeful that with all the hospitals in the city and surrounding it that he got there quickly when this happened. The entire flight Thomas asked if I needed anything, was I hungry, was I thirsty? He never let my hand go the entire flight. I was thinking about my father and hoping he would hold on as I needed to see him and make this right between us. I remember how we stopped talking for so long. I was lost in my memories and then realized that as Thomas held my hand softly that his was not the touch I needed, it was Rand's romantic caressing of my hand I so longed for. I dozed off against the seat arm and the window shade. Thomas had placed my sweater into a ball under my neck creating a soft pillow for me. I wept and slept and my thoughts carried me to Rand.

I was on his bed, he was standing above me and he was shirtless. He climbed up over me and started to kiss his way up my body beginning at my thighs. He hovered over my body and paused in between his kisses to look down to me with a look of peace, his was a calming presence. He came up over my body slowly and in closer to my lips and I could feel him without touching him and he smiled at me and assured me we would be alright; that everything would work itself out, that he was there for me. I replied, "Oh Rand, I feel you near me, please hold me." I stirred and shifted in my seat knowing I must have been speaking out loud. Thomas leaned toward me and I knew that he clearly heard my groans over and over again. Thomas probably knew in his heart what I was feeling and for whom, and he knew that there was no chance for him and I, as my sleep talking surely confirmed this but Thomas also was not one to concede.

When we landed in Philly, Thomas said he was glad I slept for a bit and he got us swift transportation to the hospital. Just as we were getting through the doors of the hospital to the critical care area, Thomas stepped back and allowed me, as my father's only family member, to go ahead first to see him. I had only hoped as I went in that I had arrived in time. As I tuned out all the sounds coming from the beeping machines attached to my father, my thoughts drifted to Austin, Texas and sounds of the band's songs played in my head. I knew the band would be traveling on in the van, laughing and looking forward to their next stop. I wanted to be there, with Rand, having him hold onto me tightly, kissing me and enjoying all their company as they headed toward San Antonio which was only about an eighty mile trip for their next concert the following night. I didn't fare too well in hospital settings, I was trying to have my mind sweep me away to some other place, I so wished my father was healthy and this wasn't happening.

I slowly stepped into the Intensive Care Unit and froze. Before me was my father, one who was an officer of the law that many looked up to, once my idol of strength and a large man who towered above me. Now he was here in this bed weak, curled up and partially paralyzed. It had been several months that he and I had not spoken and this moment was the same. In silence I stood just taking in the sight in front of me and holding back my tears. I pulled a stool next to him and gently touched the back of his hand, lightly stroking. I heard a gasp from my father as he slowly opened his eyes. I dropped his hand and leaned in and said, "Dad it's me, Maddy. I'm here." I continued to speak to him. "You didn't have to do this just to have me come to visit." He cleared his throat a bit and still held my eyes.

"Maaddyy" he spoke slowly and his eyes glistened. I didn't want him to get upset and told him we could talk later. He was a persistent man and seemed like there was something he wanted to let me know. He began, "I neevver meant to huurrt you Madison." He continued that he hoped that Thomas and I would stay together, as he had wanted with my mother, Grace. My father said he never wanted to face a day alone. That being on the police force was a risk every day and when the day was done he wanted to know he had his loved ones to return to. My father said that he knew inside that Grace was in love with his brother Jake. When my mother left him, he asked her never to return as it would only hurt him.

As my father continued slowly talking about the day my mother left, it took me back long ago to when I asked "Mom are you and dad in love?" My mother looked at me and said, "Yes, Madison, but it's a different love I feel for your dad, it's a safe love, not a passionate love. Sometimes you can truly love one person, and then be conflicted to be so in love with another." My thoughts were interrupted by my father's gasp. My father now had my complete attention and he said, "Madison I wanntt you to know that yoouu must follow your heart, and if it is not with Thomas, then find where your heart longs to go. Thomas is a good man, a kind man, I am thankful for the relationship I haavve with him, and he knows that." I followed my father's eyes to Thomas's as he had walked in and been standing right behind me. I looked up to Thomas with a compassionate smile and my father took that in.

We both remained there for quite awhile, and my father as tired as he was, he continued to speak to us both. He told me that he so often sent Grace updates about me, my writing, my column, my wedding but she only replied once. She said that she left to follow her heart, but she knew that hurt my father and me. She said that she and Jake could never face us again after that. I wondered all these years what he had told her as he never let me know until now.

The ICU night nurse came in and told us we really should let him rest. I leaned into my father's forehead, I kissed it and left my lips pressed to his head for a long moment. I rose and pulled Thomas in for a hug. I promised my father I would be back and for him to get some sleep and have pleasant dreams. I pulled from Thomas to whisper into my father's ear just as he was closing his tired eyes, "Dad I love you so much, you're the best." I turned and pools of tears overflowed the edges of my eyes.

I was going to spend the night at the hospital in the waiting area until Thomas suggested that I crash at his condo, actually our condo before we divorced that was only a few streets from the city hospital. After a lot of coaxing I agreed. I had all my luggage and items I needed with me anyway from traveling. As I left the ICU and headed with Thomas to his condo, I powered up my phone and saw that Rand had tried to call me but my phone went directly to my voicemail and he did not leave a message. I knew it was well into the San Antonio concert hour, so I did not want to call and leave a voice message. I knew that they had scheduled the next three days for down time, first to complete the five hour ride to Galveston and then another day of doing some media related gig. And I remember one conversation on the plane to Austin that Rand and Maxwell were having and Rand said he needed a half day in Galveston, but I wasn't sure for what. Right now though being so far from the band I knew where my place was and that was with my father. I knew also after the wrenching pain that I watched Rand endure over Ashley's anniversary that I couldn't put him through this with me. Feeling the need to talk to someone else other that Thomas, I dialed my phone.

"Jillian, hey how are you? I'm so sorry to bother you this late, but I need to talk to you. My father had a severe stroke," I couldn't finish speaking to her, I broke apart.

Thomas took the phone I dropped to my lap and told her that I returned with him from Austin and that I was staying at his condo. He told her what hospital my father was in. I heard him clearly as my eyes were clouding, "Jillian, it doesn't look good, please come, early tomorrow would be best." I waved at Thomas to keep the phone, as I couldn't talk at this moment. I would see her tomorrow. I knew in my heart that my father was not doing well. I felt it, and I also knew that was why he had to tell me as much as he could from his hospital bed. There was probably so much more he wanted to share with me, but he was drained in just the little time we were there. I knew tomorrow a lot of his police brothers would be by trying to see how he was doing too and that would hopefully raise his spirits.

When we arrived at the condo, my heart sank for another time this evening. First, seeing my father so helpless and then seeing my former home again, where I'd lost my heart not so long ago. As I walked through the door I took in the familiar surroundings. Thomas kept it neat and nearly the same as when I was here. I headed toward the bathroom down the hall to change and told Thomas I would sleep in the spare bedroom. He came down the hall only to pull me into him in gentle, comforting embrace. I felt his warmth and I hugged him back. He then carried my travel bag to the bathroom and as I entered it he leaned on the outer hallway wall, "Hey, you know I'm here for you, sleep well."

Early in the morning I dreamed of Rand. Rand and I holding one another, as the pad of his thumb slowly rubbed along my face and neck, inching toward my chest… that soon turned to me crying that my father didn't make it. I must have cried out loud because I soon felt warm arms envelop me. I burrowed tightly onto the arms and kissed the hands that were so near to my chest. I took the pad of his thumb to my lips and then pulled it to my chest. My cries became whimpers and then faded into a smooth sleeping rhythm.

When I awoke I was still wrapped up tightly in Thomas's arms. I slowly slid out of his hold. I jumped when my feet touched the cold, hardwood floor. Thomas spoke, "Are you alright? I came in earlier when I heard you crying in your sleep. I couldn't resist holding you until you stopped." I stood and leaned over to thank him with a kiss to his cheek and he turned to catch my lips to his, but I backed away.

I walked down the hallway and found my phone and checked it for messages. I had a few. First Jillian wasn't happy that I was here at the condo. She didn't know if I was here because we were trying to repair our relationship or if it was of my father being ill. She was coming over with breakfast shortly to get me to the hospital. The second message was also from Jillian. She said that Raeford called her early this morning asking why I left them without a word, and with my ex-husband. Kent told the band when he saw me leave I looked torn. And then there was a text from Rand, my heart jumped but all it read was –

Why?

I remembered the text I sent to him yesterday asking if we could talk. It seemed like days ago. I wondered if that was the "Why?" or if he was asking why I left. I couldn't do this with him right now…

The doorbell chimed, I knew it was Jillian, my savoir. "Oh Jillian," I hugged her and cried. "Madison, it will be alright, let's go see your father together, he knows I am his other daughter." We laughed; she really was like a sister to me.

"Madison, I hate to get you upset any more, but Raeford called me this morning. Maxwell was upset because Rand was off in his performance in San Antonio. He said Rand seemed angry. Raeford said they were heading to Galveston for a few days and then they would be back here. He asked me why you left, I told him your father wasn't doing well. I'm sure he'll tell Rand. Raeford said you and your dad are in his prayers. I told him I would keep them posted."

Thomas entered the kitchen, and walked over and gave Jillian a big hug. I know they had their differences when it came to me but they appeared to table it to keep me calm and help me through this time with my father. I was thankful they were getting along and that she brought breakfast, as I was actually able to get a few bites of food down. I needed some strength to carry me through this.

The ICU floor was mostly quiet as only family members were allowed to visit. Stepping off the elevator it looked like they were giving away something free there today in the waiting area. It was filled with so many familiar faces – my father's precinct friends and former partners. I welcomed them all and told them that I could only sneak one or two of them in claiming they were my uncles. A few of them did get the chance to see him throughout the day; he really didn't wake like last night, only tossed in his bed a bit. I sat with him and I talked to him and Thomas joined me and held my hand while I held my father's frail hand. Jillian also came in with me for a while and spoke to my father about crazy things she and I have done. With all the visitors that came to see him, no one left, the waiting room was crowded and some of the guys spoke of my father and his police days, remembering several close calls. We did break during the afternoon, Jillian, Thomas and I went to the cafeteria to have something to eat.

As nightfall came upon us, I wasn't hungry and wanted to stay close as my father's doctors revealed he was slipping. Thomas and Jillian and others went to get some dinner. I remained seated on the tiny stool that rolled about in his room, only rolling it closer to my father's bedside. I lifted his hand and stroked the back lightly. I thought maybe he would feel this and awake. Then I leaned over and kissed his hand. The monitors started to sound, I didn't know what to do, I buzzed the nurse, but she was already entering, she asked me to move back. It only took her seconds, mere seconds, to turn back to me and tell me that he passed. I was lifeless, I couldn't move, I felt panicked and I dropped my head to my hands and sobbed. I walked over to my father's bedside and bawled like a tiny child. I then passed the nurse and the doctor that had come in and thanked them for their help the past few days. As I walked out of his room and down toward the waiting room feeling numb and alone, I glanced at the wall clock it had been nine o'clock and time for one my father's favorite detective dramas on the television. I pushed past the doors to the waiting area, and as I did, Thomas saw my eyes and jumped toward me.

"Oh, Thomas, hold me please, I need you," I cried.

Thomas kept me in his arms, as he moved me over to sit me down, I saw his eyes widen shooting a look at something or someone. I glanced around the room and saw Jillian along with all of the wonderful people that my father meant something to and then I focused on the person exiting the room. Through my teary eyes, I saw the back of someone, their dark hair, just bordering at the shoulder line. Rand had been there, or I wanted him there so badly that I just though he was.

Days after someone passes are the hardest. You have to begin to make plans to sum up what their life was in one evening of a viewing and then another day of the memorial. If it weren't for Thomas and Jillian I don't know what I would have done. They helped me with all the arrangements. The viewing was done beautifully. So many flowers were delivered and as I walked that evening into the funeral parlor with Jillian before anyone was to arrive I knew it would be a long lingering evening of friends. I was saddened that my mother would not be here, and I knew so many years had passed but there was a longing to see her again. And, even my father's brother Jake, my uncle Jake, I had loved him when I was growing up, he was the fun uncle, the irresponsible one I was told, and yet he was now the keeper of my mother's heart.

I walked up toward my father's coffin as he was laid out so dignified. There were so many flower arrangements; I began to read the cards, many from fellow officers and their wives, one from Thomas that was lovely. Jillian and I chose my favorite crème roses for my father and that was stunning in presentation just above the casket, then off to the side, I saw an arrangement of deep red roses and I read the card that said: *John, we will both carry you in our hearts forever, Grace & Jake.* I held my breath. I shivered, someone told them and I knew they wouldn't show here but they knew and acknowledged him. I was happy for that. It was then that Jillian took hold of me and led me away as I was starting to tear and another arrangement caught my eye. Over the top in size, I'd never seen so many crème roses with dark pink edges, you would need a large wagon to haul it out of here. I approached the bountiful floral arrangement and inhaled the incredible aroma and read the card –*Mr. Thomas McCormick (Mick), I would have been honored to have met the man who created the lovely Madison, watch over her from above now, and I promise I will from here below. Max Rand*

Jillian held me and kept me from falling, Rand never ceased to amaze me. He wasn't even here and I felt him and hoped my father could too. She then told me, "Madison, Rand was at the hospital the day your father passed. I knew he flew in and was in the waiting room during the day. I spoke to him and he was very concerned about your father's condition and also wondered why you returned to your ex-husband."

"What, I didn't go back to Thomas, why would he think that?"

"Well all I know is Rand was there when you came out from your father's room after he passed away and fell into Thomas's arms."

"Raeford told me that he and Rand had to return to Galveston for their show tonight. I really didn't know what was going on with you, you and him, or you and Thomas. You haven't really filled me in." I looked at Jillian and said, "Nothing is going on with Thomas and me, I can't believe Rand was actually here." I broke into pieces.

As this evening unfolded, I somehow pulled it together though and was commended for being such a picture of strength. I did my father proud and stood acknowledging all the people that poured in to memorialize him. It was hours and hours and a long line, but I smiled and genuinely hugged them all. I was exhausted. Jillian took me to my home, I told her I would be fine and as she dropped me off and I entered my house, it was quiet and I was alone. I felt so awfully alone. I found comfort in my notebook that was sitting on the edge of the table and pulled it to my chest. I began to write with tear filled eyes, a love note as I curled myself into the living room corner chair.

Rand:

I smelled the aroma of the flowers you sent to my father's viewing. I read the card over and over in my head of the words you beautifully wrote. My father surely is smiling down at you knowing what a kind person you are. I too had wished you could have met him but there are many stories I can share about him that will bring him to life for you. Although he loved Thomas for me, by his bedside as he was failing he did tell me to follow my heart and if it wasn't to be back with Thomas then that was fine. I think my father had a forewarning of what lied ahead for me. I fell apart after the loss of my father and I wanted to reach for you but I could never have put you through that again after the suffering I saw in your eyes from Ashley's passing. I held in my heart that you were near and were thinking of me. I felt protected by a memory of the look of warmth in your blue eyes.

Thomas did help me in this time but truly as a friend, he wanted more, but I was beginning to carry an Olympic sized torch for you in my world. For now just know John (Mick) McCormick would have greeted you with a questioning eye and a firm handshake. He would have asked your intentions with his only daughter. Your longer hair and tattoos may have had him prejudge you but once he touched your hand through that grip he would have felt you like I did and know the true you. I thank you for reaching out to my father. I wipe the tears from my face now as this is a powerful moment for me.

Maddy xo

When I completed my thoughts, I searched the missed calls on my phone. I had dozens of messages. I scrolled through and then came to one I reread. *Madison – our hearts are with you at this time, we'll think of you as we play tonight, take care of yourself – Maxwell and Rolling Isaac's.*

That was nice for them to take a moment to reach out to me before their show. I knew though I couldn't burden anyone now with my loss and sorrow, especially not Rand. That since I was at such a low point in my life before and that months of time had begun to heal me and that now again I was faced with feeling empty and depleted inside and this would take a long time for me to heal.

Chapter Eight – Old habits never die

Sometimes time is a healer in itself. Seasons are changing and now the fall is fast approaching. I feel a slight crispness in the early morning air as I sit on my balcony having coffee. I have kept busy most days with my writing. I had some earlier pieces I was working on long ago that resurfaced in my mind to rewrite now and I still have all the gathered information I was writing on the band. Thinking of the band, they send me a text now and again which is very nice. Kent tried to send me a big kiss from him, but his lips just came cross my computer screen blurred, I laughed at that. I haven't heard a word from Rand though, since his text asking me why? I have been following them from afar, from my computer.

I knew after my father passed that they returned to Philly for a time to write some new songs. Raeford keeps in touch with Jillian so she in turn always tells me, although I try to play it off, pretending not to be interested, but inside I am waiting for tidbits of information like a dog waiting for a water bowl on a hot summer's day.

Last week while we were at the gym Jillian told me that the band was heading west for at least a month plus. They had several local shows and a friend's place to crash at for the month or two. I was missing that I wasn't going to be with them on the West Coast but figured I could just go on the internet and follow along with their travels. I knew down the road I would need to touch base with them to finalize some of the items I was placing in the book, but I wasn't even putting a time table to that just yet. In the meantime I was looking to hire a literary agent to field my writings to a publishing house.

I found Cecile Brookes by accident. Jillian and I had gotten into a routine of hitting the gym three days a week to keep me busy and her in shape although Jillian is always in beautiful shape. We had finished a work out and had gone to have a light latte. While we were ordering, we saw a petite but very outspoken girl walk in. She told the barista that she would have her usual as she approached the counter. She smiled cheerfully at Jillian and I, and then walked over to us.

"You're Madison Tierney, hi, I'm Cecile Brookes" She introduced herself telling me she was a literary agent. "I've read some of your work, and I followed your column years ago. I don't really care for the columnist that replaced you."

I was taken back as I didn't know that some people actually knew of me. As I was thanking her, she decided to just come over and join us. When you get three girls together for a chat anything and everything are topics for discussion. It didn't take long for me to warm up to Cecile; she was like a bright glass of fresh squeezed orange juice carrying you through the day, so sunny and happy. I told her I was seeking out a literary agent and you would have thought she just won prom queen. She was over the moon with enthusiasm. I discussed briefly the book I was working on about Rolling Isaac's and she hung on my every word.

"Madison, can you take me to see their rehearsal location and **The Wall**? Maybe, when the band returns I can see them play? This way once I've read your book I will have the complete picture of your work. I can get you in the door, across the publisher's desk and to print." I agreed to take her out there one day. She and I actually shook on the deal to work together giving me a nice feeling of anticipation and friendliness.

After our first meeting by chance, she was off and running to assist me. Jillian was a great judge of character and she was right on board with me taking her on to help.

Usually daily, Cecile would text me or call with a simple question about something I had written about the band. She seemed to take my work seriously. Most mornings of late, after touching base with her I would go online and catch a brief review of the band from the show the night before, or see where their tour was heading. This morning, there was a video feed that was taken by a fan. They had titled it "Randevouz." I was curious so I hit play and enlarged the screen size and turned up the volume on my computer. It wasn't the music that had me so surprised as it was one of Rolling Isaac's that played loudly, and I began to tap my finger to the side of my computer to the tune. I was hit with the visual of Rand, kissing one girl and moving his hand down the curves of her back and then leaving her and walking further down the back of the stage area and pulling in another girl and almost stabbing his tongue into her mouth and the person recording the video zooming into this as they kissed. He sat down and brought her onto his lap and as she straddled his waist with her legs, they never broke their kiss. I closed out the video feed. I was blankly staring at the monitor as my phone rang.

"Hey Madison, that Rand is one sexy guy. I just saw a video of him, the fans love him! What's not to love, he's a total package." Cecile's voice bellowed in her description of him. Not that I didn't know how intoxicating he was, but I played off the video saying I hadn't seen it. My stomach wrenched. I had seen it and couldn't shake it from my head. I could see only one way to push past this. I decided to throw myself into planning my upcoming birthday. Thomas, Jillian and Cecile had asked how I planned to spend my birthday, so I decided to focus on that. I needed to put Rand's sexual pursuits in the back of my mind.

"Cecile, Rand is Rand, that's how the band guys roll, oh by the way I have put some thought into my birthday." I continued trying to quickly change the subject with her.

I entertained years back and had dinner parties with Thomas's business associates. I decided I wanted a party to lighten my solemn mood of late and have it at my home. The guest list would be limited to close friends of mine as my family was all gone now. I told them they could choose a theme for the party, provide the food and beverages, and I would leave to give them time to put it together and surprise me. My idea went over well with them all. Thomas and I had been continuing a nice, friendly talking relationship since my father's passing and I had met quite a few people at the gym being there several days a week. Jillian took the liberty of letting them know.

They had a few weeks of planning and they did party planning justice. On my birthday afternoon I left the house in a limousine and was scheduled to be pampered and puffed at the spa for hours. It was a well appreciated treat bought buy Thomas to make me enjoy this special day from the start. After I was all refreshed I dressed in new backless black tunic-style dress and black heels, I was ready to attend my own surprise party.

As I walked up my front door, I really wanted to open it and have Rand there to embrace me and see me gaining confidence again and feel his arms wrap tightly around me as he wished me Happy Birthday. I turned the knob to my door and there stood Thomas front and center surrounded by many. Thomas pulled me in and embraced me; he lightly trailed his hand down the exposed back. Despite his touch and the warmth of his hug, this is not what my body was craving. I glanced toward the back of my living room and there stood a familiar, smiling face, Raeford.

I ran over and hugged him so tightly. I actually bypassed other close friends but once I wrapped my arms partially around him I felt a secure feeling cover my entire soul. I was so happy that he was there. I asked the dumb but obvious question with excitement in my voice, "Is Rand here? Is he coming?" Raeford said he thought he was coming, but he did not elaborate as Raeford was not a man of many spoken words. When we looked around, Rand was not there.

Thomas made his way over to me and forced his hand in between myself and Raeford to introduce himself. Thomas said, "Hello I am Madison's husband Thomas." I looked at Thomas and then he corrected himself in saying he was my ex-husband. He did say though that he was hopeful one day again we would make it legal. Raeford greeted him pleasantly just as Jillian swooped in eagerly to take her new man into her arms. Raeford turned to Jillian and said quietly, "I think it would be better if Rand doesn't show." I meant to question Raeford as I heard his words so lightly, but then I was so quickly spun around and hugged by another guest.

I drank so much throughout the evening. I enjoyed being with everyone and letting loose in my own environment and since I didn't have to be driven home or cared for, if I got to tired or felt too drunk I could simply crash in my own bed at the top of the stairs. I caught glimpses of Raeford and Jillian kissing in the hallway, the kitchen and even out on the deck although it was pretty chilly. I was thinking if Rand were here that would be us out there in the cold air, and I would have his warm lips conquering my mouth and his body embracing mine. We would hold ourselves so closely and be wrapped in one another's warmth. I faintly heard the doorbell ring, but I suppose someone answered it because when I got toward the living room the door was closed and the bell never sounded again.

In the foyer several gifts were left, I didn't want to open any until the next morning, tonight I just wanted to enjoy the evening and the company. It was later that I went to use my bathroom upstairs and I crossed the foyer to the step landing and saw a pile of floral bouquets in that area all stacked on top of one another.

There were so many. I looked to Thomas standing several feet away, "Thomas what is all this, they're lovely?"

"You had a delivery."

"But so many?

"All for you Madison, the roses are pretty but you're beautiful." I thanked him as he seemed to surely be taking the credit for this lovely gesture.

I entered the bathroom upstairs. As I fumbled for the light on the side wall, the window to the front of the house allowed me the nighttime's street view. I saw a vehicle with the headlights on and a person climbing into the front seat with dark hair just touching below the shoulder of their jacket. By the time I got closer to the window and opened it up, they had pulled out and were driving down the street. I shook my head, and told myself I was wishing something that wasn't and that I had way too much to drink.

As the party was dying down, Jillian hugged me and whispered in my ear, "I'm sorry Rand was a no show, I wasn't sure if he would be here that's why I didn't mention it to you earlier. But I love you so happy birthday! And please don't be mad at me, but I'm bailing and taking Raeford home with me now!" I didn't blame her, he was one chiseled, hot man and she deserved him. I was going to tell him to tell Rand hello or some other stupid thing since I'd had too much to drink, but I just thanked him so much for coming. I watched his ass the entire way as they left my house; Jillian was one lucky girl this evening.

Thomas stayed on to help clean up and Cecile was still talking to us as she headed out the door. I hugged her and thanked her and asked her if she was okay to drive. We decided that if the weather permitted, to go out to one of the orchards in Bucks County the next morning. We wanted to get some pumpkins and definitely pumpkin pie and then stop at the band's rehearsal studio as Raeford told me where to find a hidden key so I could get in and show her the place. Raeford said he may be there as well and he could talk to her briefly.

The house was quiet now as we stopped playing the music and I fell into my sofa and closed my eyes. Thomas had remained. He came over to me and leaned into me and kissed me slowly. I drank a lot this evening and even just the sensation of lips crossing over mine, made me tingle. I pulled Thomas into the sofa with me and continued to kiss him. He gingerly took his lips down to my neck and climbed on top of me, keeping me pinned to the flat of the sofa below. I could feel that he wanted me. Silently in that moment of us kissing, he was telling me that he needed me. I was looking up at him from beneath his hold. "Madison you are so beautiful. I should have never let you go." I pulled him in again and I swirled my tongue deep in his mouth, I was feeling so aroused, but not by Thomas, just by the act of kissing him, licking his lips and feeling him fill my mouth with his passion. I felt I was using him as a replacement for the desire I wanted to feel, and the taste I yearned for from Rand. Thomas pulled me in and I turned slightly, satisfied to have been kissed and so passionately. I closed my eyes and sighed and pretended to pass out so that he would not continue.

He rose and kissed me on the forehead and spoke, "Madison, I still love you, and I know you love me." I heard him walk away as he gathered a blanket from the other room and I felt him cover me halfway. I heard the front door shut as he left my house. I opened my eyes as I laid there and thought of nothing but Rand. I sat up for a bit and began to write another love note for Rand, in my notebook.

Rand:

In an old attic trunk you store away treasures and keepsakes. Some may be good, some maybe unfavorable and many were part of your life that made you grow. I have stored a memory away of my marriage to Thomas. That time was wonderful, but the ending destroyed me. Now one of the trunk's contents has escaped the confines, climbed out and dusted itself off. This is Thomas. He has reinvented himself to come back to me thinking I will just fold and crumble and welcome him back and become his wife again. I don't know why I am writing this to you, but I feel that you should know that had I not met you this may have been an option for me. It was meeting you that made me something more.

Time that passed after Thomas left me and then our divorce put me at the lowest point I can remember. Reaching out to you with confidence to write again and your taking me along with you and the band was a fit in my life that has made me better. I know I still have feelings for Thomas. I just can't turn them off, but it's different now. The feelings that I have for you are what I turn to in my every day thoughts as of late. I believe fate has also come from my stored trunk in the attic and become the force or principle believed to predetermine events. As I am torn with feelings that tug in my heart, I am certain you are in my life now for a reason and the timing of us sharing moments and touches and kisses may become our wonderful destiny.

Maddy xo

I fell asleep with my pen and notebook spread on my chest. I was awakened midway through the night when I heard an awful rendition of the Happy Birthday song being left on my answering machine and I heard chuckling from girls in the background. As I made my way to the kitchen for a huge drink of water and to take a few aspirins to prevent my morning hangover I hit the play button and heard the song again. It was from Rand. He was drunk, it sounded in his singing voice and I heard girls with him asking him who is Madison that you are singing to, who is she?…he simply said to them in a cold tone, *no one, let it go*. This was the Rand of late that I was seeing all too often on the internet and now hearing him not in a manner I would fantasize about. Back in my bed I turned to my side and placed my notebook on the flat of the comforter and began to write, all I kept thinking about was Rand.

Rand:

I would never want to change you as you are so different in ways that I think we complement one another. But, I don't now at this moment if I can ever really be with you or if we will ever make that step to be a couple. I see so many photos of you and fan made video clips that make my stomach turn. Not as jealousy but that we share moments together and then I see a clip of you with another in a stolen moment. It makes me believe that our time spent together may have no special meaning to you. I want to feel safe again in life, have that person as my rock, build that relationship…but you to me are unsure, the flight risk, and the wanderer.

This doesn't mean I have no feelings for you because of this as my feelings are so intense for you. But how do I get us, if there is to ever be us, on the same page. I don't think I could ever be truly intimate with you and not wonder about you off at the next concert in another city. I trust you when you are near; it is the distance that I fear. I too have been drawn back at moments to Thomas and that is not fair to you although I don't think you even know that at all. I guess, who am I to question your ethics and morals and actions when I am no better? I wish some of our habits could change or we could work on them together. Maybe one day I will have the voice to share these thoughts with you.

Maddy xo

I am not sure when I finally closed my eyes to the dark of the night, but I was sleeping very deeply under my comforter when I heard my phone sound again in the early morning hours. I reached to my nightstand and picked it up to see Cecile's name and knew she was wide awake and cheery already. Her message was –

> *Up, Up, Up. We have a nice day planned. I'll be over soon. I am so looking forward to seeing* **The Wall** *you write about and their studio.*

I dragged myself to the shower; I put it on a cooler setting and stood in the center cursing at the chill but letting it awaken my senses and banish any arousal resulting from thoughts of Rand. I was up now and knew Cecile would be eager and full of excitement today. I decided with the autumn coolness now upon us that I would wear a rust colored sweater and I pulled on my low rise jeans and boots.

Definitely not flip flop weather anymore. I grabbed a multi shimmered scarf and looped it around my neck and took my camel colored jacket.

It was the beep, beep, beep that told me Cecile had arrived. One beep I would have known she was here, but three possibly four…I heard them all. As I climbed into her car, I programmed her GPS with the address for the band's location. Before we got there we stopped at one orchard and another small pumpkin stand along the way. I actually got a cider donut and some coffee at one as I had not eaten since earlier last night at my party. As we drove along the road, the fall foliage was in full glory. The colors were so beautiful and vivid, it was almost as if they were painted rather than naturally occurring. It happens like this every season for several weeks. The leaves are beautiful and then as fast as they turn brilliant and lovely they drop and we know winter has begun. But I was soaking in the sun coming through the windshield and watching all the orange and golden colors bounce about outside from the trees as the rays pierced through the branches.

"Here we are, we have reached our destination," Cecile exclaimed, sounding too much like the GPS voice, as we turned down the winding road that led up to the barn and the house off in the distance. "This is so beautiful; it looks like a canvas painting." It did indeed, it was lovely. My eyes looked to the house and I didn't see any activity or any vehicle parked out front. At the barn there was one unfamiliar car parked there. It may have been one of the band members'. I know it wasn't Rand's. I pointed out where Cecile should park. As we walked up to the barn, Cecile pulled out her phone and was taking many photos. She even wound up getting one of me with all the autumn colored trees and the barn off in one corner of the photograph. She snapped it and showed me. It was a great photo, because I knew I was thinking of Rand, and being here at his place.

I found the key that they kept hidden but I didn't have to use it as the main door was open. When we went in I hollered. "Hello is anyone here?" as the entire rehearsal area was not lit up. Slowly coming out of the darkness was Raeford, "Hey, good morning Madison, how are you feeling? Oh, hey Cecile, nice to see you again."

"I'm feeling better, I drank too much. Hey, thanks for coming last night. Are you alone here?"

"No."

I got flutters in my belly thinking Rand was near. "I got your company now," Raeford said. And right he was, since Cecile and I arrived he wasn't alone. He told us he was gathering some things from the barn to take back to California early tomorrow. I did not question where Rand was especially after my early morning sing along. Cecile was in a sprint up to **The Wall,** examining everything and there was plenty of memorabilia to absorb. She asked if Raeford would answer some questions for her and I hit him with a stack of my own notes that I wanted him to look over as a second set of eyes from the band's perspective.

I was just walking about in the studio and I said, "Are you both okay for a bit, I want to just go outside and take a walk and get some air?" They told me to go ahead that they'd be fine.

As I opened the outer door I sucked in the cool refreshing air and it filed my lungs and revitalized me. I walked over to Cecile's car because I had left my voice recorder there and wanted to get some thoughts out. I sat in the car with the door partially open. I decided that I felt too weird being here without Rand and wanted to tell him that I was at least here as a courtesy. I pulled out my phone and sent him a message.

Rand, I wanted to tell you I stopped here at the rehearsal studio, I ran into Raeford and he said it was okay. He is still here. He and Jillian got reacquainted last night, they are very striking together. Rand…can we talk sometime soon?

There was too quick of a message received back from Rand.

Madison, I have tried to talk to you. I've texted you about three times a day for these past months. I know that's over one hundred messages.

I was suddenly confused; I knew I never received any. I replied –

I never received any of them.

Rand sent me his reply –

I never could press the **Send** *button.*

I started to cry, my tears chilled against my cheeks as the air from beyond the open car came through to me. The car door opened wider and there he stood. It had been so long since I had seen him live and in person in front of me. It was almost like a mirage. I wiped my tears with my hand, looking in the other direction as he bent down into the door and took hold of my right hand. I rose up from the car seat and suddenly locked into an embrace with him. Rand pushed me to the side of the car and rested his hands above me, trapping me in his hold. He looked down at my tear filled eyes and began to kiss me slowly, first my forehead, then my bridge of my nose, I closed my eyes. I'd wished for this to happen for so long and I felt his tender lips sweetly kiss my eyelid. He then moved to my lips, possessing my mouth as he took over.

He deeply kissed me, claiming my lips in every wet taste and lick. I had known I felt this passion for him for so long. Being away from his attention and kisses made me yearn for him and want him so much more. I didn't want this to stop. I lifted my hands up under his jacket and under his shirt to feel his naked skin that warmed under my touch. I played with each of his nipples and licked his lips as he moaned from my playful touches. He dropped his arms and reached back behind me to lift me up; I pulled my arms out and clasped them behind his neck tightly. He carried me the long way across the landscaped, autumn colored lawn and up the steps and he set me down on the porch bench as he opened the front door. With the door open, he came over picked me up again and carried me into the house, he closed the door with his foot and up the steps we went. We went to the end of the long hall to his bedroom. It was opulent and beautiful with cathedral ceilings.

I came to rest as he laid me on his king sized bed that had a beautiful atrium window view just behind. We hadn't spoken a word. I sat up slightly only to have him remove my jacket one sleeve at a time and then tear off my scarf and sweater. With him next to me, I slid off his leather jacket and took his shirt up over his head. He tugged at my boots and tossed them someplace in the room. I laid back down into the softness of the comforter. He undid my belt and the zipper of my jeans. Pausing, he took my scarf and tied my hands gently together at my wrists and placed them up above my head. He removed his boots and started to kiss me just teasingly on the mouth and then continued downward. My chest heaved, straining toward his mouth; I lifted to meet each kiss. I wanted his mouth on every inch of my body.

"Rand, I've missed you." I lightly sounded in between my catching breaths.

"You're so beautiful, so beautiful. Madison, I need you." There was desire in his voice. I knew I wanted him. Rand began to pull my jeans down my thighs. My lower body flushed in anticipation of his touch. He didn't miss the opportunity to lightly lick my belly jewel. He smiled like he had claim on that part of me too. He spread his tall, spectacular body alongside of me. With my hands still tied together at my wrists, I brought them down toward the zipper of his jeans. With one quick move on my scarf, he untied it like pulling apart a ribbon from a gift. I opened the button and unzipped his pants. I could hear his breathing become more rapid.

"Rand, I want to feel you so bad," as I reached lower in to his jeans following the zipper down with my fingers. I felt him harden and noticed how aroused I had made him. Rand then moved up over top of me and said, "I want..." he paused, "we cannot do this now, we have company and the front door's unlocked."

He was now positioned on all fours over me his jeans undone, his naked chest and he was looking out from his bed through the large window to the sidewalk that wound from the studio to his door. Approaching the house was Raeford and perky petite Cecile. I rose up to take in their arrival. I laid back in the bed for a moment savoring being here with him like this and wanting him so, and then a doubt appeared in my thoughts of him just last night singing drunk with girls.

I reached over and found his shirt and helped him back into it only I stopped to kiss his chest so deeply not wanting this moment to really end. He dressed me and fixed my hair tucking some behind my ears. We headed down the steps as the door opened. "Rand, this is Cecile my literary agent." I made the introductions and it didn't take long for Cecile to lock on to Rand's blue eyes and sexy bed-tossed look and she was like a melted chocolate bar. Rand made her acquaintance and then he and Raeford headed to the bar for drinks. I looked at Cecile to see her still unable to move. I tugged at her arm and pulled her forward with me. We joined them for some drinks, only I opted for water since I was still playing catch up with my feeling a bit hung over and now majorly love starved.

I apologized for putting Rand on the spot, but Cecile wanted to ask him a few questions. He smiled at me calmly in a way that made it obvious he expected me to make it up to him. Cecile asked him if he had any favorite towns to play in, or any favorite songs that they played. She asked him what his inspirations for songs were. During her brief Q & A session she complimented him on his talents and said she hoped to see them live in concert.

"That can be arranged Cecile, Madison can get passes anytime," he assured her.

Then she put the question out there, "Rand, I know you love music, but do you have any other love interests?" Cecile dove in without hesitation.

"Well actually I have one immediate love interest," he hesitated and then focused on meeting my eyes, "and that would be that I would love to take Madison for the rest of the day to New Hope to enjoy her birthday that I missed." With that, Raeford surely got the hint and he escorted Cecile with him to the front door. I walked with Cecile and told her we would catch up later. She looked back to Rand like a deer caught in headlights, just like most other women, she was completely awe struck.

Rand and I left the house, although I wanted to run right up the steps taking two at a time and jump right into the center of his bed again. He took hold of my hand and said, "Madison, spend today with me."

I could not offer any refusal, and truthfully, I didn't want to. There was something about the tone of his voice that directed me. It took me on a path closer to his heart. I finally saw his Hummer when we left the house; it was parked down past where Cecile was. I guess he had come up while we were in the barn earlier and I never looked around for vehicles after we first arrived. Rand held my hand and rubbed the pad of his thumb over my hand in tiny patterns. We traveled through the beautiful pallet of fall and were soon on River Road heading into downtown New Hope.

This is a quaint town of many shops and eateries and just a great place to spend a day walking about and enjoying being outdoors before the colder weather. I enjoyed this afternoon so much strolling in and out of stores and being looked at and smiled to by strangers that passed us. He held me tightly with his arm around my waist while we were in the shops, sometimes letting his fingers drop into the back of my jeans, touching my naked lower back. Then he would again grasp my hand tightly before we left each storefront, like he was worried I would disappear. We passed a furniture shop that had antique pieces inside, so we ventured in and there was a lovely old roll top desk. It was so large with plenty of writing space on the top. I sat in the chair and almost immediately felt like this desk was made for me. I wondered about the history of it. I wanted to know who once used this desk. Rand had to pull me out of the seat or I would have remained there for a long time. I traced my hands over the wood surface and told him I loved this desk as we walked on to the next store.

As we passed several shops, we came upon one that had artisan jewelry and we inside, only to see some of the finest handmade pieces. I was taken by a piece that caught my eye in the window. It was a crystal heart bracelet. The bracelet displayed a large sized heart dancing with sparkles in the afternoon sun. It was laid on a silver and leather cuff. I hadn't even shown it to Rand or made an attempt to single it out, but as we entered the shop he asked the jeweler to bring it from the window to us.

"Madison, I didn't get you anything for your birthday, I want you to have this heart. It shines just like you," he smiled as he spoke. I was thrilled. How did he know I looked at that piece? It was lovely. I also thought the cuff was similar to the one he wore to remember Ashley. I was touched. I reached up and pulled him in to give him a lingering kiss. I wanted to express my thanks but I knew words wouldn't be enough. When we finally broke the kiss, the jeweler and his assistant laughed and said, "We do have custom engagement rings too." Rand and I just laughed and I smiled happily as he secured my new bracelet on my wrist and he pulled my wrist closer to his lips and gave it gentle kiss.

We had worked up an appetite as I had not eaten too much today and my stomach needed food. Rand and I stopped earlier while shopping and sampled an autumn beer selection at one of the local bars on the main road, but I was in need of real food. Rand offered up, "Do you want to eat here or we can go pick up some food and I can cook you a birthday dinner?" Without hesitation I pulled him in the direction of his vehicle, I knew he could cook and I wanted nothing more than just his attention and to be alone with him in anyway that I could.

What a great cook he was, I was admiring him from across his kitchen island. He moved between the counter, stove, and the cutting board without hesitation. I watched every movement. I was even mesmerized by him chopping up the mushrooms. With his traveling with the band for the last month he had no food in the house, but we stopped at the market on the way back and he seemed to know exactly which isle had the ingredients to complete my birthday dinner. My only contribution to the dinner was to go to his bar and decide on a bottle of wine. That was a difficult selection process as he had many. I finally found one that was labeled *CrossBarn*, and I pulled that from the holder. Cross reminded me of his awesome chest tattoo and barn, his home. Being a writer I am always looking for hidden meaning in words and items.

This line of thinking made me want to text Jillian. I wanted to thank her for the party last night and talk with her about what happened here with Rand and me today. I grabbed my phone as Rand was busying himself in the kitchen. I sent her a text;

Hey girl, I wanted to thank you for the party last night, it was fun, I drank way too much. Also it was great seeing you with Raeford. I saw him today when I was at the rehearsal studio with Cecile. I was wondering why Rand never came last night, but I didn't want to ask him, he and I spent the rest of today together, first with interrupted passion thanks to Cecile but, I will fill you in on the details later as I'm still at his house. We went to New Hope, walked around and had a great day. He bought me a beautiful heart cuff bracelet. I am having the best time with him.

What hit me next was the aroma as Rand seared the scallops. I finished up my text to her –

I have to go; Rand is making dinner and it smells way too good to stay out here in the den.

Her reply came quickly and was brief –

Enjoy the food and him. I am cheering for you both. I was so happy to see Raeford I wish he was staying here longer. But you go girl, I don't want to keep you especially from him.

The smell from the kitchen pulled me in, and I actually snuck a fork full of the wild mushroom risotto. I could not believe how pricey some little mushrooms can be. Once I tasted it though I realized they were worth the price.

Our dinner was terrific. I couldn't have been in a more content setting. Rand's presence was awesome and I found myself captivated by even the mundane things he would do. I watched him use his fork, I watched him with every bite of his food. I could not stop watching this man. For dessert he recreated the warm apple dessert we had once in Austin only he topped his off with extra whip cream and one lit candle. He brought this into the sunroom for us to devour, again without any forks. This time the Happy Birthday song was perfectly in tune. As I made a wish before I blew out the candle, I took his hand into mine and I closed my eyes. I knew exactly what I wanted to wish for. I wished that I could fill his heart as I knew he was doing a wonderful job of satisfying mine. As we hand fed one another he looked a bit sad.

I asked, "Are you sad I'm another year older than you?"

"Madison your age doesn't matter to me, I'm just sad time is not in our favor. I have to get to the airport tonight. Raeford and I have to get back to California."

He took a huge swipe of the whip cream from the dessert and placed it right under my throat, at the top of my chest, "But I have right now and I am going to enjoy this." He began to lick the cream off me as he laid me down on his sofa.

Playfully we finished every last piece and then continued with our own type of sweetness as we snuggled there for the rest of the time we had. Our lips just could not stop reaching toward one another as we kissed, trailing kisses across one another's neck. Neither of us let the passion reignite to the level it was earlier. I knew I wanted to be with him, but still had so many uncertainties of what he wanted with me in the long term, if there was any long term for us.

Seeing the recent videos online of him while traveling, there were so many girls at his disposal. I knew that he was heading back to that lifestyle all too soon. For now though knowing he was leaving shortly I pressed my head up into the fold of his underarm and rested myself comfortably. He stroked my arm with long sweeps making me quiver for more, absently twisting my new cuff bracelet.

Chapter Nine – Turkey Day

It must be really hard to travel as much as the band does. Sleeping in another place every night, not your own comfy bed. As I sit here this evening, on my cozy bed, I am wondering where they are all sleeping at this hour. I am wondering especially about Rand. I am missing him, and as I am putting my book about the band, *Rock Notes*, in some order, I find every time I write his name I pause and a smile comes to my lips. I actually lick my lips to wet them, somehow entranced by him even now. I bite my lower lip hard to put to rest the feeling that is stirring in me for him. The band and Rand are still on the West Coast. I keep following them online, but I refuse to watch another fan made video.

The first holiday of the fall season will be here in just days, with the winter ones not far behind. Rand has been in touch with me since he returned to the West Coast but we haven't spoken about any holiday plans. He will probably spend it with Maxwell, as he is his family. I don't have any near. I had spoken to Jillian and she is heading to Atlanta to see her brother Jason. They invited me, but I like being a home body in the cooler months staying in, writing a lot and enjoying coffee or a great glass of wine near a burning fire.

Thomas has been in touch with me at least weekly to ask me to an impromptu dinner or to meet him for a drink. I haven't really committed to any yet. He called this past week to ask me to join him and his family, which was once my extended family at his condo for Thanksgiving Day for an early dinner. When we were married I used to host the day and make all of the food and the men contributed by eating it all and watching the football games on Thomas's sixty inch television. It was almost like being at the game without the weather element. I know he would not be making the dinner, I could only assume he was placing an order with one of the Philly restaurants for a pick up of an entire meal with all the trimmings.

As for the band and their plans, Raeford told Rand he was heading back for a visit in Decatur. Ron was taking the girl he was currently crushing on with him for a mini vacation to his family in Florida. Kent was heading up to upper Pennsylvania, Clarkes Summit, and offered to take Isaac if Isaac could be a little quieter around Kent's family. I had been meaning to text Kent as Cecile has been developing a major crush on him. Cecile is really a cutie, and I could see them possibly dating as she is so perky and he is hysterical to be with. I will have to make myself a voice note on my recorder to text him. As for Rand and Maxwell, I heard they were going to be working on something for the band, probably promotional work right up to the day before Thanksgiving. I wasn't sure what I was going to end up doing on that day, but settled in the comfort of my warm bed, I feel so very thankful for all that Rand has brought to me. I reached for my phone and sent –

Rand, please note this is definitely not sexting… but I wanted to let you know that I was thinking of you while I was all settled warmly in my bed. Not sure where you're all at this evening but hoping everything is going well and your shows are as explosive there as they are here. I also just wanted to see what your Thanksgiving Day plans are?

I rested the phone on my chest and closed my eyes. My phone sounded an incoming message from Rand –

Madison, why no sexting? I could really use some from you right about now it has been a long time that we've been out on the road. It's great just to hear from you tonight. I know we talk but the days drag out here, I swear the West Coast is on a slow moving pace for everything. Things are going well thus far and well everyone is heading in one direction or another for the Thanksgiving holiday. Maxwell and I have some band business first in Chicago, so we plan to leave Los Angeles and hit Chicago and hopefully get in late the night before Thanksgiving Day. That is our plan as of now, so I would really like if you and I could share a nibble of a turkey leg and pumpkin pie with plenty of whip cream on top. Maxwell, plans to head to my Aunt's, I don't go as my aunt loved my father, Paul, so I want to avoid that confrontation. Great news for you, when we get home, we'll have a break until after the New Year. I think Maxwell is trying to line up one show in Philly a small venue during the first or second week of December. But a long rest is what we need. I know our time difference makes it much later for you, so I will let you go and sleep. I'm missing you. Oh, and if you change your mind on the sexting topic, feel free and make certain you press send. See you soon.

I was getting tired, but I sent him a reply –

I know you can cook, and I want you to know that I can as well so I will try to put something simple together for us. I am looking forward to the holiday season now. I was dreading it, but perhaps this will be a thankful one for us. I think I might take you into my dreams tonight, good night and Rand, I miss you.

I fell into a deep sleep and thought only of Rand and his coming back home, well back here. It was a wonderful dream, first I was only about a step away from the top landing of my confidence ladder and new I'd grown so much personally these months. Then I recall that I actually dreamed in color as I saw so clearly the pumpkin pie I was making in a dark orange and then I saw the red wine I was pouring in the glasses. I then was dreaming of snow, a light dusting of whiteness newly fallen that accumulated enough to make snowman. I saw Rand and me at Christmas which wasn't getting too far ahead of me and I saw all the colorful presents.

I was awakened not by opening the beautiful presents that I saw all around the fully decorated tree, but by the presence of someone outside ringing my doorbell. I jumped up and threw on a sweatshirt over my cami top and still in my pajama pants I padded down toward my front door.

"Good morning Madison," Thomas spoke as he leaned in and kissed me on the cheek. "I thought I could grab a fresh cup of coffee from you and see if you've made your plans for Thanksgiving yet." I knew his stopping all the way out here was not for coffee as he passed many coffee places on the way, but he wanted me to feel guilty so I would go to his place for the holiday. I had not told Thomas anything that I was feeling for Rand, for all I know he just thought I was friends with them all.

"Actually I'll make you a cup of coffee as I need one now. As for Thanksgiving, I am staying home and maybe having Rand over. It's a day that he has no place to go to and I can go over some of my writings with him since I haven't been in California traveling with him or the band." I added, "It's not a big holiday for me anymore so you enjoy your family and maybe we can do something another time." I felt good about letting it be said like that to him.

"Madison, my family adores you and there would be no awkwardness as I told them you and I are very friendly lately and who knows where we'll go." His reply was obviously worded to get me to cave for him. But as I started to make the coffee, I just said, "Maybe the next holiday, don't push Thomas."

After Thomas left I felt renewed that I wasn't going to be put through a day with ex-in-laws. I started to get out a few turkey day recipes to see what I could prepare. I hadn't spoken to Jillian yet today and decided to catch up with her as well. When she answered my call I said "Hey girlfriend, how are you? I had a great talk with Rand last night only to open my front door to Thomas this morning. Thomas came in person to ask me to come to his place for Thanksgiving, but I'm staying home with Rand."

"Good for you girl, I am proud of you for finally making a wise decision to be with Rand. Although I'll be with my brother I invited Raeford but he said he had plans already back in Decatur. I don't want to press it. He's so quiet at times, that I'm not sure what he's thinking. Hopefully he'll be here over Christmas and we'll have some private time then."

"I hope you have fun visiting with Jason and give him a kiss from me too. I bet Raeford will be missing you as well." She was quiet there for a moment.

"Madison, I really miss Raeford already, crazy huh? But so glad that he came back for that overnight. I'm trying to get him to open up to me, but it is really hard, he keeps everything inside. Not like us women that shout out everything we feel. Speaking of feelings, Thomas really is pushing the envelope with you. I give him credit, he isn't going away easy. You're going to have to make it clear with him that you aren't going back. I think he believes you will eventually."

"Oh, that is so not going to happen. I still care about him, I can't turn that off, but I care, really care for Rand. It is so different, I can't explain it."

"Maybe it's love you're feeling again. Listen, you have fun over the holiday and I will miss you, give Rand a big hug from me. Raeford says Rand is really into you. Raeford doesn't tell me much, but he also said that you are so good for Rand. I'm flying to Atlanta tomorrow to beat the holiday rush and just staying the weekend. But I'm a phone call away if you need me. How about Monday, we'll hit the gym after eating all the holiday food?"

"Yeah that sounds good, just how many calories do you think we'll put on this holiday?

"Girlfriend probably way too many, but we could always burn some off with sex, so remember that while Rand is near!"

"I'll try to take your advice, love you." I blew her a kiss goodbye through the phone and told her to have a wonderful holiday, I was so thankful to have her in my life.

"Have a warm holiday Madison, you deserve it."

The next few days were a bit hectic for me; I had to meet with Cecile to give her more chapters of my book for her to read through as I was on a timeline to finish. She had questioned what my dinner plans were for Turkey Day but I told her I had plans already and I think she was truly fishing for an invite but I didn't want anyone to be with Rand and me. I know that sounds selfish but I hadn't seen him in quite sometime and wanted to really spend a day of quality time with him. I was also busy with getting the ingredients on my list for my Thanksgiving Day dinner. I wanted it to be perfect. I felt that being on the road for so long that all Rand ate was meals out at the restaurants or room service or the buffets they brought in before the shows, and I wanted him to have some home cooking.

Wednesday night I was in the kitchen late, rolling the pie crust and making a flawless pumpkin pie. My house smelled like an autumn candle's aroma, very warm and tasty. I was wondering what time Rand's flight would be coming in from Chicago. I had put the news on and saw that there was some snow already in the Midwest, but not enough to cause flight cancelations. My phone sounded – it was Rand.

Madison I'm stuck with Maxwell, not that he isn't a great guy but I would rather be lying with my arms around you. Our plane had mechanical failure and we're grounded until further notice. Looks like we may not leave till the morning, which is if we can get on another flight on Thanksgiving Day. Everyone in the entire world is traveling now. I'll get to you as soon as we land. I miss you.

I was so excited that he would be here tomorrow that I didn't care when he would arrive. I replied –

I was actually watching the weather channel to make certain you weren't hung up by snow. I'm looking forward to seeing you. Tell Maxwell Happy Thanksgiving and I will see him sometime soon too. I'm deep in flour and sugar baking pumpkin pies so you can take him one all for himself. I'm glad you are missing me.

Rand sent another text –

That sounds really sweet, you're making my mouth water. I can't wait to taste your pies, and taste you.

I blushed and almost dropped my phone in the bowl of pie crust. I had to regroup and then I continued to busy myself with my culinary endeavors. My skills were limited but I was determined not to have any of this meal go wrong. When I had finished all the prep work and cooking I could do at this late hour I turned in for the night and my thoughts took me away to Rand.

I woke up early enough to read a text from Rand that he and Maxwell were able to get seats on a flight midday today and he would see me later. I was thrilled. I had a spring in my step as I went to the kitchen to prep the turkey and get everything underway. Looking out from my kitchen window a few flurries swirled and stuck to the wooden planks and then evaporated. The sky was a swirl of grey, and the remaining few fall leaves were a pop of color to this ominous feeling day.

The middle of the day I looked at the kitchen clock and knew he was on a flight as he hadn't sent me any messages changing that. I was a mess from cooking and decided to take a long bath and get all cleaned up and put something nice on with a hint of sexy for him.

I soaked in the water, enjoying the exciting scent of passion berry from a bath ball. I realized that I was here naked and wanting to feel Rand in the tub with me. I wanted to feel his desirable, sculpted body and take my hands up over his wet chest and carry my fingers to his dampened hair. I wanted to pull him into a passionate hot kiss and then watch him continue to move his lips down my body till he had his head between my thighs. I could feel myself getting all wet and aroused just by thinking of him. He will be here soon. With that thought, I slowly sank lower into the tub taking the warmth from the water into my body.

I lit the fireplace and some candles around my house to make the atmosphere warm and comfortable. I was dressed in a golden sheer sleeve short dress with a black leather belt resting low on my hips and black boots that came just above my knee. The belt complemented my leather cuff bracelet that I added to finish off my look. I glanced in my living room mirror as I walked past and for the first time in so long I liked the reflection that looked back. I had sent a text to Rand earlier –

> *Rand, hoping you got on that flight or another. Happy Thanksgiving. See you soon.*

I began getting nervous as the hours ticked away and I had not heard from him. I was wondering why I hadn't heard from Rand as I had already expected him hours ago. All the food cooled off as everything was ready earlier. I poured myself a glass of wine and was quite generous with the pour. My phone sounded –

> *Madison, hey, sorry I missed your message, we got delayed again. Maxwell had indigestion from something he ate here at the airport and got very sick. I took him to an urgent facility just outside the airport to be checked out and we had to pass up our earlier flight. We hope to catch a later flight. I'm sorry.*

My phone sounded again only it was a call from Thomas – I answered it trying to be cheery and not let him notice that I was choking up from the message that just came in from Rand. I felt deflated that Rand may not make it here.

"Hello Maddy how was your day? I wanted to tell you the last of my guests have left and Thanksgiving was not the same. Your cooking was missed was the general consensus."

It took me a minute to respond. I was trying to swallow the sad lump that formed in my throat as my day was not happy as I thought it would be.

"Maddy are you there? Are you okay?" Thomas pressed.

"I am fine, just a little let down. I was actually planning a dinner with Rand and he didn't come." There I said it to Thomas, I put it out there, whether he just thought Rand and I were friends or maybe something more, I actually said what I was feeling.

Thomas responded, "Maddy pour me some wine, I will see you soon, and you'll have a wonderful Thanksgiving night. I am not letting you say no and you are not going to end this day alone."

It took Thomas less than a half hour to get to my door from the city. There must have been no traffic on the roads as everyone was surely with their loved ones still enjoying the day or he drove really fast. When I opened the door to him, I was overtaken by his compassion. He opened his arms and I fell into them. I invited him in even though I had turned him down earlier this week to spend this day with him. I offered him a glass of wine and led him by his hand to sit fireside with me. I did offer him some of my dinner that was untouched and he made me feel proud that he actually said he wanted another complete dinner, so we dined late in the night together. Our conversation during our meal turned to my writing for the band.

Thomas asked, "I have to ask but you don't have to tell me, but what are you to Rand? And before you answer me, I can see he hurt you today not showing up. I don't think he will be able to be there for you for a lot of special days in the long run."

I felt his words deep in my belly. His words and the wine I was consuming had my head swirling about too. I didn't want to tell Thomas the feelings I had for Rand. Sometimes, I felt like I was infatuated with this singer, but I knew it was so much more. The last person I wanted to share any of these feelings with was my ex-husband.

"Thomas, Rand and I are friends. I was just looking forward to spending time catching up with him and his uncle since I haven't seen them in a long time." I gave Thomas that shake off attitude like it was nothing. I just didn't want to go into the whole story with Thomas. Although Thomas and I had become friends he didn't need to know my true feelings for another. Thomas gathered up his plate and took mine from me and bent down and kissed my head and thanked me for dinner as he carried the dishes into my kitchen. It was a nice sight to see him taking care of me. I joined him in the kitchen and put the coffee on and offered up some pumpkin pie to him. I didn't have to sell him on it saying it was homemade, as he knew I made pumpkin pie and he loved it.

It was uncanny and comfortable as we both made way to getting the dessert plates out and forks and making the coffee knowing how each other took theirs. This was a relaxed, familiar feeling. I felt calm and at ease with him here, although I longed for Rand and his touch. I doubted now with all the interruptions that kept occurring that Rand and I would ever progress as more than what we were.

Finishing up our desserts, I smiled at Thomas and he licked his lips with satisfaction. I saw something more in his gesture. I walked over to him and took his hand to my cheek and held it there and thanked him for being with me tonight and the past few months since my father's passing. I was reflecting on my past with him looking into the flames of the fire that danced behind him in the fireplace hearth. I leaned into him and took his mouth into mine. I kissed Thomas hard and strong. I didn't stop. I pressed his lips until he took mine back and as we opened and accepted each other's tongues that tasted of coffee and pumpkin, it was so sweet. We traveled toward the sofa and curled up next to one another and kissed for a very long time. My phone sounded and I broke the moment abruptly – It was from Rand

Madison, I really tried to see you today, sorry we could not get together. Do know that I'm thinking about you.

After reading this, the moment with Thomas was broken. I knew it was wrong of me to ever have started to sway to that direction. I was so confused, I had this need and craving for Rand that I could not shake although so many times it has gone nowhere and then I have the safety net of Thomas always there always ready to reach for me and catch me and hold me. I didn't know where my heart was heading. I told Thomas that I was so glad he came again to my rescue but I was tired and wanted to call it a night. He, like a gentleman, did not press me for anything more, and as I walked him to my door, he gently kissed me goodnight. I kissed him back actually wondering if I should explore romance with Thomas again. I shut the front door and rested against the back of it. Lost in my thoughts I went to answer Rand's message. I was going to take the high road and not let him know it broke me up earlier and wasn't going to tell him Thomas came to save me on this holiday.

Rand, I understand things happen. I hope Maxwell's feeling better. I have plenty of leftovers if you're around the next few days. I wish we could have been together, goodnight.

Rand sent back –

Tomorrow's open how about you? I love cold turkey sandwiches and cold slices of stuffing. You better have saved me pie. Can you come by the rehearsal studio? I'll be there all day. There's so much to put in order from our California trip. Also Maxwell wants to stop to see me about doing a local concert next week in Philly.

Round two, here I go again, his pull is too much for me, I want to not be so reeled in by him and yet I jump at his words he sends. *Rand, I can come by in the afternoon, we'll do a post turkey day lunch.*

His response seemed apologetic –

I'll be here and I am looking forward to seeing you and holding you…near me.

That did it for me, just the thought of him holding me once more I weakened. I would actually prefer to not have another around us but then again I was too uncertain about being with him alone, I guess something was imbedded in my head telling me that Rand could possibly break my heart, just at Thomas suggested. But I had missed him and was looking forward to it being tomorrow already. As my head hit my pillow, not knowing where my life was heading again, I was feeling torn in my relationships. I drifted to endearing thoughts of Thomas and then to sexual thoughts of Rand and I; wet, hot sexual thoughts where I slept well, very well.

What a crazy afternoon and wow, traffic to all the malls was horrible as I drove and drove and tried to take back roads instead of the main ones to avoid the crazy shoppers on this unspoken holiday. So many women venture out all day to shop their hearts out for bargains for the kick off to the Christmas season. My arrival to the barn was filled with excitement as I did not see any other vehicles there except Rand's Hummer. Checking myself in my car mirror once more before heading in to see him I adjusted my scarf around my neck. I had chosen to wear one this morning thinking about how he tied my wrists together the last time I wore one. Before I could get the handle, my door opened and it was like a vision, the sun glowed behind this truly awesome looking man. I was mesmerized by the way his hair hung messy and his blue eyes penetrated right through me.

"Madison, let me help you." He spoke as he started to gather my bags of food in one of his strong hands. It looked like I was a food delivery person with an order he had placed. But before we even got past my car, he took hold of me with his empty hand and tilted my face up. He was smiling so blissfully right before he stole a kiss from my longing lips.

Without ever even getting out a hello to him we had placed the food carriers down and took over each other's bodies, hands roaming everywhere. He licked at my lips, but obviously wanted more. We held onto each other so tightly that I could feel his heart beat even through his jacket. I could not believe I was here with him, this striking looking man of such physical perfection. I wanted to eat him up. I had such a desire to take his clothing off slowly, one piece at a time. I felt his tongue so deep into my mouth and my lips pressed against his not wanting to release. We could have stayed like this, but he broke apart from my lips and tossed his head back shaking his hair and said in a low tone, "I wanted this so bad and here you are. I have missed you." My eyes started to tear in the corner as I leaned down and picked up the food bags.

"I missed you too, I missed not spending yesterday with you" I spoke but began to choke up and didn't want him to see me cry. I was so afraid to scare him off and have him slip away.

"Did you really?" The way he asked made his doubt clear. I was wondering why I felt that way. I had so missed him yesterday, if he had only known how I longed for him.

We had laid out the food picnic style on the floor on a woven blanket in the rehearsal studio near **The Wall**. I took several of the pillows from the couches to the floor. Rand said all their music equipment was coming back here today and tomorrow from their trip and he had some business to handle with Maxwell. But just sitting with him now and enjoying his company, seeing his body in front of me was enough.

He caught me up on most of the West Coast trip. He told me funny stories about each of the band members' crazy behavior. I took a few notes on a nearby notepad as he spoke wanting to capture some of the visuals of the band that he described. He told me about the place they stayed at in California that it was awesome and they had a great panoramic view of the ocean. Each morning he would rise, look at the view and think about me all the way here on the other side of the country. I smiled and my belly fluttered as he spoke and I found myself studying his features with every breath he released.

As he got up to go grab us a beer, I watched his back and just past him I caught a glimpse of something on **The Wall**. It was a new addition on Rand's corner, there were many new photos of him with female fans from the California shows, each one had written across it the city…but then there was a large photo of one woman in particular. A fan looking bright eyed at Rand from the very front row, she was staring at him, so consumed in her thoughts, so reined in, and lost in thought. It was a photo taken without the person knowing it and so it captured her raw and real and you could draw a dotted line exactly from her lips to Rand's eyes on stage. There was no missing the smile on his singing face and the endearing look from hers. It was a picture of me. I don't ever remember it being taken. How could I as it looked like I was in a trance, focusing on the stage? It had been taken on the very first night that I went to see them play in Philly.

"You look beautiful in that photo," Rand said returning with his drink. "I wonder when I look at it what you were thinking at that moment."

"Rand, I think maybe I was hoping this singer takes me on to write about him, and I am sure I was thinking about how that would be. Look at us now, who would have thought we would be like this…" I stopped speaking as I didn't know what to call us. There was an undeniable passion but what else did we give to one another.

"Yeah look at us, hungry for food and one another," he said as he sat down next to me and started to feed me.

After we ate the Thanksgiving leftovers, we settled in each other's arms on the sofa for long nap as the turkey surely tired us out. Or was that just a myth? He was on the sofa and I was lying between his legs with my chest resting just across his stomach. I could feel my body rise and fall with his every breath. He played with my hair, twisting the strands and tugging softly at them and then he began to stroke the lightest touches across my throat with the pad of his thumb. He undid my scarf and slid it away from my neck exposing my skin further to his touch. Like an artist with a delicate paintbrush going over and over an area of the canvas, he continued to work his fingers sensually until he reached the edge of my sweater.

He slid his thumb down over my nipples going back and forth under my lace bra, over and over in an up and down motion. Rand releases an intense moan and it feels like he is playing air guitar across my nipples hardening under his touch. Without even moving I could feel his chest move as he sighed, and I could feel him hardening against my hip. Rand splayed his fingers out across my stomach. His hand pressed harder to my belly as it stimulated my every nerve ending. He passed his hand down over my music note charm and circled my belly button with his thumb, and then he lowered his hand into my jeans and pressed hard to my abdomen.

I moved with his rhythm, still lying on him but letting him continue to travel down my body, enjoying all this pleasure from the ride. His hand was now the lowest it had ever been on my body and I felt like I was going to explode just at the thought of him touching me. I wiggled turning onto my side, trying to encourage him to continue. I wanted to feel his fingers deeper. I was unbuttoning the fly of his jeans and slowly taking my hand to him to pleasure him as well. The door to the rehearsal studio flew open and we looked down to see a smiling and well feeling Maxwell.

I caught myself first wanting to scream as Rand was on the verge of taking my body further, and that again, we were interrupted. I hated that our timing was off and that we never completed what we started. I sat up fixing myself. I just wanted Rand to take me and finish touching me and release all this pent up lust I was carrying. I was frustrated to have this moment end. But then I was happy to see Maxwell, just wish it was an hour later. I shouted down an invite to him to come up and join us saying how much food I brought up here and made him feel comfortable as I told him I knew he would be joining us. Up in the loft area near **The Wall,** Maxwell was unable to see what moment in the making he had just cut short. We both sat up and held each other, arms and legs entwined as Maxwell climbed the stairs to us.

I enjoyed the rest of the afternoon with Maxwell and Rand. I had fed these two fine men and they enjoyed it. As much as I wanted their company, especially Rand's, I could tell that they had some work to get to. I didn't want to hold them up so I told Rand I would see him soon. He walked me to my car.

He said, "I hope, soon we will be alone together." There was a moment of hesitation in his voice and I was uncertain what brought that on. I had hoped his words would come true. I only wished it was today and that I could feel him touching me again, finishing what we started. I pulled at his shirt collar to tip him toward my face and kissed his nose and then had to kiss his lips again and again.

As I drove away, I glanced in the rearview mirror and saw him returning to the studio. I watched every step of his walk until he wasn't visible anymore, and then what I did see was my neck. It was red from his kisses and exposed as I had left my scarf on the sofa. I wasn't cold though as a different kind of warmth tingled through my body like that of a furnace igniting. My heart burned and pumped and I knew this heat I felt was entirely caused by the memories of what was interrupted on that couch.

Chapter Ten – Where We Began

The remainder of my holiday weekend passed very quietly. I was glad it was finally Monday. While most people dread the beginning of the week, for me, the mere fact that Jillian would be returning from her weekend in Atlanta put a pleasant smile on my face. I was also meeting with Cecile this week and I was looking forward to the distraction from my feelings. I couldn't wait to tell her that I got us tickets to a very small gig at the 2nd Street Coffee Café where the band actually started playing together. Maxwell had set up a one night limited ticket engagement for the pre-holiday season. It was definitely going to be a tight fit in that coffee house.

It was only nine in the morning and my phone started jumping, first Jillian –

> *Hey Maddy, I'm getting in later today than expected, let's definitely hit the gym tomorrow and catch up and ask Cecile if she wants to tag along too, I have a guest pass. Missed you and hope you had turkey and all those Rand trimmings…*

She had no idea what actually happened but tomorrow I would fill her in. I sent her –

Jillian you can't go away the next holiday, I missed you. Mine was different, I'll fill you in. Hey keep Saturday night open the boys are playing in Philly.

Jillian was quick to reply –

I'm on that guest list thanks to none other than my new man Raeford…I really missed him over the holiday. I can't wait to see him this week. Oh, yeah and you too! Ha-Ha.

I finished up our conversation letting her know that I was going to reach out to Kent to give him a heads up that Cecile would be joining us. She really seemed to like him and I hoped the interest was mutual.

My phone sounded again before I could get a message typed out to Kent. It was Rand.

Good morning beautiful! I woke this morning again with visitors coming up my sidewalk. They weren't intrusive, just a few deer hanging out. They probably feel safe here on my property from the hunters. Well, have a very busy week with Maxwell. I like the holiday season. I like to play Santa, and give people presents they would never ask for. Have you been a good girl this year? The guys usually go home for their holiday. I'm staying here and will have some professional help to decorate. I want you to come, and you can be Santa's helper.

Rand I have been a very good girl this year and would love to be your helper. As for your the holiday invite, I will check my calendar as it usually is so very full...but I will adjust it and I would certainly love to be there. Thank you,

Madison, the holiday party will be at the rehearsal studio before everyone heads out of town. Isaac usually can't keep his mouth shut but has about what they got you. I play host on Christmas day with an open house. I would really like if you could come then too. It starts at noon and ends whenever the food or alcohol runs out. I'm planning to have a New Year's Rocking Eve in the barn complete with a dropping ball. It's a lot of fun since we normally don't play cover songs; we all pick a favorite and perform it. Since I missed Thanksgiving I want you to ink me into your calendar and also voice me into that recorder of yours for these dates. Hey I will see you this Saturday at our show. Hope we can get some alone time, wouldn't that be nice? I'm thinking of you right now as I can smell your lovely scent.

I love it when he calls me beautiful because he is beyond handsome. I paused a moment, how can he smell me? My mind flickered to thinking how it would be wonderful to spend Christmas with him, and replied –

Good morning Deer. I'm really looking forward to Saturday and was just sending a message to Kent to let him know about Cecile. Maybe you can put in a good, nice word about her. You have given me many holiday invites to think about, they all sound fun. I miss you.

We ended our conversation and I finally was able to send a message to Kent –

Hey Big Guy, haven't seen you in awhile but will see you on Saturday. I'm bringing along my adorable agent, who has her eyes on you. Her name is Cecile. You cannot miss her, she will be the bubbles in the champagne, the fizz in the soda pop, she is very outgoing, so cute and shapely. I think you may just like her; unless that is you already have someone you're seeing?

Kent slammed a reply – I could practically feel it through the phone.

Hell yeah I'd love to meet her! We've all been missing you Maddy. I thought you left to go back to your husband. I wanted to stop you like a big overbearing brother. You looked sad. Sorry about your dad, I found out later. Raeford led us in the prayer so he gets the credit, but we said it with him. See you this weekend! I will look for this Cecile chick.

Finally the morning was moving along with all the conversations. I thought I was done on the phone when I heard a ring, but it was my doorbell. Now who? I was thinking as I opened the door. Standing there was a floral delivery truck with a large Rosemary Christmas Tree. It smelled wonderful. I thanked the driver and brought it in to read the card.

Madison, I want you to remember this smell. You once had one in our condo and seasoned the holiday with it. Please join me this holiday for a Christmas Brunch. I think we really reconnected on Thanksgiving and I wanted to give you some space so I haven't pressed you. You don't have to let me know now, just come Christmas Day and I'll know your answer.

Please remember, I don't want you to be let down yet another holiday. Love Always, Thomas.

I stood in my foyer for so long, trying to take in these invites from two totally different men, two very adoring men each in their own way. I was going to have to choose where to spend the holiday. I wanted a better holiday for myself this year than what I last had. I would make it better, I was determined. I smiled as I took the tree into my kitchen and gave it some water, within minutes the house was filling of the scent of Rosemary and a smell of the holiday season ahead.

I didn't want to be on the phone again with Cecile at this moment, as her conversations could get lengthy so I sent her a quick message asking her to join us tomorrow at the gym to catch up and we would chat. She quickly sent a yes message back.

The rest of this day I was shifted into great holiday memories, from the delivery that Thomas sent. I remembered my mother putting me in my red pajamas before going to bed for Santa Claus and saying he would see them and know I was one of his helpers. I would put out plenty of cookies for him and his helpers and always sneak one for myself under my pillow. I remember, being an only child, how my mother and father made Christmas special for me and that way I didn't feel I was missing anything. They always made the comment I was their best gift ever, that Santa need not bring them anything more.

When I got older and married Thomas, we continued to include my father in any festivity that we had whether a dinner in the city or the holidays themselves. With my mother not here, and not reaching out to us, we made sure he was never alone. Thomas would always make the holiday grand by buying expensive presents and always letting you know that they came from the finer stores. We were very different as I would make some simple gifts for some that came more from my heart. Like a written piece in a frame, or a photo taken that was memorable. All in all, grand or simple, my holiday memories were filled and fun.

We all met at the gym the next morning. It was like a chat session rather than an actual work out as we sat three in a row tying up the stationary bikes for over an hour and a half when the allotted time is thirty minutes per person. We didn't pay attention to that rule today. Jillian was happy she saw her brother and was more excited to be seeing Raeford this weekend. Cecile was excited when I told her that I'd told Kent how cute she was and that I wanted them to meet. She almost fell off the bike. She did actually miss the pedals, but regained her stride and was thrilled. She asked dozens of questions about him and I only knew some of the answers but told her to find out the other answers so I could include it in my writings of him.

We all decided that we would go together like a girl's night out on Saturday. I told them it would be best if we met and drove together. I invited them to come to my house and offered to be the driver to the show and they jumped on that idea. We left the gym much later than planned and hugged each other looking forward to this weekend out.

Well here it is already Saturday afternoon and my closet is thrown all over my bedroom floor. I cannot decide what to wear. This is a really small venue and I want to look nice. I picked up a sheer blue top that I knew matched Rand's eyes and a black cami from the pile of clothes I pulled out. I put that on along with a pair of low rise black jeans and boots. I added hoop earrings that had a few diamond chips in them that sparkled and complemented my heart cuff bracelet. I looked at the mirror, walked away, ran back and looked in the mirror again and then looked over at the mess I would have to deal with in the morning. I never spent this much time deciding what to wear while married to Thomas; I would just put something on and be done. I was always ready in no time at all. Today I think I spent three hours getting ready and changing outfits.

My doorbell sounded and I knew the ladies were arriving. I went down and greeted my good friends. I had opened a bottle of wine for us to start with and take the edge off before we went to the show. We all began to make a toast but then they geared it to me.

Jillian and Cecile said, "To Madison, we're all together because you are such a wonderful person. And we thank you for our introductions to these fine, sexy men." They both laughed. It was funny though, oddly we all were heading into different relationships or introductions with one of the members of the band and all since my whim to write about them.

Getting into the city is hit or miss with the expressway and this evening it was not too bad, but there was no parking to be found anyplace close to the café. I rode around the streets several times and then decided to park in one of the garages as we were all in heels and I didn't want us to walk too far. As we began to approach the café the band was just arriving and still standing outside talking to Maxwell and it was quite chilly. I gave a wave and Rand met my eyes and left the pack and came trotting up to us.

He slid his hand into mine and his head down to my ear. "I've told you that you're beautiful, but you're absolutely stunning tonight." He continued to speak gently as he also licked and kissed my ear giving me a chill. "I got a table up front for you ladies. I want to see you, only you in front of me while I play. Now that you're within reach, I don't want tonight to end without you near me."

I felt so warm inside and was tingling just by his adoring look at me. His hands never left me until we were seated and then he leaned over me and tilted my head back and gave me a kiss in front of everyone that was quite lasting.

Cecile gasped, "How dreamy."

He had to leave us as they needed to get set up for the evening, and we three girls would be just fine. I then felt a tap to my shoulder seconds later and thought he returned. But it was a quick, friendly kiss on my cheek from Raeford. I was thrilled to see him. He left me quickly after that to kiss Jillian. That was a much different, much longer kiss! Rounds of drinks were brought to our table without any hesitation, and we couldn't pay for them as Rand took care of everything for us.

Right before the band went on Rand walked back up to me at the table and asked me to hold his wallet and phone. Since this was a small venue they didn't have the luxury of a dressing room back stage for all of their stuff and he had tight jeans on with his microphone pack in the back pocket.

I smiled at him and put his wallet in my tiny purse and laid his phone on the table next to mine. While Rand and the band were doing their final quick sound checks, his phone displayed an incoming message. I took the phone to make sure it was silenced for the performance and my curiosity got to me, I glanced quickly at the message –

> *Your letter and surprise contents arrived to me today, thank you. I have thought about nothing more than our first meeting over the past few months. You are amazing. I have been listening to your music over and over. I wanted to tell you yes, I look forward to this holiday season and getting to know you so much better. I will see you soon. G.*

I stared down at the text and reread it twice. Who was G? I was just starting to feel that comfort zone with Rand and trusting that perhaps he was feeling things for me as he was surely acting like he cared. Could this all be an act? And when was this G person coming, was I going to meet someone he met on the road or someone from his past that he invited here to start to date? I didn't want to look at any more messages, I felt bad that I looked at this one. Perhaps this was a sign to me where not to head on Christmas day.

I didn't want to ruin the night for the girls, so despite the fact that I volunteered to be their designated driver, I started to drink. I thought if I couldn't drive home we could always hire a cab or someone in the band would get us home safe. I drank my first drink without a pause. The band had taken the stage, and I was front and center to Rand, only about four feet away. He smiled. I drank him in as I was on my second cocktail and he was so unbelievably handsome, I really was star struck with his body, his face, his eyes and now he just blew me a kiss so I smiled back thinking sarcastically, "G" was that really for me or for show? We girls were having a fun night and I was starting to loosen up and forget, well not entirely but I put the message to the back of my mind for now. I couldn't get too upset as I did violate his privacy by reading his message.

Throughout the show I felt like I was the only one that was in the audience with Rand. He never swayed far from me even though he had room to roam across the stage. As he would pick up his guitar for some songs and then place it back on the stand for others, he had in the beginning brought the stand over to be closer to him so he didn't have to leave my sight. He sang to me on so many of the songs. At one point Cecile was waving her hand in front of my face like one of us, or both of us was in a trance.

I continued to keep the drinks coming to the table, not sure of how many I consumed. Cecile didn't need any loosing up, she was a funny girl and drinks only made her sillier. I caught Jillian looking at Raeford often and he would send her a wink now and then. It was toward the end of their playlist that Kent was spotlighted. The band and Rand gave way to Kent to take his bass and play his heart out. He positioned himself in front of Cecile's chair, again only few feet away and played. Everyone got to their feet to clap when he was done. Only he jumped off the stage and picked up Cecile and spun her around. I don't think he kissed her, just spun her and I was hoping she wouldn't get sick. He put her back down into her seat and he spoke closely to her ear. She beamed. As he jumped back up on the stage, I could only imagine the words Kent said to her because he then licked his lips and smiled directly at Cecile. I could definitely see something developing between those two.

After their show, which was so good, Rand and the band all came off the stage and talked with everyone in the crowd. Most patrons this night were close friends or family. It was nice to see them play such an intimate venue as we so enjoyed it.

I had gotten up and left the table for the first time since the show started. Jillian and Cecile remained seated. As I planted my feet to walk I was a bit unsteady. I felt a gentle on the side of my hip helping to keep me standing straight, and it was Ron. I gave him a hug and said that I must have stopped counting the drinks at some point. He directed me to one side to introduce me to the girl he had been crushing on since long ago. Her name was Dahlia and, yes, she was pretty as a flower. She was so polite. I did notice that it was well into the late night hours and she had, sunglasses sitting on top of her head. I guess she and Ron had a lot in common. Tonight though he did not wear his at this show, I guess the lights weren't as powerful or bright as the other stage sets, or perhaps he wanted to see Dahlia without wearing his sunglasses indoors. I talked to them for a few moments and then was picked up by Isaac and his loud roar of a hello. I told him I had to hit the restroom and I would be back and he could introduce himself to Cecile at the table.

As I walked to the restroom which now had a line forming, a hand came around my waist and I knew through the sheerness of my top exactly whose touch this was. I was led to the upper portion of the café and down a small hall to the end door. It was another tiny one person bathroom without even a window. I smiled at Rand, and asked him to excuse me since I really had to go to the bathroom. I drank a lot this evening. He stayed outside the door like he was waiting to go in next, but since the venue was staged downstairs; no one was even up in the top section of the café. The coffee shop had it roped off as this is where most people hang with their coffees and computers during the day.

As I came out of the bathroom relieved to have finally gone, I saw Rand had not left. In fact he pulled me back into the bathroom and locked the door and turned out the light. In the darkness I could only smell and feel this sensational man in front of me. I felt him as he gently lifted off my sheer top from my jeans and rolled up my cami and bent to kiss my stomach. I twirled my hands in his hair and pushed his head and lips tighter to my belly. I felt him lower and kiss my jeans and continue downward kissing the fabric that separated my lusting body from his wanting lips. He rose back up in the dark and took my mouth with his. One long sweep of his tongue at a time.

"Madison, I so want everything we could be, I watched and thought of you all night from that stage." I immediately softened toward him. I knew I wanted him so badly, but I also knew that we were in this tiny bathroom and it wasn't going to happen for us here. I also knew I was getting a little dizzy. I wasn't sure if it was due to emotions or the drinks I had. He leaned me up against the wall and continued taking my mouth with his, controlling the kiss and positioning himself tightly up against my body. His hands were now so firm on my hips. We were moving with each other getting even closer if that was possible. I suddenly felt claustrophobic.

"Rand, I need air, I can't breathe. There's no window, I need to breathe." I reached for the doorknob and it was locked, I pulled at it again. Rand reached down and unlocked the door and I stepped out and inhaled a huge breath. I turned to him as I was sorry I stopped our moment this time but I felt trapped in there. He came to me, held me. I think it was then that I told him I felt ill from drinking too much. I ran back to the tiny bathroom and found the toilet in the dark and began to throw up.

Rand helped me through this embarrassing ordeal. He left me only to head downstairs and get me some water and to tell the guys he was taking me home. When Rand returned to me, he told me that Jillian hadn't overdone the drinking like I had so she was going to drive my car back to my house and make sure Cecile would get home if Kent would let Cecile leave his lap anyway. I figured Jillian and Raeford and Cecile and Kent would surely hang for another several hours. Rand brought me my purse and had given my car key to Jillian.

Rand helped me redress as he slipped my sheer top back over my head and held me tightly. I told him that his phone and wallet were in my purse. He took out his belongings and I watched him slide his phone into his front pocket and that's when I remembered the message from "G' and another wave of nausea threatened at the top of my throat. Quickly, I ran back to the bathroom.

This was not the ladies night I had thought we all were going to have. Rand took me so carefully to his vehicle and drove me home, asking the entire way if I was okay. He smoothed my hair and gently touched my cheek. When we got to my house he carried me into my bedroom and sat me on the edge of my bed. Behind me hung our selected piece from the art gallery in South Beach, "Separation" and in front of me was the hottest, most sexy man on the earth.

He lifted my arms up and removed my sheer shirt leaving my cami on. He let his fingers slide under my cami in the back and, like playing music he very effortlessly opened the clasp of my bra. He slid it off of me, lifting the cami straps and replacing them back onto my shoulders. He then laid me back and slowly removed my boots. He unzipped my jeans and although I was getting excited just by watching him undress me, I let out a groan. It wasn't a moan of arousal, but that of illness I laid there as he slid off my jeans, but made certain that my tiny string panties remained on me.

Carefully he removed my earrings and kissed each lobe afterwards. He laid them next to my cuff bracelet that he slid from my wrist and placed them on my night stand with the heart facing my direction. He moved over and placed a pillow under my head and grabbed a blanket off the side chair. Before covering me, he looked down and laughed at the mound of clothes he had to climb over to get to the blanket. He then covered me and sat beside me. He kissed my forehead. I passed out.

When I woke up I remembered a few things of yesterday. The first was I had totally forgotten to eat anything as I spent hours, too many hours, deciding what clothes to wear. The next was that I drank way too much and the next hit me like a brick. It was the scent of Rosemary that made me leap out of the bed to again throw up. When I returned to my bed from my bathroom, I saw in the chair in front of my closet, Rand all curled up, sleeping with a few items of my clothing as a pillow. I'm not sure if the sound of me getting sick or the feeling of me staring at him woke him.

I walked over to him and said I was so very sorry for ruining his evening. I was feeling horrible for what happened and horrible for how he slept in here with me. To lighten the mood I asked, "So how was your night sleeping with me?" He laughed. I went back to the bathroom to freshen up and I padded down the hardwood to the kitchen. There was some plain toast made and a tall glass of ginger ale waiting for me to drink.

He pulled me it to him and hugged me tightly. "I didn't make coffee yet because I was afraid the smell would set you off." He was still fully dressed just as he had been on stage last night. I could smell his sweat and I snuggled into him and kissed his chest. I knew that his scent would not upset my stomach; he had cared for me last night and stayed with me. I felt that I let him down though; I read his personal message, got myself sick from drinking. I figured I wasn't a good thing to be looking at right now. I thanked him and told him that I would be fine and to get going. I was sure he had something to do, but he kicked his shoes off and stayed.

I tried to eat a little bit and then told him my head really hurt so I took a few aspirins and sipped the ginger ale and headed back to my bed. Later in the afternoon I heard him on the phone a few times and I heard the television. When I reappeared from the bed later into the afternoon, he was watching football with the volume low. He had brought his journal in and was writing in it, probably music or maybe what a nut case I had recently become. He was making himself comfortable on the sofa, he had the fireplace lit and warming, and he had removed his shirt and looked like he had taken a shower. He smelled of soap and freshness to me from across the room. I had slept through Rand taking a shower in my home. I couldn't believe I missed the opportunity to have joined him with no one around to interrupt us.

I could not take my eyes off of his chest, his bare, beautifully inked, chiseled abs and chest. I was feeling better with every stare. He told me he had some phone calls as everyone had called to see if I was doing okay. He said he wasn't leaving me. It was Sunday and most Sundays are lazy days for me. I curled up next to him and put my head to his naked chest and remained there until sometime later, my stomach rumbled with desire for food and he grabbed the phone and we called for a pizza delivery. We talked about our favorite kinds of pizza, and surprising enough after I ate a few slices and drank some Coke that seemed to do the trick. I felt worlds better. Being with Rand the whole time may have helped too.

As we were seated together on the sofa a message came to his phone, he grabbed it and I just caught a glimpse of it.

I didn't hear back from you and wanted to know if you got my message from last night? G

I watched him quickly glance at his messages from last night and then he typed a quick message back.

I was busy with a show last night here at home, and today I got tied up, but I got your messages, we will talk real soon. L, Rand

I saw that he signed it with an L, and I felt saddened. I wasn't sure how to ask him about this as I read it over his shoulder. I didn't want to get upset in front of him.

"Hey, I really feel exhausted. I want to get some more rest so I'm going to head back to bed." I smiled at him with sincerity. "You spent way too much time taking care of me. I know I wasn't the best company but I feel much better."

"Madison, I enjoy being in your company and caring for you, but I'll take off so you can get to bed."

I slowly started to get myself up and moving toward my bedroom, and I looked up into his eyes, "thank you for everything today, and being here."

"No place would I have rather been." He kissed my head and I walked him to the door. As I watched him leave, I saw him grab his phone and get on it. I shut my door and headed to my bed. I pulled the covers up over me and wondered who G was. I heard my phone sound.

I want you to sleep and feel better. I have a busy week, I'll check in on you. By the way did you know you talk in your sleep? When you passed out you kept repeating something like gee, gee who are you? And gee where are you? Then you said Rand please don't leave me, so I stayed. I miss you already, sleep well.

I never thought I talked in my sleep, I hope he never hears the other dreams I have about him, especially the sexy ones. I was glad he was here but was assuming the worst again. I was too tired to fight off the sleep and think. I sent my last thoughts of the night to him.

> *Rand, thank you for staying with me. This is sort of where we began when I met you and saw the first rehearsal, only I stayed at your home and then too we never made it past first base. Let's try one day to hit ourselves to second or third base? I am going to rest; I am tired, good night.*

Chapter Eleven – Joyous Occasion

The entire world is busy although Christmas comes the same time every year. Why do people get crazy this time of year? They get stressed and panic like they have a deadline they cannot make and yet it is the same date on the calendar year after year. Well, the past few weeks had been crazy. I was drilled by my girlfriends over and over to make certain everything was alright with me. They were worried that I was upset or depressed because of the holidays. They figured that was the reason I drank so much at the show that night. It took some convincing but I assured them I was fine.

Cecile and Kent have hit it off so well. He was actually planning on staying at Rand's this week to hang out and spend time with her and then leave just before Christmas Day to head upstate to his family. He was coming back though for the big New Year's party at Rand's.

I found Jillian and Raeford together at her home. He even answered the phone when I called her. The good news I found out is that Raeford was staying here through Christmas and into the New Year, and I think at Jillian's the entire time. He told me this when I got him on her phone and she didn't deny any of it. I heard from him that Isaac and Ron were staying until later in the week. We all planned to meet at the rehearsal studio for some drinks and see each other on Thursday afternoon. We could hang out for a bit together, toast to the holiday and then everyone could go on to where they have to travel with a few days to spare. Rand and Maxwell had been busy with each other and I received a few messages and calls from Rand but most were that he was thinking of me and looking forward to the holiday season. He also told me to come by Thursday to the studio for a get together with everyone. I still felt bad for getting drunk and sick at the 2nd Street Coffee Café after their show and the message he got that evening on his phone that I read, I had a weird sinking feeling about all that.

I had to push this all aside in my mind since now I have to begin to dodge the holiday rush, and meet with all the mean shoppers to select the few presents that I had to purchase. I wrote myself a list of what I had to buy. First stop was back to a shop in New Hope. I enjoyed returning to the shops there and I had seen some jewelry that surely Jillian and Cecile would like. While I was in the Artisan jewelry shop, I noticed the window display had a man's cuff with a cross on it and it was similar to the one Rand bought me for my birthday. I asked the jeweler to let me see it. As I touched the cross on the leather strap, a shiver ran through me. The jeweler asked me if I was okay, as I drifted off in thoughts of Rand looking at this piece. I shook my head to him that I was fine, and I knew I was more than fine, for here I was feeling the holiday spirit and new found joy in my heart. I knew this was going to be a wonderful holiday season. My shopping travels then took me to the longest line at the liquor store in search of the perfect port wine for Thomas, as he often enjoyed a glass of port after a fine meal.

I had spent almost an entire day shopping and my feet were tired, but I got it done. As I carried my bundles into my house, I had messages showing on my answering machine. The first was from Thomas saying he wanted to tell me he really was looking forward to Sunday and seeing me for Christmas Brunch. Although I hadn't given him an answer, I know from his voice he was hopeful. The next was Cecile saying that she was invited by Kent to their little party on Thursday and she was screaming in excitement about it. Finally, Jillian wanted to get away from the whole crazy shopping to have some alone gym time with me in the morning. That was fine, I sent her a message I would meet her there. I thought I might fess up to her about reading that message and the other ones I saw that day at my house.

Contently, I was sitting wrapping my gifts and really taking the time to make them look extra special. I loved putting in the extra effort to make them stand out and look really festive. I got up and made myself a cup of pumpkin spice coffee. It only becomes available certain times of the year and since the autumn season had just passed I could still enjoy it.

As I stirred my cup, I drifted to thinking about where I would be heading on Sunday, Christmas day. Last year was a mess for me; I was lonely and saddened that my marriage was erased in a divorce document, even though Thomas and I had filed for the divorce many months prior it took some time to be final. I wasn't looking forward to holidays or any other day of the week at that point. Although Jillian had warmly invited me to join her and her brother, I declined.

This year, what a difference time has made. Thomas and I are friends, but he wants more. With Rand, I found something I feel so wonderful about with him, but then this could all be one sided. I was hoping for happily ever after. I didn't do any holiday shopping last season and I was so enjoying this year and the holiday spirit I was feeling. I hadn't felt this way since I was younger and my mother and father were together. My mother let me help her with all the trimmings and making the cookies, which was so much fun. As I reminisced, I decided to make some cookies and I pulled out an old recipe from my kitchen drawer. It was for my mother's special Christmas cookies. It was nothing more than chocolate chips, but she said they were special, that Santa loved them. I guess they were my father's favorite.

I began to locate all the items needed. I first found the flour, brown sugar, eggs, and vanilla. I left some butter on the counter to soften. As I was reaching down to lift my mixer to the countertop my phone sounded. It was from Rand –

> *Madison, I'm thinking about you looking forward to seeing you Thursday. My holiday decorators have done great work with the barn and my home. You'll see for yourself it looks like Longwood Gardens during the holiday. Hey, is everything alright between us? I haven't had a moment to see you lately and talk with you and I felt a distance with us lately. Miss you.*

Rand's reference of Longwood Gardens brought a smile to my face. When I was a child we went there and it was filled with lush gardens, dancing fountains, and opulent architecture. During the winter holiday season they display brilliant light shows of holiday colors and brightly lit holiday trees. It is a true winter wonderland of lights. As soon as night fell the lights illuminated to present a beautiful sight to behold during the holiday season. Since I didn't want him to know I felt upset by the texts he had received from "G", I didn't call him to talk to him directly. I wanted to sound upbeat. I sent him a reply –

We're good, and I'm so in the holiday mood. I was just remembering all the sparkling lights from the gardens when I was a child. I'm now busy baking cookies and looking forward to seeing this holiday wonderland on Thursday. I finished all my shopping and wrapping and so tomorrow I'm catching up with Jillian at the gym in the morning and will need that as I will probably eat most of this cookie batter. Miss you too.

I think he was waiting to reply as his fingers sent me a response so quickly –

My we are smart, extremely beautiful, a talented writer, a health enthusiast and now a baker. Madison there's so much I don't know about you, but you better save me a few or I will have to nibble on your ear and proceed downward if there aren't any cookies left for me. See you soon.

Rand, if you mean what you say, I will throw all the batter in the trash. Only kidding, I will make plenty and have them for us all. Let me get baking, the ovens beeping that it is ready.

Madison you have me hot already. You have no clue what you do to me and now there is this added sweetness I crave from you. The end of this week cannot come soon enough.

My baking turned into a many hour event. What started with getting a cup of coffee earlier in the day had me refilling it as I made dozens of cookies. When I was finally finished in the kitchen it looked like a cyclone hit that swirled flour everywhere. After cleaning the entire room and packaging the cookies I was tired from standing there for so long. I took a long hot bath and turned in early. Before I hit my pillow I sent Rand a message –

House smells yummy like hot baked cookies. The warmth had me thinking of you, Goodnight.

I never got a reply from him. I slept.

Jillian was up and ready to hit the gym and we had a great workout and, yes, our jaws were tired too from talking. We had so much to catch up on. When she said Raeford's name it was like she was off into the puffy clouds. It was so wonderful to see my friend this way. She actually left him at her place to come meet me for a bit. Those two seemed further along in a dating relationship than Rand and I, and that made me think that Rand and I weren't really progressing and this is what it would be. I waited until she caught me up on all her juicy items of Raeford, how he kisses her, how he touches her and she sounded so captivated by him. I was so happy for her, but then I wanted to share the uncertainties I was feeling about Rand of late.

I asked Jillian, “Should I feel horrible for reading a text that Rand received? I actually read it when it came over his phone when they played at the 2nd Street Coffee Café.”

“Madison tell me what it said.”

“Well, first that message is why I kept drinking so much that night.”

“So what did it say, tell me?”

“It was obviously from a girl who is looking forward to seeing and being with him over the holidays. She signed with only her initial. The next day she emailed him again while he was taking care of me. Usually whenever someone texts him or calls he tells me in passing who it was. He never said anything about this one.”

Jillian stared at me, “I really like Rand with you, I think you should ask him when or if it happens again.” I wanted to ask him but I didn’t want him to think I was crazy, jealous, or insecure.

“Jillian, my dilemma is where am I going on Christmas?”

“It’s about time that you think with your heart and not your head. Follow that on Christmas day.”

“Hopefully, I will figure it out by then.”

“Madison, when I first met Raeford I never thought I would really begin to feel what I do now for him, but I opened myself up and let him into my heart. You need to let love in again.”

I was silent a moment thinking that I had completely given my heart once so long ago and had it torn apart. I think she knew what I was thinking because she said, "Oh no you don't! Don't you even go backwards when you've come so far. Let's just look forward to Thursday and enjoying the holidays wherever we end up."

We did just that as Rand's Thursday afternoon gathering began. I got there slightly after everyone else had come and Rand appeared in the doorway of the barn as if he had been waiting for my arrival. With plenty of cookies in tow, I brought them in and he helped me as I made a tin for each of the guys, including Rand. Before we entered the barn he licked my ear playfully, he was in a great mood. I got to hug Kent and Raeford as soon as I came inside. It was so nice to see my gal pals there as well. Cecile looked like a holiday ornament, all dressed in a sparkled sweater and Kent wasn't too far from her, always looking at her. Jillian and Raeford were already holding hands.

Rand announced that he had food and drinks set up in the loft above and for everyone to go ahead up there. Isaac and Ron were already started on the drinks up there. Rand had moved over to me and placed his hand on my lower back, after putting the cookies in a pile near the tree by the stage. We were the last two that stood down below as everyone went up the steps.

I was taking in all the decorations, they were definitely professionally done. It looked so classic Christmas, with beautifully hung balsam fir greens and berry sprigs. It smelled awesome. There were three holiday trees all decorated. A large tree stood at the entrance of the barn that blocked the view to the loft as it was so tall and full, filling the entrance way nicely. There was one down near their rehearsal stage, and a very large one up on the loft near **The Wall.** Behind that one up above was something with a large drape covering it. There were giant ornaments hanging down from the ceiling on beautiful velvet ribbons. The ornaments were musical notes. On every tree there were musical ornaments of glass, metals, and carved woods. It was so impressive.

I turned to him to comment on how festive this looked but he wrapped his arms around me from behind and I couldn't turn. He then pulled me into him tightly just so that we were along side the one tall tree, he nuzzled into my neck. I loved that he did this so I had picked an off the shoulder sweater in encouragement to go with my short holiday skirt with boots. With his lips resting on my shoulder, chills traveled through me. I felt his hands release my waist only to slide down to my thighs and with us just out of the sight line of the guests he took his hands up under my skirt. It was quite arousing to be there with all these people and yet have Rand's tender fingers traveling over me.

I inhaled and held my breath. He turned me back toward him and kept his hands under my skirt and leaned in for a kiss. He pulled my hips just enough toward him that I could feel his growing excitement. Our kiss lasted for sometime as I had missed him so much more than I wanted anyone to know and it appeared by his romantic gestures only minutes after I arrived that he had been missing me as well. He was so playful with his kisses and licked my lips and then looked up.

"Do you see something you like?"

"I see you and I like that," I commented as I was still so focused on his hands smoothing over my hips underneath the fabric of my skirt and he was lightly stroking my silk panties, and I was focused on his obvious bulge pushing hard into me that it took me a moment to notice what was above. I looked up to see we were under the mistletoe.

"Do you stop all the girls at this spot?" I asked and he started to laugh. We stayed there for a little bit and continued to kiss with a longing in our lips since we had not gotten enough with our earlier kisses. Then like a fog horn on a boat, the noise sounded. "Hey you two get up here and have fun!" Isaac shouted.

We joined them all and I was really having a nice time. Everyone was having a drink, some of the holiday food that was spread out lavishly. The guys said Rand does this each year. Maxwell was to be there soon too. I was told he had to go to the airport to pick up someone coming in for the holiday. I wondered who that would be but didn't ask. There were a bunch of people I didn't know in the loft, they were briefly introduced to me as they were the road staff that helped them at each location with equipment and such. I got a big hug from Ron and he told me Dahlia couldn't come today but I told him I looked forward to seeing her at another time.

Isaac came up to me like a kid and took hold of my hand and led me over to the tree. I thought, oh no, I hope there is no mistletoe in this tree. He told me he needed a Santa's helper and I was the one chosen. With that he handed me three heavy boxes to give out. The first tag was for Jillian and the next Cecile and then me. We opened them at almost the same time. The band gave us all leather jackets made with *Rolling Isaac's* across the back. That was really nice. Cecile put hers on immediately. Then Isaac said, as Rand grinned standing across from him, that they had another present for me. I hadn't expected anything here today.

Isaac said that he saw how cramped I looked up here in the loft trying to write and would watch me go from couch to chair and back. At this time, Maxwell arrived and gave me a quick hug too. Isaac, like a magician, went to the covered item near the tree in front of **The Wall,** and pulled off the fabric covering. I let out a gasp. It was the writing desk I loved so much from my day in New Hope with Rand. Above the desk was a Post-it note attached to an empty brick area of **The Wall** that read "Madison's Place." It was so cute. I felt like I was surrounded by family they had been so warm and nice to me. I went over to Rand and placed my hands into his rear pockets, pulling him close to me. I heard, "What about me?" coming from Isaac who was so proud of keeping this secret and his unveiling of it today. Everyone laughed.

Rand told me that we could have it delivered to my house any day after they all came back from the holiday season or keep it here if I chose to. I quickly sat in the chair and felt the wood in front of me and felt such a connection to this piece of furniture. It was, I thought, too grand of a present for me, but I think they all wanted to make certain that I was writing nice things about them and this would surely bribe me.

"So are you having a nice start to the holiday?" Maxwell asked me.

"Yes, it's the best since I can remember." I replied excitedly. Rand stood next to me and I saw him reach into his pocket as his phone sounded. He pulled it out and read his message and smiled.

I arrived safe and sound, I got to meet your uncle as he was my driver which was nice, we talked on the ride, mainly about you. I could have easily taken a cab but I gave in to your insistence. I will see you very soon, I am nervous. G.

I didn't want to ruin this moment. I had been feeling cheerful, but I read that message. Then, I went over it again in my mind. I was starting to get upset, but this was not the place to ask him. I simply asked, "Rand is everything okay?"

He smiled and said, "Couldn't be better." He pulled me in for another kiss. As I returned the kiss, I wasn't thinking about or really feeling his sensual touch during this moment. My mind was questioning was it better because I was here or better because she was now here? I let myself go, enjoying his kiss feeling that I may not have many more of these moments with him going forward.

The rest of the afternoon was fun. Rand and the band that never play covers at their shows, took the time to perform one for all on their rehearsal stage. Rand got things started as he jumped up on the stage, pulled his jeans down even lower than where they hung and removed his shirt. His ink gleamed in the lights like a kaleidoscope of colors. He swung his hair back a bit and I was breathless. I stood and thought I was going to climax right there in front of everyone. He must not know how sexy and stunning he looks. I licked my lips and he caught me just as my tongue cornered the side of my mouth, he then pursed his lips and sent an air kiss to me.

His choice of cover song was perfect, "Do you think I'm Sexy" and everyone had their eyes glued to his body. Right then and there I wanted that body. I watched his moves and wanted to take my hands and explore every inch. His song ended too quickly and so did my hot thoughts. Next, Kent grabbed the microphone and sang "Miss You" and he looked at Cecile the entire time. It was Ron that was dead on with his choice of a cover. He stood at his keyboard, paused a moment and then the classic "Piano Man" sounded from his side of the stage. They wrapped it up with some Christmas tunes, Isaac had the band doing a rendition of "I Saw Mommy Kissing Santa Claus" and we all laughed joyously.

Then a powerful moment came when Raeford keyed the guys for the next song. When he was done, we all had tears welling in our eyes. Raeford soulfully sang, "Oh Holy Night." Rand too, who had his hand dipped into the waist of my skirt resting just between my waistband and my skin. He took his thumb and rubbed away a tiny tear that formed in his eye and then attended to some of mine. He asked me if I needed a drink or more food to break the teary mood and even suggested a walk out in the cold. I decided a walk would be good. I went and gathered my new band jacket and he grabbed his coat and we stepped outside.

As I left the barn, I walked into a holiday light show. From the barn to his home holiday bulbs outlined every corner of his property. The front fences were draped with lights and greens. The trees had snowflake lights hanging in all different places and it was so picturesque. It looked like a holiday greeting card.

"It's so beautiful! I cannot believe you do all this, why?" I asked.

Rand looked at me and said, "First you are so beautiful, and why I do this is to see everyone smile. It makes you smile. I like to show them appreciation at the year's end for all their hard work."

"I'm sure they're thankful, it's very nice to do all this."

"Yeah today was nice but when I host the New Years Party it gets a bit crazy."

"Oh, how crazy?"

"Just about as crazy as I am for you Madison."

As I pulled him in to warm me from the chill that crept up my spine, I had to ask, "Rand who is G, I accidently saw that on a text message you received?" I did it, I put it out there, and I waited for him to reply. I waited.

He pulled from me and simply said, "Madison, I cannot go into this with you right here and now, let's talk about this later."

"Why won't you talk to me now about this?"

"Madison you need to trust me, can you do that? I know we are getting closer to one another but I'm sure we don't share everything yet." With that response I knew it wasn't good, I felt the blow to my insides. I felt weakened, but I didn't want to continue to feel something more that wasn't there and it appeared he had something else going on, shutting me out. I told him I was too cold and we headed in to everyone else. I kept a small distance from him for a bit, talking with Jillian and I told her another message came from

"G" tonight and I asked him about it and he didn't want to go into it with me. I was very upset but masked it with a cordial smile.

Jillian told me, "I asked Raeford if he knew anything and he said he didn't know. He did say though that many nights on the road, Rand would not head out with all the guys to bars and such, but always seemed to be occupied or roll in late."

"Oh I can only imagine where he was or what he did." I gave Jillian a very sad look. This wasn't settling with me well. As the festive day continued into the evening, several left to get their packing finished, shopping done or traveling started to get them to their loved ones for Sunday. Rand had told me that he wanted me to come to his house, and see the decorations. I wasn't up for another let down and didn't want to go there tonight, knowing someone else was in town to see him after me. I wasn't going to do that to myself as much as I wanted to be with him. I told him I was getting tired and that I hadn't drank much and was simply going to head home.

"Is everything alright Madison?" he questioned. I told him I was fine, he didn't push. I had wanted him to push because honestly, part of me wanted to cave and stay with him. But I walked around and said goodbyes to all and hugged it out with each person that was still there. I thanked him and the guys again for the desk. I was definitely going to have it relocated to my house soon. I put my new leather jacket back on and Rand took hold of my hand and walked me toward the door. Once past the corner of the large tree, he dipped me back for another lasting kiss and looked up yet again to the mistletoe and smiled. I looked up too, but was looking beyond it to the vast ceiling above and wondering what was going on that I didn't know.

I hadn't even gotten into my bed when my phone sounded and it was Rand –

Merry start of the Christmas Holiday, glad you came by and loved the smile on your face as you sat at your new desk. I look forward to seeing that smiling face on Sunday. Remember you better have been a good girl as Santa is coming. Good night, sleep well.

How could I sleep well, I was in an awful state of mind. Who was "G" and what was he keeping from me. He could easily tell me that we aren't anything to one another. Why dip me back into another unwavering kiss, why invite me over and compare me and her if she is possibly coming there? No I could not do this to myself. I sent him a message –

I'm looking forward to Christmas. Thank you for today, I love my desk. I'm going to sleep and remember all the lights that danced outdoors this evening.

I never did though tell him where I was going to head on Christmas just that I was looking forward to it. I had to decide and I needed a solid night of sleep to make the best decision.

Christmas morning was lovely, as outside a dusting of snow had fallen. It just coated everything with a winter white and made the day seem more special. I awoke content in knowing where I was heading today and with whom I would be spending the day. I showered and dressed and hummed to myself this morning and let the sounds of the season fill my house from the radio as I took a little time to pick out an outfit to wear. I had this long black skirt and I put boots with it. I found a festive looking top that was sleeveless and just skimmed the top of the skirt, actually you could see my skin through the lace cuts, but it looked like a holiday outfit. I pulled out my long coat and gloves as it was chilly today. I packed up my presents and gently carried the bottle of port. I drove out of my neighborhood with ease as the light coating of snow parted as my tires passed through it. The weatherman said some areas got a coating of snow and others received several inches.

I parked my car and began to walk toward the elevator door. I pressed the button for the 27th floor. I let out a huge sigh. I watched the floors tick past. I felt like I was walking back into my past. I reached the door of the condo and as I paused, I felt the door open before I actually pressed the bell. Thomas stood looking so happy that I had arrived. I was actually early for his brunch and wanted to see if I could help him with anything. He took the bottle bag and smiled when he saw the cookie tin that I had made for him. He set them down near his tree that looked just as it did when I lived there, same ornaments, familiar trimmings. I left that all for him when I moved to my townhome. I was in a very bad way and wanted to leave everything behind. I wanted all new items that had no memories of him attached at that time. Today seeing his tree, actually once our holiday tree, brought back a smile to my face. I felt the comfort of home again. He pulled me in and gently embraced me, treating me like glass. He was careful not to hold me too tightly.

Since I was early I sat on the sofa near the tree and we talked a bit about what had been happening with us lately. I told him two friends of mine were hooking up with the band members to which he said, "Oh only two?" I laughed and played that off, I knew what he was saying, but didn't comment further. I told him I had so much of my writing done and felt it was going to be a good book. I left out telling him that the band had just bought me the most awesome desk. Thomas looked so content with me just being there that I didn't want to say that. It would feel like throwing mud in his face.

Thomas had already begun to pour me a glass of wine, telling me about a few more financial conventions he was attending in the New Year. He wanted to know if I would still be traveling with the band in case they crossed into a state he would be in. I told him I was unsure how much more time I would be with them, I knew he was fishing for answers.

He started to get up and he reached toward the back of the tree for a gift box. Thomas smiled brightly at me, and commented how lovely I looked today. I sipped the wine and felt at ease, he was not pushing me. We were talking about safe subjects, and the conversation made me feel warm and welcomed in the condo and with him. I reached over and handed him a bottle bag and he smiled and said thank you to me as he knew I had gotten him his favorite bottle of port. He leaned in to me and kissed my lips, but didn't press.

He then sat very closely to my right and set a gift box on my lap.

"Madison, this is for you, I want you to open it before everyone comes here today."

"Thomas I didn't expect a present from you, do I need to remind you that we're just friends." Even telling him this he seemed to not hear me. Before I reached to open the box, he took my right wrist to his lips and kissed my hand gently and then he twisted on my cuff bracelet. I took my hand down and opened the box and there was a diamond tennis bracelet, clearly made up of too many carats. I was stunned. I wasn't going to take it.

"Are you crazy, this is way too much?"

As he took it out of the box he shared, "I'm crazy in love you with you, let's get this cuff off your wrist and put this beautiful bracelet on." He continued, "I'm so sorry I didn't realize what I had with you and screwed it up. I will not take you for granted anymore; I will spend every day making it up to you."

My eyes started to tear and Thomas reached up and dabbed the corners of my eyes catching the moist droplets, but my tears weren't what he thought. I couldn't stay here, just the touch of him twisting my cuff was like a tug to my heart. I had not been able to get Rand's explanation of "G" yet, and needed to find out what was happening there before I could ever walk away from him. I needed to hold Rand and figure out what had made things awkward recently.

I needed to get out of here, out of my old condo, my old life. I couldn't breathe. I felt suffocated; Thomas looked at me like I was having a panic attack. He got up to go to the bathroom to get me a wet wash cloth and when he returned I had fled. He called my cell phone moments later; I could not take his call. I got in my car and sank in the seat and closed my eyes and took a huge breath, I felt so much better. Follow your heart I told myself in my head. I opened my eyes and was looking down at the shimmering heart on the cuff bracelet, and I was going to have that lead me back toward the person whose heart had given this to me. As I drove from the parking lot to Rand's my phone rang several times, all from Thomas that I let go to voice mail. I silenced my phone.

I parked at Rand's and there were several cars here already. The gathering was already under way since I was late. But a ride and visit to the city and then a drive back out of the city took time. Rand was sitting on his porch when I arrived and stood as he saw me approach. He came toward me immediately. As I rose out of the car, he picked me up and twirled me around in the snow. I was afraid we were going to tumble and be making snow angels on the ground. When he stopped his twirling he began to kiss me and muttered, "Merry Christmas Madison."

He didn't have to tell me how happy he was to see me. His enthusiastic greeting said it all. "I'm so happy to be here," I said softly. After several minutes, he was able to pull himself away and we headed into the house.

I stopped to take in the lovely decorations on the porch itself; there were lighted pathway topiary trees and a giant wreath that hung on the front door again from a velvet ribbon. Inside a sleigh was in the foyer with presents and bottles for guests. I stared to count the decorated trees and from the three at the barn to the two more in the foyer alone, my count was up to five lavishly decorated trees.

"Rand this is amazing, I fell like I'm at the North Pole."

"You're amazing Madison, come here." Before I could even remove my coat, he was pulling me upstairs. He pushed past some of his guests which were mostly neighbors and close friends. He promised to introduce me a bit later. When we reached the second floor, he took me down the hallway to his bedroom. "Madison, close your eyes."

I wondered if he was going to take me there and now upstairs while all the guests remained below us. My thighs trembled and my heart rate increased. I felt the exciting tingle in my lower body just as I did a few days ago with Rand behind the holiday tree. The tree then hid us from the band while friends were just above in the loft. I kept my eyes closed with anticipation. He led me slowly and carefully forward, pulling my hand lightly. He stopped me and turned me toward the direction he wanted and said, "Merry Christmas Madison, you can open your eyes."

As I opened my eyes I first glanced to him and looked puzzled and then he pointed. I looked forward. Hung on his wall in front of me was a painting "Embrace" by the same artist that we liked from South Beach. The other artist's painting was in my bedroom "Separation." This painting was beautiful. It brought the two images of the lovers in the first painting together and it was huge, covering a large portion of his wall. He already had it professionally hung and a light that illuminated the placard that read, "Embrace."

"Rand, it's beautiful, I love it." With that Rand took me into his arms, touching his lips to mine.

"I think of you every time I look at it." He passionately kissed me, and after a moment I opened up for him. I reveled in the moment as our tongues danced together. When he set me down, I had to speak.

"Rand, it's lovely. I didn't know there was another painting in the collection." He was smiling glad that I truly liked it. I then had to finish conveying my thoughts to him. "Rand I'm sorry I came here late today, I wasn't going to come."

"Wait, did you just say you weren't coming?"

"Yes, I felt like I was being dishonest to you because I read a message you received when you played at the 2nd Street Coffee Café. You're definitely keeping something from me."

"Madison I asked you to trust me, can you do that?"

I completely ignored his question and kept right on speaking. "I drank so much that night at your show because of that message and then I saw some of the other messages."

"Do you think I am keeping something from you that will hurt you, would I ever hurt you?"

"I don't know what you're hiding, but I really need to know, Rand who is "G"?"

Again, there was a long pause before he spoke, "Madison I should talk to you about her," he pulled me to sit on the bed. My head started to reel and I felt this wasn't going to be good, but I needed to hear this. Rand was about to speak when he heard Maxwell calling for him from downstairs. Maxwell also sent a message to his phone that he had returned from picking up very important guests and for Rand to come down to greet them, right now. I stood behind Rand as he started down the hall to the stairs as I was about to dart off into the bathroom to cry. I was so frustrated at not finishing our conversation.

He stopped and turned to me and smiled, "I promise I will never hurt you and we'll continue this conversation later, but please trust me." I was a big girl so I sucked it up and followed behind him and wondered what he would have just told me had we not been interrupted. I figured before the night ended I would know.

As we reached the bottom of the stairs, Rand went ahead and I heard him say, "Welcome!" I heard a female voice lightly speaking telling Rand that she was so thankful to him for getting her here. I came around him to see who was here and froze. Rand looked at me, then to his guests then back to me, and I hadn't even blinked yet then he looked back to his guests. Rand broke the stunned stares. "Madison, this is "G", you know Grace, your mother."

I stood and tears filled my eyes, I didn't know what to do. Should I hug her? Run upstairs and pitch a fit for him not telling me and throwing me to her here and now? I thought "G" was a girlfriend, so many things raced in my head. Before me now standing was an older vision of myself. I never thought it was my mother he was getting messages from. I noticed that my Uncle Jake was holding on to her, standing at her side and keeping her steady as she looked so nervous and just as stunned as I did. Rand walked to me and held me up as well.

He whispered in my ear, "Madison I'm sorry I didn't tell you sooner. I didn't mean to have you not trust me. I wanted to surprise you. I found her after your father died while I was in Galveston and looked them up. I went and met them with Maxwell. I told her your father passed away and I kept in touch with her hoping she would accept my plane tickets and visit you on Christmas."

"I can't believe you did all this," I quietly said to him.

"Well, Maxwell and I made all the arrangements for getting them from the airport to a hotel stay the past few nights. You can thank Maxwell he brought them here today, so I could stay to see you first."

I glanced at Maxwell and mouthed thank you.

"Madison, I know you've missed her and I wanted to help you be reunited." He was done whispering and lightly kissed my cheek. I was shaking. I was so scared to do the wrong thing. I turned and hugged him and cried and didn't want to take my arms off him. I asked if I could talk to him for a moment.

We walked down the side hall toward the sunroom. I noticed that there were yet two more decorated holiday trees in the sunroom bringing my silent count to seven. I told him I was frightened. I didn't know how to act, that there is no book written to tell you how to handle something like this. He told me he would be right there with me and not leave my side. He wiped my face and then kissed it all over to clean up any remaining wetness and said for me to go say hello to my mother. I held his hand so tightly. I walked with him step by step.

I hugged my mother with my other arm since I never let Rand's hand loose. I then held my Uncle Jake gently too. My mother started to cry. I told her in between my sobs, "Mom we need not relive the past and who did what wrong or right, I'm so grateful to have you standing here at this moment."

"Madison, you are lovely, I never thought I would see the day with us together again."

"It has been so long Mom." It was a giant step that she and my uncle came all this way for me, and a greater step that Rand had put this all together for me. I felt sad that I had doubted him thinking the worst. My heart hurt. I had hoped that someday perhaps Rand would feel this ache too. It was a good hurt, perhaps one day his father Paul would return or find a way to him.

"Madison, I love you so much," my mother said as she again hugged me and I still had not released Rand's hand. I think he had lost blood to it from my hold as it felt chilled.

This day could not have gotten any better, we all hugged and cried and ate and drank and it was truly a family holiday. Maxwell was very kind to have helped Rand with all this and he enjoyed conversation with my Uncle Jake a lot. They both liked discussing music. My mother and I shared moments of conversation, first about how long it has been since we have seen one another. We then focused on the present. A lot of our talk was about Rand.

"Madison he is so gorgeous and so kind, he has my approval, and I so happy you have found someone."

"Mom, he is great on the eyes, but I'm really unsure what we are to one another, but I'm hopeful."

Rand left us alone to reconnect for quite awhile. When the day turned into the evening, I slipped out to my car to retrieve Rand's gift. I brought it in to share with him while I left my mother and uncle talking with Maxwell and other guests that Rand invited. I took his hand in mine and lead him to the living room and where there were, yes, three more decorated trees all different sizes each with so many colorful decorations and hanging musical note ornaments. Truly at this point I had lost count of the many trees that he had professionally decorated, but the holiday decorations were so beautifully orchestrated.

We sat of the sofa near the fireplace and surrounded with this fresh cut tree line view. I handed him a gift box. I spoke as I was dazzled by his blue eyes.

"Rand I didn't know what to get you for the holiday, but then I stumbled upon this and I knew it was meant for you. I cross my heart that I have so enjoyed every moment since we've met." I leaned in and took hold of his face and pulled him in to kiss his lips tenderly.

Rand opened the box and looked so happy; there was a cuff bracelet like mine but this one had a cross that shimmered and picked up all the light from the Christmas trees. It was mesmerizing. He hadn't worn the cuff for Ashley on his wrist since I learned of her story. In fact, that cuff was now on the memorabilia wall in his corner. So he removed the cuff from the box and let me fasten it tightly to his wrist, and I kissed it when I was done. He pulled me closer and we kissed, staying in that embrace for some time without any mistletoe near us.

We joined the others and Rand had one more holiday surprise up his sleeve. He announced, "Thank you all for coming today. I hope you're having fun. I would now like to play a tune I've been working on. It's called *Our Holiday*. And Rand began to play–

I could live all my holidays
If I could spend them along with you.
Every breath of this lifetime,
Is another moment I wait to come true.

As you are a beloved gift for me
I'll wrap you delicately in shades of love,
I'll tie us with a thick bow of wonder
For us each to thank our maker above.

Because every holiday is nothing without you,
Every moment everyday is celebration in my heart
Cheerfulness surrounds me as I reach a touch of you,
Every moment everyday keeps building from the start.

I was the one, who saw you just below my stage,
Something unspoken was captured deep in your look.
I never knew what could be ahead of us.
But I am certain of the passionate path we took.

Here it is now the whitening of wintertime,
Let us make our festival together,
Savor my gift of my words and song.
Please stay wrapped within our holiday of forever.

Because every holiday is nothing without you,
Every moment everyday is celebration in my heart
Cheerfulness surrounds me as I reach a touch of you,
Every moment everyday keeps building from our start.

Everyday is a holiday as long as you are near.
Everyday is my holiday as long as you are near.

He sang this with so much emotion. We were hanging on at the end of the song wanting more. He lifted his head several times while playing his guitar and caught my eyes and sang. I was so teary that I wasn't sure if I could ever cry this much in a day again. I realized that I had become his inspiration behind this song and he felt something very deep for me. I was now going to need something to drink. I think I'd dehydrated myself from all of the crying. When he finished everyone clapped loudly and went up to him with a warm hug. I cannot believe watching all this love overflowing in this house today that I almost didn't come here.

Chapter Twelve – New Year's Rocking Eve

With one of the best Christmases behind me ever, I glanced at my notebook that remained open to the page I wrote the morning after Christmas Day. The read over the love note I wrote as I pulled a tissue from the box to wipe my eyes several times.

Rand:

In so long, for so many years I cannot remember my holidays ever being as special as they were this year. I can only hope that in the years to come that possibly we will make many great memories. If we do not make it as a couple then I will forever treasure the holidays we shared and store them in my head, like tucking your favorite things in an attic. I will pull those memories when I need to go to my happy place. Besides the gift of you in my life, there has been no greater gift than that of you bringing my mother to reunite with me. I am so filled with joy of having her and my uncle back close to me. I hope that she will come to love you as I do and get to know you, remember I will be at the same time getting to know her all over again. Sometimes in life the best things are new beginnings.

You are my new start and I am ready to begin to move forward and take many steps with you. I think there is a reason for most happenings in life and I believe there was one that pulled us together.

I am sure there is a cheering section in the heavens pulling for you and me. I am so blessed to have you every day.

I hope I keep you challenged and hope I keep you intrigued and know you will build my confidence and make me a much stronger person.

As the fireplace burns and mesmerizes me with its formations, I am just as captivated by you. Your warmth surrounds me and it feels like home. I feel the comfort of having a glass of milk and holiday sprinkled cookies. Happy Holidays to you my love. Maybe one day I will call you my love out loud.

Maddy xo

With Christmas day behind me, I had a full next few days. First, I had to do damage control and return one of the many voicemails that Thomas left me after I abruptly left his condo Christmas day. I inhaled deeply and dialed his cell phone. Mentally I was praying for his voicemail. Thomas answered his phone before the second ring started; he could see it was me calling in.

"Madison, it is about time you called, I left you so many messages and thought that I did something wrong that made you run. I only wanted to make your day special."

"Thomas you didn't deserve me fleeing the condo, but I felt panicked and needed to get air and there was someplace else my heart had to be."

"Did you run to Rand's? Never mind, I already know the answer, but tell me, don't you think you ran to the wrong arms as his will never keep you safe? Madison he will never love you like I do, he will not stay true to you, he could never. I know how he is; you will come back to me when he fails you."

"Thomas wasn't it you that left me, failed me?" Thomas' outburst shocked me but I continued anyway. I knew I didn't need to share any of this with him but I did. I told him all about all of the things that made my holiday great. "I met my mother again thanks to Rand. I don't know what lies ahead for Rand and me, or if there even is a Rand and me, but I need to be with him now and see where this is heading."

"I didn't mean to upset you, I just thought we'd always be together, I guess you have plans for New Years too?"

"Well, I'll be spending time with my mother for the next several days, and I have New Years plans and plans to move my life forward. Happy New Year Thomas, you should crack that bottle of port wine open and enjoy."

"Madison you and Rand will not last, you will fade like the lights after his concerts," he had to get in the last word. I did not respond. I knew I had to breakaway and step forward without him and I knew that I had grown and would definitely survive. I focused on what brought me inner strength and a smile, it was seeing my mother again after so many years and having Rand in my life. "Goodbye Thomas," was all I could give him to close our conversation.

My mother and Uncle Jake wanted to stay at the hotel that Rand had set them up in to not cramp my style even after I repeatedly asked them to join me at my home since we left Rand's on Christmas night. They did come over and stay for the entire day yesterday and then I had to return them to the hotel. I knew I would be busy this week as they were staying for a few days and wanted to visit my father's gravesite. I wanted Rand to know just how special all this was but knew he was planning a huge party for New Year's Eve and was busy with that. I offered to help him but he said he had it all under control. I sent him a quick message –

Rand, hey, I'm thinking of you. I'm spending such good new moments with my mother and uncle. I plan to visit my father's resting place with them tomorrow and then having lunch. I want to thank you for the BEST holiday I can remember. See you New Year's. I have to think of a great resolution. Let me know yours.

Miss you and by the way, my mother is now a fan of yours, she adores you. See you have a pull with the older women too.

He replied –

My heart is smiling for you all. This has been a long time coming. Let me know if you want me with you at the cemetery. Plus since your mom likes me so much I would get another time to see her. Hey, the New Year's gig is going to be awe-some. A lot of people are bringing more people, it keeps grow-ing. By the way, Russ from Bejeweled is flying in for the party and hopes to do some New Year's inks. Is there anything you want tattooed by him?

I remember my body piercing and that shiver of excitement and rush of sensations, but that was hard enough for me to get through, I sent him –

Don't you recall my body piercing fright? Multiply that by 100 and that would be how I'd be with a tattoo. I'll pass. How about you? Getting anything new added to your stunning collection? And yes, please come along tomorrow. I will text you the address of the gravesite and the time later as I have to check it with my mother. That is really weird writing to you saying my mother…Miss you.

Perhaps Rand was missing having his family, his mom, his sister and his dad so I didn't want to cut him out of tomorrow with my family. My phone sounded –

I don't have anything new to ink on this body just yet. Hey that will be my New Year's resolution to have the next tattoo I put on my body in the New Year to be the best one ever drawn and the last one applied. See you tomorrow. Thanks for letting me come along.

It was an odd feeling meeting at the cemetery. I picked up my mother and my uncle and we rode over together. I had sent Rand a message telling him when we would be there so he could join us. As we drove the skies were grey and the clouds were looking heavy and there was that distinct smell in the air of snow. My mother was here with me, this was so hard to believe. I thought after so many years had passed that we would never know one another again. I was so thankful in my heart that Rand brought us together.

I glanced at her as I drove and saw myself in her as she spoke to me and my uncle. Her mannerisms were similar to mine in her laughing and speaking. I smiled at her and took her hand in mine as I drove with my other. She told me on the drive that she never meant to hurt me or my father, but she loved my Uncle Jake so much and could not stop their connection. She told me that people told her that the age difference between her and my uncle which was about the same as my age difference with Rand would not work out. I guess she proved them all wrong as they have been together for so long. I see in my uncle too how he hangs on her every word and is always by her side. I have seen him kiss her and hold her hand and it just flows out of them, the love they have. And all these years they have never married.

She talked about Rand and his kindness, she kept calling him Max which is his real name, but I don't hear anyone call him that but his fans. As we turned into the cemetery I saw the first snowflake dance down and land on my windshield. I saw Rand in the parking lot looking as handsome as ever. He held in his hands a bouquet of crème roses. My heart twisted inside my chest.

It was a short walk to my father's resting place. The snow had begun to swirl about more but with the lightest touch to our hair and face. We stood and said our silent thoughts to my father and Rand held onto my hand. Rand then knelt down in front of my father's headstone and spoke.

"I promise I will watch over her now."

I got tears in my eyes. My mother was crying and my Uncle Jake spoke, "Brother Mick, I will miss you always, I have for so long. I am so sorry I hurt you and Madison for the love of Grace, but please know I love her so much and will always take care of her."

My mother reached and hugged my uncle and we all turned to leave and the flakes started to become more steady and thicker. My mother and uncle got into my car and I walked Rand over to his Hummer. We stood there and looked into one another's eyes and kissed in between the snow flakes that appeared glistening on our faces. I tilted my head to the side and Rand found an exposed part of my neck, just above the collar of my coat. He gently flicked his tongue on my skin tasting the wetness of the fallen, melted fleck. I wanted him to keep licking and I felt my breathing increase. I tilted my head back further and stuck out my tongue to catch the flakes. Rand came toward the edge of my tongue and met it with his and then took in my lips only to stop and tell me, "Hey we aren't alone, let's get them to lunch. Madison you know what's ironic?"

"What's ironic is kissing here at the cemetery getting a rise from the dead?" I smiled.

"No, not that, I don't think there is going to be much snow coming but it started snowing the moment we arrived. I think your father knew we were all here."

"If you believe that then I'm glad he knows you were here and he saw you kissing me. If he is watching us from above then he surely must know how happy you make me." We left there not with sadness but smiles in our hearts.

We had a wonderful lunch that followed and I noted mentally how much my mother was interested in Rand's music and she carried on so much conversation with him. He felt very comfortable with her. My uncle talked about so many things he hoped we would be able to do going forward. We discussed me coming to visit them in Texas and of course they would come back up here to see me. After lunch Rand had to leave us as he had too much to do at his home for New Year's preparations. He hugged my mother closely and kissed her cheek. She seemed star struck; I saw it in her eyes. He shook Jake's hand firmly and took him in for a man hug. As for me, I felt his breath skim past my face and the heat of a quick kiss that sparked something inside of me. He said goodbye and he'd see me in a few days. My mother said she knew he liked me. She knew she liked him for me, in fact she believed he could be in love with me. She said Rand looked at me as my Uncle Jake looked at her. After all these years my mother finally meets a man that I want in my life, she missed out on my entire married life with Thomas.

As quickly as Rand said goodbye, it seemed like I was telling my mother and uncle goodbye again as they were heading to the airport to fly back to Texas. I refused to cry at their departure. I knew we would keep in touch and I felt so happy for the time we had just spent. As I waved and turned I reached for my phone that had an incoming message. Rand sent –

Hope they got off safely and hope you are not crying, be happy that you saw them and I enjoyed getting to know them. I know when you age you will always be beautiful as your mother is still such a lovely woman. See you soon.

I replied –

I was about to cry but didn't, I was a big girl. As for my mother, watch it as I know you like us older women. Besides she thinks you are so yummy, I say hot, she said yummy. I caught her gazing at you several times. Anyway don't get me started on thoughts of gazing at you, I have to drive home on the expressway, I cannot be sexting… so I will see you at this grand party real soon.

I knew he would respond for sure and then it came –

Oh Madison please do some sexting, it has been way too long for us to not have had a long uninterrupted moment. Please send me something sexy and hot. Make me think of you more until the party. Please.

I cannot believe he was begging…I took my phone lifted up my shirt, snapped a photo and sent it to him. His response was quick –

My secret music note belly gem, nice, not entirely what I had in mind, but it will have to do and I will be thinking of what I will be doing around this little gem when I see you. Drive safe, no photo taking on the road.

My ride home from the airport was mixed with emotions that I hadn't felt in so long. I had a love that poured into my heart for my mother and I accepting one another and I also had a yearning desire for Rand to have him give me love if he could. Yes, he was always playful with me and kind, but was that all he would ever offer to my heart? I wanted him so, but so much more of him that I wasn't sure was there.

My mind was busy the next two days getting ready for this party, and making certain I called and talked to my mother and uncle once they got back to Texas. I had made yet another pile outside my closet on the floor trying to put together the perfect New Year's Eve outfit. I think I finally found something that would work. I selected a long black skirt that actually was completely sheer from the thigh down. I decided on a shimmering silver halter top and that way my heart cuff bracelet would stand out on my wrist. I chose heels even though the weather was still a little icy out from a recent dusting of snow.

As I laid my outfit on the corner of my bed, and was beginning to dress, I remember playing dress up as a child with my mother's wardrobe. *"Mommy does this look good on me?"* I would ask her as I was too small to fill out her high heel shoes and her necklaces hung to my young little hips. I do remember some of the early memories of her and I. She would come over to me at the mirror where I stood admiring myself in her accessories and she would apply simple lip gloss saying, "*There, this completes the outfit.*" I would smile brightly into the mirror all dressed up like a big girl. Like my mother would look. I did look up to her. I really had missed her for so many years, too many. I am so glad she is back in my life and now.

New Years Eve was finally here. I was thinking about how much fun I would have tonight with everyone. I was also thinking about my resolution since I hadn't decided on one that I thought I could stick with. So many of us state a resolution and succumb to failure of it only days into the new year. As I was placing the finishing touches to my makeup which I usually wear very lightly, my phone sounded. I glanced down it was Jillian, she wrote –

Hey girl, wow you've had a whirlwind week with your Mom here and gone and if I know you, you are right now knee deep in clothes getting ready, see you tonight, Raeford is picking me up shortly. This is going to be fun! Who would have thought that we all would be celebrating this New Year's with new men in our lives. Raeford talked to Kent and he's back in town from visiting his family and he'll be getting Cecile there tonight. I guess since you're driving yourself that you will surely stay the night at Rand's. What a great way to start your New Year. By the way Thomas called me this week and left a message, I'm glad I missed his actual call. He said he's worried you're acting on a whim. He said you're trying to get back at him with Rand by falling for this young, attractive guy when in the end it will never work out. He asked me to talk to you to make you see reason. I know that you care about Rand and I see Rand cares about you. Who knows where this will lead, but I just wanted to be honest with you that Thomas is still not giving up on you two. See you in a bit.

I wanted to keep getting ready so I sent her a quick see you soon too response. And then I thought about what she had just told me, I wanted Thomas to understand that I felt love for Rand that did not feel like the love I had felt for him in our marriage. I know that sounds strange, but I didn't want to hurt Thomas as he hurt me and throw that at him. I would just stay friends with him and hope in the New Year that we could remain just that. As for tonight I had to get moving. I decided to drive myself in case I wanted to get home without having to rely on anyone. I didn't want to assume that Rand and I would stay together in the late night hours, but just in case I wanted to be prepared.

I pulled out a nicely wrapped bundle from my lingerie drawer. As I undid the tissue I held up the sexiest black lace panties and matching bra. There wasn't much material to either piece. As I slipped these onto my naked body I felt aroused just thinking about Rand looking at me in these. I pictured him sliding his hands over each piece and then his tongue over me and eventually stripping these from my body and taking me over. My phone sounded again breaking my new heated thoughts. It was Rand –

> *Looking forward to seeing you tonight, the barn is decorated and looks like Times Square. The event planners did a great job. Sorry I didn't get to spend time with you the past few days, but I thought you needed some private time with your family. Hope you're wearing something sexy for me and I know you will be the most beautiful girl at the party tonight. Let me know if you change your mind I can come get you, although if I come for you, we may never make it back to this party.*

I replied to Rand's message, I always found myself instantly replying to any of his messages. I wanted to always stay connected with him –

Funny I just had thoughts of you and I will be wearing something very sexy, you will have to imagine what it looks like as it will be under my outfit all evening. I will drive myself and if you let me finish getting ready I will be over shortly.

Rand's response was heated in his wording and came fast –

I'm looking forward to having you, all of you this entire night. And you're killing me Madison as I stand here with a house filling of guests I have to duck behind the bar area to block my hard on that's growing in my jeans. I guess I will help out the bartender with the ice to cool my self down. Get here soon.

Wow, is what I thought as I pulled up to the barn. Rand had a valet service set up to park. I guess with the amount of cars, it is important to do it right. There was plenty of room as his property was large, but he didn't miss a beat in the planning of this evening. The young valet attendant was very nice when I pulled in and as I got out of my car, he actually left my car and took my hand into his and helped my walk carefully across the parking area to the sidewalk of the barn so I did not slip on the surface. He smiled at me in our short walk and just when I was about to thank him and release my hand, Rand was in front of us, taking my hand into his and telling the valet that he could take me from here. The valet nodded at Rand and it made me wonder if Rand set this up and telling the young man to walk me to the door. The other guests came and I didn't see any other valet person assisting them. My heart pinged at this notion.

Rand looked so amazing this evening. He had on a black slim fitted shirt with fancy cuffs flipped up and black pants that hugged his body well. I saw the black cross cuff on his wrist that looked so fine with his outfit. Rand leaned into me before we crossed the front doors and kissed my lips briefly, too briefly, he just skirted over them and then he nibbled at my ear.

"I just calmed my body down, but I can feel I'm already in trouble again."

I pulled him into my body and although it was so cold outside, I only wore a wrap jacket as I was only going from the car to the barn. I felt the heat from his body at that moment and as others passed us to enter the barn, I felt like we were alone in the moment; I felt his hardness press into my hip. I reached up and pulled his head into my face and released a lust filled kiss that parted our lips, swirled our moist tongues and sent shivers through my body settling at points much lower than where my mouth touched his. This was going to be an amazing evening if this was the start of it.

The barn was transformed incredibly, as it had skyscraper buildings done with illuminating lights across the stage where they rehearsed. There was an actual mock skyscraper on the stage with a sparkling ball ready to drop at midnight on a set countdown timer. There were so many people, many I had never met. Rand pulled me from one person to another introducing me as Madison Tierney who was writing about their band. I felt like his girlfriend, but he never introduced me like that at all, he remained very professional as we shifted from one person to another.

I was pulled off guard and it was Cecile that hugged me tightly and she looked so cute. She was wearing a shiny deep purple dress although it was so short it could have been a long top, but Kent didn't seem to mind as his hand rested right on her shoulder. I received a big solid hug from him. I paused to talk with them as they were the first familiar faces I saw. Kent said he had a nice holiday at home but missed Cecile. She just looked at him and beamed. Then Rand tugged my fingers and took hold of just one finger and led me to some of Maxwell's friends that were there. They were older but any friends of Maxwell's were surely good people and I got into some conversation with them and Maxwell brought over some drinks for them and joined in small talk for a bit.

Isaac I saw off to the front of the stage surrounded by a few young, very skimpily dressed ladies. He seemed to be in his element talking to each one and putting his arms around one then another. Rand tipped into my hair and nuzzled there breathing me in and then he said he would be back he was going to bring us a drink. When he left me standing there in the midst of this cluster of people I stood nervously for a moment and then I saw a head of red hair and followed that direction to reach my Jillian.

As I found her I felt more comfortable and we hugged and Raeford was right by her side. I smiled up to him. I really liked Raeford. Better yet I liked him with my best friend. They made a nice couple. Jillian had shared with me recently that they slept together many times already and that he was such a romantic always taking slow care of her in the bedroom. I could visualize this as he was always such a gentleman. I hoped this New Year would bring goodness for them both, actually for all of us. I felt that shiver from Rand's touch as he passed a drink into my fingers. We clanked our glasses and sipped the drinks. I know I was thinking of where I wanted his lips and he looked at me and smirked as if he could read my mind.

Walking about the party and mingling, a familiar voice startled me, "Madison, great to see you again, will you be getting anything done?" Russ asked. Quickly I turned and shook my head no as I certainly was not getting drunk this evening nor was I getting any tattoo. He laughed back at me but did let me know he brought all his supplies should I change my mind. Rand chimed in that Russ would certainly be busy with some inks later tonight. Rand reached down in front of me and let his fingers grace the inside of my skirt's waist band and he lightly fondled my belly piercing and he winked. I saw the glow in his eyes. I know my eyes reflected that same glow.

Ron came up behind us and he had Dahlia with him. She looked nervous just as I had once felt when I first met the band. But now I was feeling much more confident in my life and definitely around all of them. Surely, there were a lot of new people for her to meet. Ron told us he hoped we had a nice holiday and we all talked for a bit. I had to leave the conversation midway as I had to find the ladies room. Dahlia joined me. It was nice that she looked up to me enough that when we headed down the hall that she asked, "Madison, can I ask you how you handle all the fans?" She continued, "I really like Ron, but I have such fears that all these girls are so pretty and they throw themselves at the entire band. It worries me."

I told her beautiful doubt filled eyes that I don't handle it well at all. "I try to not watch it, not hear it and not get into it." I shared with her the one fan made video of Rand while they were out west in the summer touring that was called Randevous. I told her it broke me up. I told her that this was real here with them and that what they do with the fans that is their performance, their job. Hopefully, she would be able to separate the two. "Dahlia, I know Ron cares about you, I remember when traveling with the band that he was crushing on you then. She smiled. We hugged and it was nice to share this moment with her. I felt older and wiser with her. I felt like I was looking out for her. There was probably an age difference of more than 12 years between us. I felt like an older sister. I knew at this moment I would always feel a bit protective over her as she hugged me tightly.

We returned to our men a little later than we planned and they looked worried, like they were wondering what we had been talking about for so long. Women go off to the ladies room and can spend so long there striking up conversations over reapplying their lipstick. Men, they go in the bathroom, do their business and are out in a blink.

We all were having such a great evening. The music played loudly over the sound system which was incredible. I was certain after the ball was dropped on the stage at midnight the band would surely jump up and start playing songs. For now many were eating the catered food that was being served by a hired wait staff and the beverages were continuously being poured. Everyone was enjoying the celebration and dancing on the floor in front of their practice stage. Rand pulled me to the floor. I had never danced with Rand, I knew I could dance but never saw his moves except when he danced across that stage in a performance and those moves alone made my toes curl. As we took to the floor, the fast paced music got him started and it received many cheers and claps by his surrounding friends as he truly lead the dancing and danced circles around me. A few females tried to pull him in their directions and tried to get in between our bodies and not in a spiteful way, but they tried to include themselves in the fun, but Rand closed that gap between his body and mine. He was obviously responsible for the entire party playlist, and was familiar with it. Each time the tempo changed, he effortlessly matched it. His breaths that were fast one moment became controlled and he inhaled and exhaled, forcing his breathing to calm. He wrapped his arms around my body and kissed my cheek.

He pulled me over toward the corner of the dance floor, while there were still many people moving side to side and we stopped near another of the many decorated holiday trees. We remained there like we had our own private piece of the floor. As the music slowed and the lights dimmed, he right there on the dance floor, slid his hand down the back of my skirt. I felt his grazing touch searching my naked skin and he caught himself on the elastic of my black lace thong panties and tugged lightly. He pressed his lips to mine deeply and explored the depths of my mouth with his tongue. His firm hand explored my backside and traveled deeper. I could feel myself getting wet between my legs. Here we danced together and our bodies were having a moment of pure wanting and longing for one another while so many others still surrounded us. This just increased my excitement.

When the song stopped, and it seemed like the longest playing song, the lights came up brightly. We stood and parted our moist, kiss swollen lips and Rand glanced to the clock on the wall, it was eleven o'clock. He removed his hand from my rear and trailed it slowly to the center of my back. He said, "Let's get out of here, and go someplace private, I think I know the perfect place. Do you trust me?" I smiled and did not say a word as I nodded. I knew my expression told him, that I not only trusted him but told him what my body wanted as well. I did not expect what happened next. He left me there briefly and talked to most of the band members quickly. He grabbed my wrap and put it around me and led me out the front door where the hired valet had his Hummer waiting all warmed and ready to go.

I only asked as we got into the Hummer, "Where are we heading to?"

"To your house for some uninterrupted privacy and if we time it right we should be there before the midnight countdown. Maxwell and the guys will handle the party outcome and make certain everyone gets home. If they can't drive they'll all be crashing in my house, even Russ is staying there tonight, so we wouldn't have the chance to be alone." He looked into my eyes and asked, "Are you okay with this last minute change of plans?" I nodded yes to him and parted my lips to take in his tongue before we drove off.

We made it to my house in record time. At each stop light along the way he placed his right hand into the front of my skirt and traveled down only to be stopped when the light changed. The roads were still a bit icy so he kept his focus on driving safely but also kept me excited with each anticipated touch. I was hoping all the lights would be red and stay on extended red as we approached them. Finally we were at my house. Rand stopped before we entered to remove from the back of his Hummer two bottles of chilled champagne. He didn't miss a beat, as we hurried in from the winter's cold.

I kicked off my heels and gathered two champagne glasses. We poured the champagne in very large pours overflowing the glasses and drank and refilled it immediately and drank some more. We laughed, we kissed each other playfully. Rand lifted me onto my kitchen counter, and hiked up my long skirt and positioned himself underneath like he was wearing a veil. I laughed as I poured another glass of the bubbly and drank. I felt his soft kisses and little nips press along the flesh of my inner thighs and I giggled. I felt his tongue continue to sweep the skin on my thighs and he licked the bottom of my lace panties. He removed his head from beneath the tented skirt and told me that he could not take this anymore and filled his glass and drank.

It was now that I blurted out to him, "I'm on the pill" and his response came to me with a smile.

"And you are telling me this why? Are you assuming something might happen between us?"

I responded, "I was hoping, finally…"

Rand looked at me with such intensity. "Good because I don't want to have to wear a condom with you, I want nothing between us." He carried the other bottle and our glasses, leading me as usual by one finger toward my bedroom. The clock was a moment from striking midnight. Setting the bottle and glasses next to the bed, he quickly gathered me and tossed me back to the bed. As the east coast was now counting down the time, ***Ten, Nine, Eight, Seven***, he was pressing passionately into my lips, ***Six, Five***, he was tearing at my top and unzipping my skirt, ***Four, Three***, he was ripping off his shirt and pants and his shoes went flying toward my massive clothing pile on the floor. ***Two, One***, ***Happy New Year***, the rushed passion between us halted, he paused and looked at me and said, "Let's take this slow, no one's coming to interrupt us, we have all night."

Rand dipped into the lower folds of my body. It was the slow, deliberate steps like one would take on the first day of the season at the beach where you gently touch the water's edge, tentatively testing. Slowly inching in further. Rand took his time savoring me at the entrance of my body. Slowly, watching me and pausing a moment to breathe us in. Then he entered me deeper, pausing again and then he dove in and filled me completely with his length. We bobbed together and rocked back and forth like a traveling, forceful current in the ocean and waves of ecstasy rose up cascading through us. We made love to one another over and over until I was boneless and exhausted and smiled from my release and he was very, very tired.

I watched him drift as I was resting comfortably in his arms. I watched the rise and fall of his chest as he took each breath. I leaned on my side and I took the tip of my finger and traced the cross tattoo on his chest with the lightest touch. I crossed it over the heart and said in a whisper, "I love you Max Rand, I was never getting back with Thomas, because you Max Rand fill up my heart. I fell in love with you with you the very first night I met you." I looked at his closed eyelids and I kissed his chest and he slept. As I drifted off I thought I heard—

"I am sorry, I have to leave you. I must leave now; I can't tell you I love you…

Snow had started to fall outside lightly and I looked out my bedroom window taking in the beautiful virgin whiteness falling downward. I awoke to find Rand gone, and I believe what I heard while I slept was real, I hear it again in my head, *I am sorry, I have to leave you, I must leave now. I can't tell you I love you…* I know it was his pattern, I should have seen this coming, and I was so stupid. I cannot believe I finally told him I loved him as he slept. I don't think he heard my words and yet he slipped out this morning and left unable to face me. I wrapped a bed sheet around me and walked past my writing room and glanced in to see all the work I had written this year with the band in a different area than I had last placed it. Rand must have wandered in there as one his journals was an arms distance from my writings. Several pages of my written work was scattered on the floor. He had probably started to read *Rock Notes*, and Rand saw that at some point I began to write another piece titled *Love Notes.*

This other piece was my soul, my passion, my making it back to love again, and to love him. There were only a few of the love notes there but I had begun to write so many and they were actual love letters to him. Oh no, I freaked him out. I wish he hadn't read how deeply into him I was and that I was ready to move on with him and make him feel loved. I poured my heart out in the love letters that he made me love once again and it was a real love, like none before. Oh I wish and hoped that he did not read my hidden secrets and feelings that I had not shared with him yet and wasn't sure if I ever could. I blew it, I scared him, and he ran off as this was too much for him.

I got to the door like so long ago and slipped to the floor beneath me and wept.... Broken again, emptiness overcame my body and I broke down weeping for being so swept up and so naïve...repeating my life's pattern. I laid and cried for some time. I thought Rand would have accepted me and that his passion and touches and kisses were evidence that he could let me in his heart or I could rebuild his heart. Especially after last night I believed that he could make love to me, really feel love for me and I knew I could love him, I had for so long. Oh how I prayed for last night to finally happen between us and just as I released my whole soul to him, he had to leave, leave me...

Hours have passed and the snow has piled outside now and somewhere in the pounding of my head from crying I hear a slight knock. It wasn't really a knock on the door, but a fragile tap. I silenced my crying and slid to one side to open the door. Rand was standing, towering over me covered in glistening snow, with a very sad look on his face. I looked up in my pathetic frame of mind and wanted to replace all the doubt and fear that I just absorbed. But I didn't know if he had come back to grab the remainder of his clothes on the bedroom floor and his journal and then leave. He slowly joined me on the floor, reaching over me and cradling me in his sturdy arms he knew without speaking, he knows that I thought he left for good, as I assumed he used to with all the other girls he met. I didn't want to ask what he read; I figured he read it all, every page of my raw emotion.

We stayed together like that for so long and I kept running my fingers over his arm and didn't want to speak or leave the floor. He lifted me up into his arms and carried me to the bedroom where we had just spent the night before of making amazing love and wonder. The night before was so powerful, from the moment I gave in and let him take me over completely, love me, want me and let me release what I'd felt for so long. He made me think that I could feel whole again and experience something so intense with him.

He now tenderly laid me flat on the bed and leaned up and brushed my bangs away and kissed my forehead. He lingered there for a moment only to then move from me to where he sat at the very edge of the bed and there he remained, silent. I thought he was just being compassionate in this awkward situation, I assumed he was feeling sorry for me and then he started to remove his shirt with his back facing me and slowly he pulled it up over his shoulders and head. My eyes were so sore from crying, still unsure if he was just changing his shirt that I had cried all over. Then I thought he would leave with a fresh shirt on. He turned to me briefly and in a low tone said, "Madison I am so very sorry" and turned back. "I went back home this morning because last night was too much for me, for us, I think something is missing."

The words plunged into my stomach as this had been the same scenario with Thomas so long ago. I was frozen and unable to speak; I looked up at him as my eyes filled in the corners and seeped to the sheet below. He leaned further forward bending toward the floor in front of him reaching for his clothes and belongings. I leaned up slowly to look at him one last time. I started to stare at his perfectly fit shoulders, then my eyes traveled down his back, and then my eyes widened and fixed on a new tattoo. It was freshly inked with shiny ointment coating it. Under the sheen I saw a heart, severed in half. There were dark crimson blood droplets cascading downward. My eyes blurred. He had a broken heart tattooed and I was saddened. As I followed the path of the redness and each newly drawn drop, I then saw the long, green stem of a rose. It was a single long stem rose that was crème in color with and a trace of the deepest pink trim. It twined, and climbed like green ivy across the naked skin of his lower spine and reached to a large red solid heart. It was the words in the heart that stunned me……

Beautifully inked within that heart were two written words………***Madison Rand.***

He was not leaving me, he was committing himself to me, Max Rand was here with me now as I had never seen him, so certain of himself and us, he was inked with the permanence of his commitment. Rand turned slightly toward me and caught my tear filled eyes trying to focus on his back. He spoke lightly, "Madison, I'm so sorry, I never wanted you to doubt me. I should have known that you would think I left, but I had to take care of something first, but you can see what that was."

I then raised, my body tired and weak from crying, and climbed across the bed toward him. I completely threw my messy crying self on his back actually hurting his newly inked tattoo. I say smiling into his eyes, "Yes, Yes, YYYYEEESSSS." I said it over and over and over. I inched up to the rim of his jeans on his back and spoke aloud "Yes" to his skin and kissed it gently. Tears streamed from my eyes. Rand stood up and came down over me with the kind of smile he so often has and he wrapped his arms tightly around me, so tightly to not let me go. I think I saw a shine in his eye that was beginning to tear.

He whispered lightly in my ear, "Madison I love you, I'm not going anywhere" and then he continued, "I tried to meet you years ago when you wrote the column about our band, but I was stopped in my tracks when I was told you were happily married. I always kept your photograph and studied it and hoped and wished. When you contacted my uncle Maxwell to write about the band and you were never answered, it was because he brought your request to me. He had known that I had once tried to meet you. I knew you were married and that in some cosmic way I felt for you something intense without ever knowing you. It was like being a fan of an idol or movie star that you think of all the time. Please understand that I couldn't reach out to you to offer you the opportunity to write for the band and have you so close to me when I was then suffering so much love lost in my life then. It was the wrong time. Then it was you, my eyes caught sight of as I entered the stage, in the front row of our Philly concert when you turned my world upside down, my empty heart pumped."

"No it was you Rand that took my breath away as I watched you from that front row."

"Well I'm glad I make you breathless, you made me completely love struck crazy. I became so consumed that very night to find out everything about you, I read on the internet gossip that you left the newspaper column at a high point in your career to write other things and I also read you had gotten divorced. I figured I had received my sign of hope."

"Rand, I am so glad you looked for me, I mean into me, and about me. I often listened to your songs and thought of you singing them to me alone."

"Well I tried so many times to get closer to you and get you alone while you were writing for the band, but there were too many times your ex-husband Thomas returned and I wasn't sure where you were heading. He was at the concert all the way in Austin, Texas, then at the hospital when your father passed away; he was again at your house for your birthday. I actually met Thomas, it was at your home at your birthday party, I had flown in with Raeford, a last minute red eye flight decision, to surprise you for your birthday and Raeford to see Jillian for the night and I came to your house, not expecting a party to be going on. Raeford and I separated when we landed as he went to see Jillian and I went to buy you as many roses as I could find in short notice and at that late evening hour."

"Rand all I thought of on my birthday was the wish that I would see you when Raeford told me you returned with him."

"Madison, all I wanted was to see you, I wanted to hold you so badly and Thomas answered your door and said he was throwing you a private birthday party. I could see he did not want me to cross the threshold and he even came out to the front step to talk to me. He made it crystal clear I was not welcome, he then asked me what I was to you; I told him my true feelings about you, I told him I was totally in love with you."

"You told Thomas you loved me?"

"Yes and he didn't take it well, Thomas said that I would hurt you and leave you, funny coming from the man that did just that. I knew then I would never leave you, I would find a way to you. I handed him all the different bouquets of roses, there was no note to any of them, as I intended to be speaking from my heart what I would have written on a card, and Thomas took the flowers and went back to your party and closed the door to me."

"Rand I thought he had those flowers delivered to me, I never knew."

"Well I will continue to bring you many more now that you're mine."

"I am yours, all yours."

"Madison I also tried to get to see you on Thanksgiving Day, despite Maxwell getting ill and having to take him to the doctor, once he was out of the woods health wise, we flew in on the next flight we could get and I did get to your house and it was late and as I walked up the edge of your driveway to surprise you and feel that Thanksgiving warmth of you in my arms after such a long time away, I saw you and Thomas, you were pulling him into a tight embrace and into your front door. I stayed outside to see you both walk past your front window enjoying a glass of wine near your fireplace; again this time it was clearly not my place to intrude. I felt I let you down."

"But, I never knew you were there," I let out a shocked gasp. I was still was reeling from all that Rand was saying. Rand reached down and cupped my chin and said, "Madison, I have always felt something so deep for you, beyond the scope of love. I was so glad to see you the day after Thanksgiving; at least we got that time together. You had forgotten your scarf and it smelled like you. For days I would hold that scarf to my nose, inhaling your scent, closing my eyes and imagining that you were close. The scent faded but I still managed to get the feel that you were with me almost every day."

"Now I know what you meant when you said you could smell me. I was wondering about that."

"I know that many times that we were apart you assumed I was having sex with fans. I am sure you watched some of the video feeds from our travels that would surely imply that. Madison, I swear on my sister Ashley that I have never been intimate with another girl since I met you. The nights I never returned until dawn I was writing music, all about you, or thinking and dreaming only of you. Last night making love for the first time to you blew my mind, and as you told me you loved me and crossed my heart with your fingers, I knew your feelings were true. My heart began to feel again."

"I thought you were sleeping, that's why I confessed my love."

"I heard your words and felt your gentle touch, the letters that spell love were simply not enough of a commitment for me to say back to you."

"I had to leave, I had to find Russ back at my house, knowing he would be there from last night's party. My New Year's resolution was to give you a permanent proposal tattoo for all that you have given back to my heart. I thought I had no love left to give, and I don't care who has been in your heart before, but you have given me so much more love than I could ever ask for. My heart aches for you. Madison will you please become Mrs. Madison Rand please marry me and stay with me…forever, always be in my front row, hell jump on my stage and stay with me by my side forever?"

I finally sobbed and caught my breath, nodding yes to Rand as I continued to shake. I was found and Rand had truly become my rock, my solstice, my world. I had written so many love notes for him with the hopes of this possibility of Rand and me falling in love. I was so complete and my love overflowing with the hopes and dreams now for our future together. He then began to climb up over me as I laid back on the bed. I think laying there on my bed on the fluffy white comforter, I had gone to heaven and as he came close to kiss me and I felt the heat between us.

I was left completely breathless. I let him take me over, he entered me. He filled me and completed me, and I realized he found love again, and we found love again in one another. It was much more powerful this time around. I rested my head on his upper body next to his cross tattoo and closed my eyes mentally thanking whatever force had brought us together, and I felt each and every heartbeat that played from within his chest.

Epilogue – Starting Line

We have crossed the starting line into a relationship between Rand and me. So much has begun since I kissed "YES" to his permanent proposal. We spend a lot of time at his home although I still visit my townhome sometimes. My mother and uncle occupy it now since they have relocated back to Philly from Galveston, Texas. My *Rock Notes* has been picked up by a publishing house thanks to the persistence of one little charming young lady, Cecile. My *Love Notes* I still continue to create with each new memory we make. It is all the love that pours into my heart that keeps me inspired. Rand remains firm that he has not read any of them but will want to someday when I am ready to share them with him. His love travels through my blood and pumps into my heart, a constant invigorating feeling.

I never did have my awesome writing desk delivered to my home as I occupy that corner of writing space at the rehearsal studio in the barn often. I have my own tiny brick space on **The Wall,** where the band and Rand has let me gather some of my own memorabilia. Most of which are Post-it notes for future writing pieces attached there and I have added a photo of his naked back with his marriage proposal tattoo.

Rand, he has been so busy with song writing and will hopefully soon release his first solo album. Maxwell has been a great coach to him, but told him it will happen but all good things take time. It is titled "Simply Mad" named after me, Madison. His cover is being created and he wants it to contain my original column photograph. His song playlist that he has written all the songs to and may add more, I have only heard him play two thus far.

New Album, "**Simply Mad**" *for Madison*
This is his song list:

- My Front Row
- Sweet Nervous One
- Secret Musical Note
- Simply Mad
- Empty Heart
- Always Interrupted
- Embrace Us
- Our Holiday
- Cross Your Heart
- Permanent Proposal

At the concert Thomas and I attended in Austin, Texas he had tearfully sang to me *Empty Heart*. And on the joyous holiday we all shared and the loving reunion of my mother and uncle with me he unveiled his song *Our Holiday*. I have peeked at his lyrics and new songs for the album. Here is one where it all started:

My Front Row

I feel you in the crowd,
Or am I just imagining?
Oh, I need you right now,
Or am, I just wishing?

I know where you have been,
I want to keep you near.
I am blessed you are my front row,
But without your love I fear.

You don't know where I've been
You can't see what's ahead
You don't know how I feel
You just look where you're lead.

I'm so glad that you came
I have needed to understand you
You're the vision from my front row
And I don't know what to do.

You don't know where I've been
You can't see what's ahead
You don't know how I feel
You just look where you're lead.

I want to find a hopeful place
Where I can lay you down
I want to be with you always
So amazed my heart's been found.

You don't know where I've been
You can't see what's ahead
You don't know how I feel
You just look where you're lead.

So, look at me,
Please, look to me,
From the front row,
I can see,
We will see,
What you don't know.

Also here is another that warms me –

Embrace Us

Take hold of me in your arms
There is no place else for us to go.

Let's move against one another
Hold tight and move nice and slow.

Embrace Me
And you will look no more
Embrace Me
And you will taste for more
Embrace Us, Embrace Us

Feel the passion in the air
Breathe in the love we have found.

Feel our heated energy ignite
Cling to strengthen our hold that we are bound.

Embrace Me
And you will look no more
Embrace Me
And you will taste for more
Embrace Us, Embrace Us

So hold tight, so pull me in,
No release, we are suddenly locked together.

This is right, so let's begin,
Inhale, move in each others steps forever.

Embrace Me
And you will look no more
Embrace Me
And you will taste for more
Embrace Us
Embrace Us, Embrace Us

And finally I guess the song that started all his inspiration and that he was crazy in love with me as I am now with him –

Simply Mad – (For Madison)

I am Simply Mad
Without you.
I am Simply Mad
I turn to you.

As I break down,
You comfort me.
I cover my eyes,
You make me see.

Without you
I am Simply Mad.
I turn to you
When I am Simply Mad.

I am Crazy,
dancing in my head.
I am going crazy,
singing out your name.

I see you everywhere,
I hear your voice.
I see you everywhere,
I hear your voice.
I see you everywhere.

I am Simply Mad
Without you.
I am Simply Mad
I turn to you.

Without you
I become Simply Mad.
I run to you
When I am Simply Mad.

I see you everywhere,
I hear your voice.
I see you everywhere,
I hear your voice.
I see you everywhere.

Somewhere in our busy phases of creativity, Rand's writing music and my writing about him. We both are going to need to carve out some real time because right now the most important thing is ***I've got a wedding to plan!***

Author's Notes

Readers:

I want to thank you for purchasing **Rock Notes***. I loved writing this novel and hope you enjoyed reading it. Please feel free to reach out to me with a comment.*

My website is: www.reneeleefisher.com *or email me at* author@reneeleefisher.com

Also, note there are five books planned in the Heartbeat Series. The next to follow is **Love Notes, coming fall 2013***. Continue to follow the story of Madison and Rand who have now just became a couple and have committed themselves to one another, but will they take the next step, will there be a wedding? Will doubt still be there, and will they be able to forgive one another? Life can change in a moment. Accidents happen…what moments will alter their course? Will Madison and Rand ever get their happily ever after?*

By: Renee Lee Fisher

Definitions

In geology, a ***Rock*** is a naturally occurring solid aggregate of one or more minerals.

Rock music is a genre of popular music.

My ***Rock***, is often used in the phrase, you are my rock, meaning someone that can be relied on.

Notes are often study guides on various subjects.

In music, ***Notes*** are used as a notation to duration and pitch of a sound.

My ***Notes*** were something I had written down to assist my memory in the future.

By: Madison Tierney

Follow the "Heartbeat Series"
By Renee Lee Fisher:

ROCK NOTES (Book One)
LOVE NOTES (Book Two)
MUSIC NOTES (Book Three)
FIRST BEAT (Book Four)
FIRST BASS (Book Five)

29111300R00152

Made in the USA
Middletown, DE
08 February 2016